Praise for
Mathias Énard

"Homeric in its scope and grandeur, remarkable in its
detail, Énard's American debut, *Zone*, is a screaming
take on history, war, and violence. . . . Mandell's
translation of the extravagant text is stunning."
—*Publishers Weekly* [starred review]

"A tremendous accomplishment. . . . Énard's *Zone*
is, in short, one of the best books of the year."
—*Daily Beast*

"With its historical sweep and grand moral import,
Zone is an epic of modern literature."
—*Bomb*

"Like Flaubert and James Joyce, Énard seems to have
found a model for his omnivorous novel in the Homeric
epic, while Ezra Pound's ghost also haunts *Zone*."
—*New York Times*

"Énard's brilliant fourth novel seeks to escape
'the memory of emotions and crimes.' . . . Form
and theme fuse powerfully in *Zone*."
—*World Literature Today*

"The novel of the decade, if not of the century."
—Christophe Claro

Also by Mathias Énard
in English Translation
ZONE

STREET

OF

THIEVES

MATHIAS ÉNARD

OPEN LETTER
LITERARY TRANSLATIONS FROM THE UNIVERSITY OF ROCHESTER

Translated from the French
by Charlotte Mandell

Copyright © Actes Sud, 2012
Translation copyright © Charlotte Mandell, 2014
Originally published in France as *Rue des voleurs* by Actes Sud, 2012

First edition, 2014
All rights reserved

The newspaper articles quoted in the novel come from the *Diario de Cádiz*, dated
February 17, 2012 (p. 137 in the book) and from the news site www.yabiladi.com (p. 144-145).

Library of Congress Cataloging-in-Publication Data: Available upon request.
ISBN-13: 978-1-940953-01-4 / ISBN-10: 1-940953-01-4

With Support of the Centre national du livre.
www.centrenationaldulivre.fr

Avec le soutien du

*This project is also supported in part by an award
from the National Endowment for the Arts.*

Printed on acid-free paper in the United States of America.

Text set in Garamond, a group of old-style serif typefaces
named after the punch-cutter Claude Garamont.

Design by N. J. Furl

Open Letter is the University of Rochester's nonprofit, literary translation press:
Lattimore Hall 411, Box 270082, Rochester, NY 14627

www.openletterbooks.org

STREET

OF

THIEVES

CONTENTS

"But when one is young one must see things, gather experience, ideas; enlarge the mind." "Here!" I interrupted. "You can never tell! Here I met Mr. Kurtz."

—*Joseph Conrad,* Heart of Darkness

I

STRAITS

MEN are dogs, they rub against each other in misery, they roll around in filth and can't get out of it, lick their fur and their genitals all day long, lying in the dust, ready to do anything for the scrap of meat or the rotten bone they want someone to throw them, and I'm just like them, I'm a human being, hence a depraved piece of garbage that's a slave to its instincts, a dog, a dog that bites when it's afraid and begs for caresses. I can see my childhood clearly, my puppy dog's life in Tangier; my young mutt's strayings, my groans of a beaten mongrel; I understand my frenzy around women, which I took for love, and above all I understand the absence of a master, which makes us all roam around looking for him in the dark, sniffing each other, lost, aimless. In Tangier I would walk five kilometers twice a day to go look at the sea, the bay and the Strait, now I still walk a lot, I read too, more every time, a pleasant way to trick boredom, death, to trick thought itself by distracting it, by distancing it from the truth, the only truth, which is: we are all caged animals who live for pleasure, in obscurity. I have never gone back to Tangier, but I've met guys who dreamed of going there, as tourists, to rent a pretty villa with a view of the sea, drink tea at the Café Hafa, smoke kif, and fuck natives, male natives for the most part but not exclusively, there are some who want to bang princesses from the *Arabian Nights*, believe me, I've been asked so many times to arrange a little stay for them in Tangier, with kif and locals, to relax, and if they had known that the only ass I ogled before I was 18 was my cousin Meryem's they'd have fallen down laughing or wouldn't have believed me; they so associate Tangier with sensuality, with desire, with a permissiveness that it never had for us, but which is offered to the tourist in return for hard cash in the purse of misery. In our neighborhood, nobody ever came, not a single tourist. The building I grew up in was neither rich nor poor, my family likewise, my old man was pious, what they call a good man, a man of honor who mistreated neither his wife nor his children—aside from a few kicks in the backside now and then, which never harmed anyone. He was a man of a single book, but a good one, the Koran: that's all he needed to know what he had to do in this life and what awaited him in the next, pray five times a day, fast, give alms, his only dream was to go on pilgrimage to Mecca, which they call the Haj, Haj Mohsen, that was his sole ambition, it didn't matter if he worked hard to transform his grocery store into a supermarket, it didn't matter if he earned millions of dirhams, he had the Book prayer pilgrimage period; my mother revered him and combined an almost filial obedience with domestic servitude: I grew up like that, with suras, morality, stories about the Prophet and the glorious times of the Arabs; I went to a totally average school where I learned a little French and Spanish and every day I would go down to the harbor with my buddy Bassam, to the lower part of the Medina and to the Grand Zoco to check out the tourists, as soon as we sprouted hair on our balls that became our main activity, eyeballing foreign women, especially in summer when they wear shorts and miniskirts. In the summer there wasn't much to do, in any case, aside from following girls, going to the beach, and smoking joints when someone handed us a little kif. I would read old French detective novels by the dozen, which I bought used for a few coins at a bookshop, detective novels because there was sex, often, blondes, cars, whiskey, and cops, all things that we lacked except in dreams, stuck as we were between prayers, the Koran and God, who was a little like a second father, minus the kicks in the rear. We would take up our places on top of the cliff facing the Strait, surrounded by Phoenician tombs, which were just holes in the rock, full of empty potato chip bags and cans of Coke instead of ancient stiffs, each of us listening to a Walkman, and we would watch the to-and-fro of the ferries between Tangier and Tarifa, for hours. We were bored stiff. Bassam dreamed of leaving, of trying his luck on the other side as he said; his father was a waiter in a restaurant for rich people on the seafront. I didn't think much about it, the other side, Spain, Europe, I liked what I read in my thrillers, but that's all. With my novels I learned a language, I learned about other countries; I was proud of these novels, proud of having them for me alone, I didn't want that oaf Bassam to pollute them for me with his ambitions. What tempted me more than anything at the time was my cousin Meryem, my Uncle Ahmed's daughter; she lived alone with her mother, on the same floor as us, her father and brothers farmed in Almería. She wasn't very pretty, but she had big tits and a round ass; at home she often wore tight jeans or half-transparent house dresses, my God, my God she aroused me terribly, I wondered if she did it on purpose, and in my erotic dreams before I fell asleep I imagined undressing her, caressing her, placing my face between her enormous breasts, but I would have been incapable of making the first move. She was my cousin, I could have married her, but not felt her up, that wasn't right. I made do with dreaming, and of talking about her with Bassam, during our afternoons spent contemplating the wake of the boats. Today she smiled at me, today she wore this or that, I think she had on a red bra, etc. Bassam nodded, saying, she wants you, no doubt about it, you turn her on, otherwise she wouldn't put on that act. What act, I replied, isn't it normal for her to wear a bra? Yes but it's red, you idiot, don't you see? Red is for arousal. And so on, for hours. Bassam had a stolid peasant's head, round, with little eyes. He went to the mosque every day, with his old man. He spent his time devising incredible plans to emigrate secretly, disguised as a customs officer, or a cop; he dreamt of stealing some tourist's papers and, well dressed, with a pretty suitcase, of calmly taking the boat as if nothing was amiss—I asked, but what would you do in Spain without cash? I'd work and save a little, then I'd go to France, he'd reply, to France then to Germany and from there to America. I don't know why he thought it would be easier to leave for the States from Germany. It's very cold in Germany, I said. And also they don't like Arabs over there. That's wrong, said Bassam, they like Moroccans, my cousin is a mechanic in Dusseldorf, and he's super happy. You just have to learn German, and they respect you like crazy, apparently. And they issue papers more readily than the French.

We would exchange our castles in the sky, trade Meryem's breasts for emigration; we would meditate this way for hours, facing the Strait, and then we'd go home, on foot, him to evening prayers, me to try and catch one more glimpse of my cousin. We were seventeen, but more like twelve in our heads. We weren't very clever.

A few months later I got my first real beating, an avalanche of blows the like of which I had never experienced before, I ended up half unconscious and in tears, from humiliation as much as from pain, my father was crying too, from shame, and he was reciting phrases of conjuration, God protect us from evil, God help us, There is no God but God, and so on, adding hits and belt lashes, while my mother moaned in a corner, she cried, too, and looked at me as if I were the devil incarnate, and when my father was exhausted, when he couldn't hit me anymore, there was a great silence, an immense silence, they both stared at me. I was a stranger, I felt that these looks propelled me outward, I was humiliated and terrorized, my father's eyes were full of hatred, I left at a run. I slammed the door behind me, I could hear Meryem crying from the landing and shouting through the door, the sound of slaps, insults, bitch, whore, I ran down the stairs. Once outside I realized I was bleeding from my nose, that I was in my shirtsleeves, that I had only twenty dirhams in my pocket and nowhere to go. It was the beginning of summer, fortunately, the evening was warm, the air salty. I sat down on the ground against a eucalyptus tree, I held my head in my hands and I bawled like a baby, until night fell and there was the call to prayer. I got up, I was afraid; I knew I wouldn't go back home, that I could never go back, it was impossible. What was I going to do? I went to the neighborhood mosque, to see if I could catch Bassam as he came out. He saw me, opened his eyes wide, I motioned for him to give his father the slip and follow me. Shit, have you looked at your face? What happened? My old man caught me with Meryem, I said, and the mere memory of that instant made me clench my teeth, tears of rage filled my eyes. The shame, the terrible shame of being discovered naked, our bodies exposed, the burning shame that paralyzes me even today—shit, Bassam hissed, what a beating you must've got, yep, I said, yep, without going into detail. And what're you going to do now? I have no idea. But I can't go back home. Where'll you sleep, asked Bassam. No idea. You have any money? Twenty dirhams and a book, that's it. He passed me a few coins that were in his pockets. I have to go. We'll see each other tomorrow? As usual? I said okay, and he left. I walked around the city, a little lost. I walked up Pasteur Avenue, then down to the edge of the sea by the steep little streets; there were red lights in the hostess bars, seedy-looking guys sitting in front of the windows. On the promenade, couples were strolling calmly, arm in arm, it made me think of Meryem. I went back to the harbor and climbed up to the Tombs; I sat down facing the Strait, there were beautiful lights in Spain; I pictured people dancing on the beaches, freedom, women, cars; what the hell was I going to do, without a roof, without any money? Beg? Work? I had to go home. The thought immediately destroyed me. Impossible. I stretched out and looked at the stars for a long time. I slept until the cold of dawn forced me to get up and walk around to warm myself up. I hurt everywhere, from the blows, but also from the ache of sleeping all night on the rock. If I had known what was to come, I would've gone meekly back home,

I would have begged my father for forgiveness. If I hadn't been so proud, that's what I should have done, I would have avoided many more humiliations and wounds, perhaps I'd have become a grocer myself, perhaps I'd have married Meryem, perhaps this very instant I'd be in Tangier, dining in a fancy restaurant by the sea or giving my kids a thrashing, a whole litter of bawling, starving pups.

I was hungry, I wolfed down some rotten fruit the market vendors left for beggars, I had to fight for gnawed-on apples, then for moldy oranges, fight off all sorts of nutcases, one-legged men, retards, a horde of half-starved wretches who prowled around the market like me; I was cold, I spent nights soaking wet in the fall, when storms beat down on the city, chasing away beggars under the arcades, in the far corners of the Medina, in buildings under construction where you had to bribe the guard to let you stay dry; in winter I left for the south, finding nothing there but cops who just roughed me up in a crumbling station in Casablanca to encourage me to return home to my parents; I found a truck headed for Tangier, a nice guy who slipped me half his sandwich and a doughnut because I refused to play the girl for him, and when I went to see Bassam, when I dared set foot again in the neighborhood, I had lost God knows how many pounds, my clothes were in rags, I hadn't read a book in months and I had just turned eighteen. Not much chance I'd be recognized. I was exhausted, shivering. I was half clean, I washed in mosque courtyards, beneath the disapproving eye of the custodians and Imams, then I was forced to pretend to pray to warm up a little on the comfortable rugs, I took a Koran into a corner and slept sitting up, the volume on my knees, with an inspired air, until a real believer would get annoyed at seeing me snoring over the Holy Text and would throw me out, with a kick in the ass and sometimes ten dirhams so I'd go hang myself somewhere else. I wanted to see Bassam so he would go visit my parents, tell them I was sorry, that I had suffered greatly, and that I wanted to come home. I remember, I thought often of my mother. Of Meryem, too. During the hardest times, the horrible times when I had to humiliate myself in front of a parking lot guard or a policeman, when the atrocious stench of my shame escaped from the folds of their clothes, I would close my eyes and think of the perfume of Meryem's skin, of those few hours with her. I was stunned by the speed at which the world could change.

You become the human equivalent of a pigeon or a seagull. People see us without seeing us, sometimes they give us a few kicks so we'll disappear, and few, very few, imagine on what railing, on what balcony we sleep at night. I wonder what I thought of, at the time. How I held on. Why I didn't simply go back after two days to my father's house and collapse on the living room sofa; why I didn't go to the town hall or God knows where to ask for help, maybe because there is in youth an infinite force, a power that makes everything slip by, that makes nothing really reach us. At least in the beginning. But then, after ten months of being on the run, three hundred days of shame, I couldn't bear any more. I had paid my dues, maybe. And no poems came to me, no philosophical considerations about existence, no sincere repentance, just a mute hatred and a deeper mistrust of all that was human.

Before I went to see Bassam, I remember, I took a swim. It was a fine spring morning, I had slept in a crevice at the bottom of the cliff, toward Cape Spartel, a few miles away from the center of Tangier, after downing a can of tuna and a heel of bread, sooty from a fire made from a wooden crate and some newspapers. I had wrapped myself up in the long wool coat stolen from a market that had accompanied me all winter, and I had dozed off, lulled by the surf. In the morning the Mediterranean was calm, calm and dark blue, the rising sun gently caressed the sandy places between the rocks. I was freezing, but I desired this beauty, this liquid rest too much. The water was terribly cold. I warmed up a little by swimming fast to the north, a few hundred feet maybe, the current was strong, I had to struggle to get back to the coast. I collapsed on a stretch of sand, in the sun; there was no wind, just the warm caress of the silica, I fell asleep again, exhausted and almost happy. When I woke up two or three hours later, the April sun was beating down and I was starving. I ate the rest of the bread from the day before, drank a lot of water; I folded the coat up in my bag, put my clothes into some sort of order—my shirt was torn in the armpit, and it had grease spots on the back; my pants were completely threadbare at the cuffs; you could no longer make out the stripes on my grey jacket, which I got from an Islamic solidarity center for the poor. I felt in shape, despite everything. Bassam would slip me a clean shirt and a pair of pants. I hadn't seen him since the end of December, since I left for Casa; he had helped me as much as he'd been able, by giving me a little money, some food, and even, once, news of Meryem: her mother had sent her to live at her sister's house in the remote depths of the Rif. Might as well be in prison. Bassam was still making castles in the sky about going to Spain, and the last time we'd seen each other, still in the same place, facing the Strait, facing the unattainable Tarifa, he had said to me Don't worry. Go to Casa and when you come back I'll have found a way to get us to the other side. I still didn't see what we were supposed to do in Spain without papers and without money, aside from begging, ending up getting arrested, and deported, but still, it was a nice dream.

I went to his house around noon; I knew his father would be at work. Rediscovering the neighborhood streets stung my heart. I walked very quickly, taking care not to pass by the family grocery store, I reached Bassam's building, ran up the steps and knocked on his door like a madman, as if I were being followed. He was there. He recognized me right away, which reassured me about my looks. He had me come in. He sniffed me and told me I didn't stink too badly, for a bum. That made me laugh. That might be true, but

I'd still like to take a shower and eat a little, I said. I felt as if I had finally arrived somewhere. He handed me some clean clothes, I stayed maybe an hour in the bathroom. I'd never have thought that having as much water as you wanted could be a heavenly luxury. In the meantime he had prepared breakfast for me, eggs, bread, cheese. He was smiling the whole time, with a conspiratorial air. He barely asked me what I'd been up to these last three months, just: So, how was Casa?—without insisting. He was excited, he kept getting up and sitting down, still with a smile on his lips. Come on, out with it, I ended up saying. He made a face as if he'd been caught stealing a chicken. What do you mean—out with it? Why are you saying that? Fine, okay, I'll tell you, I think I found something for you, a place where you can lay low, where they'll take care of you. He resumed his smiling, conspiratorial air. What kind of place is it, an asylum? I thought that behind it all was a plan for a crazy adventure, one of those Bassam affairs. No no, my friend, not an asylum, not even a hospital, even better: a mosque.

What the hell do you want me to do in a mosque, I asked.

It's not a place like the others, Bassam replied, you'll see, the people are different.

It was true, they were different. Bearded, dressed in immaculate dark suits. Aside from that, they really were quite nice and generous, those Islamists. Sheikh Nureddin (he called himself Sheikh, but he couldn't have been over forty) asked me to tell him my story, after Bassam introduced me: This is the one I spoke to you about, Sheikh, he's a real believer, but he's in need. Then God will provide, replied the other. The mosque wasn't really a mosque, it was the ground floor of an apartment building, with rugs on the floor and a brass plaque on the door that read "Muslim Group for the Propagation of Koranic Thought." Bassam looked very proud for bringing them a stray lamb. I recounted everything down the smallest detail, almost. Sheikh Nureddin listened to me attentively, looking me straight in the eyes, without looking surprised, as if he already knew the whole story. When I finished he sat silent for a bit, still staring at me, and asked: Are you a believer? I managed to reply yes, without seeming to hesitate. You haven't sinned, my young friend. You let yourself get caught in that girl's trap. She is the one responsible, and your father was not fair. You were weak, that's true, but it's your youth that spoke. Your father is the guilty one, he should have better supervised the women of his family, should have enjoined decency on them. If your cousin had been decent, none of that would have happened. Bassam interrupted him: Sheikh, his father is proclaiming to the whole neighborhood that he no longer has a son, that he disinherited him.

Nureddin smiled sadly. These things might come right with time. The important thing is you now. Bassam tells me you are pious, serious, a good worker and that you like books, is that right? Yes sir. Well, I mean for the books, I mumbled.

In five minutes I was hired as a bookseller for the Group for the Propagation of Koranic Thought; they offered me a tiny room that looked out onto the back and a salary. Not a huge amount, but still a little pocket money. I couldn't get over it. I thanked Sheikh Nureddin effusively, all the while expecting some unforeseen thing to make the whole affair fall through. But it didn't. A real miracle. They gave me some dirhams in advance, to buy some clothes and shoes; Bassam went with me. He was very proud and smiled the whole time. I told you, he said, I told you I'd find you a solution. You see that going to the mosque pays in the end, he said.

He had met the Group of Thought at Friday prayers, with his father. After seeing them for a while, they had gotten acquainted, and there you have it. They're the right kind of people, said Bassam. They come from Arabia and they're loaded.

We crisscrossed the center of town like nabobs to buy me three shirts, two pairs of pants, some boxer shorts, and some black shoes slightly narrowed at the tips, slightly pointed, very cool. I also bought a comb, some hair gel, some shoe polish, and once again

I was penniless, mostly, but happy, and Bassam as well, for me. He was so pleased that I had gotten myself back on my feet, it made me happy to see him. That warmed my heart at least as much as the shiny shoes. I hugged him and ruffled his frizzy hair. Now we'll go change and afterward we'll walk around, I said. We'll chat up some girls, hit on a couple pretty tourists and show them around Allah's paradise. And maybe they'll even buy us a few beers afterward in thanks. Bassam muttered something, then, yes yes, good idea, why not. He knew very well: barring a second miracle on the same day, we'd never come across two welcoming miniskirts, but he played the game. When I went back to the Propagation of Koranic Thought to don my new threads, it was crowded; it was time for afternoon prayers and people were there in force. I made four prostrations behind Sheikh Nureddin; the time seemed very long to me.

IT was just that I lacked the habit. Over the course of the two years that followed, I had all the time in the world to get used to it. My work at the Thought was the quietest sort, which left a lot of spare time for study and prayer. Being a bookseller comprised receiving boxes of books, opening them up, removing the plastic wrap, putting them in stacks on the shelves and, once a week, on Fridays, setting up a table at the mosque's exit to sell them. At least, "selling" them is a big word. Most of them (small paperback booklets, a little like cheap textbooks) cost 4.90 dirhams. The hellish thing was you had to have cashboxes of coins to make change, almost as many cashboxes as booklets. At that price we could give them away, I said to the Sheikh. No no, impossible, people have to be aware that this paper has value, otherwise they'll throw them out or use them to light barbecues. So then maybe we could sell them at five dirhams, that would help with the change. Too expensive, the Sheikh replied. It has to be accessible to everyone.

These manuals were enormously successful. Our bestseller: *Sexuality in Islam*, I sold hundreds, no doubt because everyone thought there'd be sex in it, advice on positions, or weighty religious arguments so that women would allow certain practices, but not at all, the act was called "coitus," "lovemaking," or "the encounter" and the whole thing was an annotated compilation of phrases of great medieval lawyers that wasn't the least exciting—a rip-off, in my opinion, even at five dirhams. The people who bought the manual were 99% male. Our bestselling book for women was *Heroines of Islam*, a rather simple and effective pamphlet on the contemporary world, the injustice of the times, and how the only thing that could save the world was if women returned to religion; the pamphlet drew from the examples of the great women of Islam, especially Khadija, Fatima, and Zaynab.

The other part of our catalogue was more expensive, 9.90 per book. These were bound books, usually in several volumes, heavy as a dead donkey. The collection was entitled *The Heritage of Islam* and was comprised of re-editions of works by classical authors: lives of the Prophet, commentaries on the Koran, works of rhetoric, theology, grammar. Since these mammoths had beautiful imitation-leather bindings in colored calligraphy, they were used mostly to decorate the neighborhood's living and dining rooms. It should be said that the Arabic of a thousand years ago is not the easiest thing in the world to read. We also sold CDs of recordings of the Koran, and even a DVD of a Koranic encyclopedia that was pretty interesting—if only because you didn't have to lug around the fifty volumes of various commentaries that it contained. The bookseller's dream, in fact.

The Thought was open all day, and my bookstore as well, but there weren't many customers. Some came by sometimes to buy one of the books that I wasn't authorized to put out on the tables. I asked Sheikh Nureddin if they were forbidden by censorship, and he told me of course not, they're just texts that require a greater knowledge, which could be interpreted the wrong way. Among them were *Islam Against the Zionist Plot* and pamphlets by Sayyid Qutb.

One of my tasks (the most pleasant one, in fact) consisted of looking after the association's website and Facebook page, and of announcing activities (not many), which allowed me to have access to the Internet all day long. I took my work seriously. Sheikh Nureddin was pleasant, cultivated, sympathetic. He told me that he had studied theory in Saudi Arabia and practice in Pakistan. He recommended readings to me. When I got tired of the porn on the web (a little sin never did anyone any harm) I would spend hours reading, comfortably stretched out on the rug; little by little I got used to Classical Arabic, which is a sublime, powerful, captivating language of extraordinary richness. I would spend hours discovering the beauties of the Koran through the great commentators; the simple complexity of the text astounded me. It was an ocean. An ocean of lights. I liked to picture the Prophet in his cave, wrapped in his coat, or surrounded by his companions, on his way to battle. Thinking that I was reproducing their gestures, repeating the phrases they themselves had chanted helped me put up with the prayers, which were still an interminable chore.

I felt as if I were making amends, as if I were undoing the stains of months of vagabonding. I could even imagine meeting my father or mother without shame. That thought revolved often in my head, Fridays as I stood behind my table; I said to myself that a day would come when I would meet them, it was inevitable. I knew that they refused to even mention my name in public; I had this disconcerted feeling that Bassam was hiding something from me, he avoided talking to me about my family. When I questioned him he'd reply: don't worry don't worry, they'll get over it, and would change the subject. I missed my mother.

Evenings, I'd go out for a walk with Bassam. We spent much less time than before contemplating the Spanish coast and much more time staring at girls' asses in the street. Tangier had the advantage of being big enough so that we could feel free outside our suburb; sometimes we'd treat ourselves to a couple beers in a discreet bar; I had to negotiate for hours until Bassam agreed, he'd hesitate till the last second, but the prospect of mingling with foreign girls ended up deciding it. Once in the joint, he would vacillate for another five minutes between a Coke or a beer, but he always ended up taking the alcohol, before getting angry with himself for hours afterward and swallowing a kilo of mints to mask the smell. Not far from the bar there was a beautiful, completely renovated French bookstore where I liked to hang out, without ever buying anything since the books were much too expensive for me. But at least I could eye the female bookseller a little, after all we were colleagues. I never dared say a word to her. In any case, she wore a wedding ring and was much older than me.

Afterwards, invariably, I'd walk Bassam back to his place, then go back to my tiny room at the Propagation of Thought, pick up a thriller and read for an hour or two before falling asleep. The neighborhood bookseller had an inexhaustible stock in the back of his shop, I don't know where he got them from: Fleuve Noir editions (the cheapest), Masque editions, Série Noire editions (my favorite), and other obscure collections from the 1960s and '70s. All these titles on the metal shelves composed an immense, incomprehensible, mad poem: *The Dining Room of the Ready-to-Bleed / The Carnival of the Lost / Pearls to Swine / Mardi gris / Sleep of Hot Lead*, I never knew which to choose, even though I had a preference for the ones that took place in the United States rather than in France— their bourbon seemed more real, their cars bigger and their cities wilder. The bookseller must not have been raking it in; in fact, aside from his stock of thrillers that I must have been the only fan of, he sold old textbooks, outdated newspapers, decrepit Spanish journals, and a few soft-porn Egyptian novels. He was a pretty funny guy who spent his time tippling in secret in the back of his shop, a freethinker with Nasserian leanings, a fixture in the neighborhood. He often told me that barely twenty years ago the surrounding hills were empty, just two or three houses here and there, and that from where we were to the airport it was all countryside. Me, I'm a real Tangierian, he'd say.

After reading, four or five hours of sleep until dawn prayers: Sheikh Nureddin came, and with him a large part of the Group (except Bassam, who said he prayed at home, which I had a hard time believing). When they left I would go back to sleep until eight or nine, then breakfast, and at 9:30 sharp I'd open the bookstore. Often the Sheikh would return around noon, we'd talk for a little, he'd ask me to add this or that to the webpage, would check the state of the stock, usually ordering the books that were running out himself (one box of *Sexuality*, one of *Heroines*, the complete works of Ibn Taymiyyah in twenty volumes), and would leave again on his own business. The books usually took a month to reach us from Saudi Arabia, so you had to plan ahead. Then I had peace all afternoon. I stayed there quietly studying, as Sheikh Nureddin said. Paradise. Room, board, and education. After evening prayers Bassam would come by for me, and we'd go out on the town, and so on. A healthy routine.

I had only one fear, or one desire—meeting my family; they knew where I was, I knew where they were; I saw my mother, once, on the sidewalk across the street—I took cover, my back turned, my heart pounding. I was ashamed. So were they, even if I still didn't know to what extent, or why. I'd have liked to see my little sister, she must have changed a lot, grown a lot. I tried not to think about it. I'm still trying. I wonder what they know about me, today. There are always rumors, gossip that reaches home; they must surely cover their ears.

Often, I thought of Meryem—I told myself I could have found the courage to take a bus to the village to go see her secretly. I wrote to her, and these letters always ended up in the trash, out of cowardliness mostly. Meryem already belonged to the realm of dreams, to the rustling body of memory.

The year passed quickly, and when the demonstrations began in Tunisia I'd already been at the Thought over a year. My tranquility was a little upset by these events, I have to say. Sheikh Nureddin and the whole Group were like madmen. They spent all their time in front of the TV. They prayed all day for their Tunisian brothers. Afterward they started up collections for the Egyptian brothers.

Then when the list extended to the Libyan and Yemeni brothers, they began organizing actions "for our oppressed Arab brothers."

When the uprising started in Morocco on February 20th, they couldn't stand still anymore. They took turns in sit-ins, demonstrations. My bookstore had become campaign headquarters: the group saw the Arab revolts as the long-awaited green tide. Finally, genuine Muslim countries would stretch from the Atlantic Ocean to the Persian Gulf, they dreamed about them at night. According to what Sheikh Nureddin told me, the idea was to win as many free, democratic elections as possible in order to take power and then, from within, by the conjoined forces of legislature and the street, to Islamize the constitutions and the laws. Their political projects didn't matter much to me, but the incessant and noisy activism turned my life completely upside-down. They stopped letting me have constant access to the Internet (they needed it all the time), and I could no longer read quietly. There was always some activity, some demonstration to take part in, some broadcast to watch on TV. So I would spend more and more time downtown. I'd go read a detective novel over a cup of tea on the Place de France all afternoon. Sheikh Nureddin blamed me a little for my absences; he'd look at me reprovingly and say, you could take a more active part in our struggle.

They took some blows. The cops had received orders to disperse the tail end of demonstrations not with tear gas or rubber bullets, but in the old style, by hand and with clubs, and they did pretty well for themselves: you'd see blue uniforms swarming over the bearded men. Since young people had to be in the forefront of the Movement, Bassam had been the first to sustain some injuries near the Place des Nations, late one night, and to return a hero, his chest streaked with bruises, a bandage on his nose, his eyes purple, still chanting "For God, Nation, and Liberation." The model for all this was Egypt. That was the only thing on their lips, Cairo, Liberation Square. Egypt is an advanced society, said Sheikh Nureddin, the Brothers will carry the day. He almost cried with emotion. I remember, when we heard a French specialist on Arabic society on the TV saying there are no Muslim Brothers on Tahrir Square, Sheikh Nureddin was incredibly upset at first. Lies, he said. May God destroy these miscreants. What bastards these Frenchmen are, they respect nothing, not even the truth. Ready to do anything to keep their power, those assholes. And then he got hold of himself, saying after all it's not bad to stay in the shadows, it gave an even more legitimate feeling to the uprising. What's more, the news from Egypt was excellent: the Brothers were confident of emerging the great victors in the free elections when they took place, and of forming a government. The first one since the Algerian swindle twenty years before.

It was chaos in Tangier for at least a week, but Sheikh Nureddin could clearly see that it wasn't taking the Tunisian or Egyptian path, that the Palace was more clever or more legitimate (after all, isn't the King the Commander of the Faithful?) and that they'd have to form an alliance with a party already in place if the reform of the Constitution were to take place.

A few weeks later, the King granted amnesty to an entire contingent of political prisoners, among them members of the Group who had been languishing in government jails since the massive roundups after the attacks on Casablanca years before. The Sheikh was euphoric. He welcomed these companions as if he were Joseph himself returning from Egypt and finding his brothers again. The Propagation of Koranic Thought became a hive of bearded men.

I was impatient for all this agitation to be over so I could resume my reading and regain my tranquility. The Group was like a pack of caged animals—they kept pacing in circles, waiting for night and the time for action. They had decided to take advantage of the disorder, the demonstrations and the cops to undertake a "neighborhood cleanup" as they called it. Bassam, anxious to avenge his broken nose on the first person to come along, was on the prowl for fights. They went out in bands of a dozen each, armed with cudgels and pickax handles after a belligerent, eloquent sermon by Sheikh Nureddin, which talked of the campaigns of the Prophet, the Battle of Badr, the Battle of the Trench, the fight against the Jewish tribe of the Banu Qaynuqa; about Hamza the hero, the glory of the martyrs in Paradise, and about the beauty, the great beauty of dying in battle. Then, very heated after this theoretical warm-up, they would move out into the night almost at a run, with Bassam's nerves and cudgel in the lead. I heard nothing about the result of their first engagements, except that they would come back happy, out of breath, with no wounded or martyrs. Sheikh Nureddin thought that for safety reasons it was important he not take part in this holy war himself, but would look at me in surprise when I said I preferred to keep him company at the Center. After two nights of fights without any losses, he wanted to lead his troops to victory himself; I was finally prepared to stay alone and peaceful in front of the computer, but one glance from Sheikh Nureddin was enough to convince me that I'd better join them; I was given a club which I hid, like everyone else, under my caftan.

The expedition could have been amusing; our band, hoods on their heads, beards, long coats, haunting the dark sidewalks, wouldn't have looked out of place in an Egyptian comedy.

I hadn't been warned of the goals; the sermon had mentioned fighting against impiety, sin, and pornography, but nothing more precise. The night was cold and damp. There were six of us, we walked in rows, it began to rain a little, which took away whatever charm the expedition had. The struggle against drunkenness and materialism was not a pleasure outing.

When I saw that we were turning left two hundred meters from the Koranic Thought, I began to get a little worried; there was one possible target, at the end of the avenue, which I hoped was not ours. But it was. It couldn't be anything else. Everyone seemed to know where we were going but me; Bassam in the lead, the group advanced unhesitatingly. We reached the bookseller's shop; he had closed the display window because of the rain, but light seeped through the door, despite the late hour; I imagined he was in the process of knocking back one or two bottles of cheap wine while leafing through old Spanish or French magazines of naked girls. And he was in the back of his store, with a bottle of red; he raised his head from his *Playboy*, looking furious, recognized me, and smiled timidly, disconcerted. Sheikh Nureddin's eyes were full of scorn, he uttered a brief sermon in classical Arabic, you are the shame of the neighborhood, our neighborhood is respectable, respect God and our neighborhood, Infidel, we are the punishment of Infidels, the ruin of miscreants, leave our neighborhood immediately, respect God, our wives, and our children, the bookseller rolled his wild eyes; they darted very quickly from right to left, rested on Bassam, on me, and returned to the Sheikh reeling off his anathema. He still had his glass in his hand, and his incredulous look, wondering if I was playing a bad joke on him or something of the kind. Then the Sheikh shouted The wrath of God be upon you!, and turned to me, Bassam opened his coat to take out his pickaxe handle and looked at me too. All three of them stared at me, the bookseller said in a toneless voice, what kind of joke is this?, Bassam looked as if he were begging me, as in, come on, for God's sake, what are you waiting for, shit, go on, go on, the Sheikh was sizing me up, I opened the panel of my coat, took out my club, the bookseller looked terrified, surprised and terrified, he got up all of a sudden from his chair, skirted around the desk on my side, very quickly, as if to flee, I didn't want to hurt him, he tried to seize hold of my club, he began insulting us, bastards, dogs, assholes, I fuck your mothers, then Bassam hit him hard, on the shoulder, it made a dull sound, he shouted in pain, collapsed while clutching my coat and my legs, Bassam pummeled his ribs with his cudgel, very spiritedly, the bookseller shouted again, swore profusely, Bassam started up again on his thigh, aiming for the bone, the man began groaning. Bassam was smiling, brandishing his stick. I wondered for an instant if he was going to smash my face in as well. Sheikh Nureddin leaned over the bookseller, who was on the ground groaning, said to him I hope you have understood, then gave him a kick that made him cry out even louder. Tears were running down the poor guy's face, I couldn't look any more, I put away my weapon and went out. Bassam followed me, then the Sheikh; I heard him spitting on his victim before leaving. I ran back to the center, the others behind me. When we reached the Group for the Propagation of Koranic Thought, I threw my axe handle on the rug and locked myself up in my room. I was trembling with hatred, I could have cut Sheikh Nureddin and Bassam into pieces. Me, too. I could have cut myself up into pieces. Sitting on my bed I wondered what to do. I didn't want to stay there. I was full of superhuman energy, an incredibly powerful anger. I took all the money I had and left. The Group was at prayers again, I crossed the large room without trying to be discreet, Bassam raised his head from his prostrations to motion to me, I went out and slammed the door.

I had 200 dirhams in my pocket, enough to buy myself a few drinks. I thought about giving the money to the bookseller in restitution, but I was too ashamed to go back there. Plus he was probably in the hospital. I hoped Bassam hadn't broken anything, I should have turned my cudgel on Sheik Nureddin, it would have done him good, getting a few thumps. Bassam's look had frightened me. It was a test. And now what the hell was I going to do, leave the Group, go back to the street, look for work? I'd see tomorrow. For now, I'd forget my misery.

I crossed Tangier until I reached the little bar on Avenue Pasteur; I went in, greeted everyone like the regular I wasn't, sat down at a table, ordered first one bottle, then another, and things began to look up. Why did life treat me this way? Maybe I'd been cursed because I had dishonored my father, who knows. Maybe God himself was angry at me, pushing me toward a greater despair at every step? What do I know. At least the beer was good. Maybe I should have thrown myself into prayer, instead of alcohol, but what the hell.

There were just four Moroccans in suits in the joint, talking and drinking whiskey, no lonely female tourists; I began to get a little drunk, and felt like crying. Meryem came to mind, she was sleeping at that hour no doubt, over there in the Rif. Maybe she was dreaming of me, who knows.

The TV was showing the demonstrations in Egypt, in Tunisia, in Yemen, the uprising in Libya. It isn't over yet, I thought. Arab Spring my ass, it'll end with beatings, stuck between God and a hard place.

I regretted not having brought a book with me, it would have taken my mind off things.

When the guy came into the bar, I was still busy watching TV; I barely saw him. It was he who approached me. He walked over, leaned on my table, stared at me with a mean smile. Little eyes, brown moustache going grey. I immediately turned to him.

"Well, if it isn't my little fag," he said.

I turned to the bartender with an offended air, as in customers can't be insulted like that, my heart was pounding, my cheeks were on fire. The bartender was observing us with a surprised look.

"You remember me?"

Impossible to forget that face, the dim light and the smell of piss in the back of the parking lot.

My knees began to shake, I wanted him to disappear, as if by magic, and the shame and memory to vanish along with him.

I'd have happily smashed in his face with an axe handle.

He left in a great burst of obnoxious laughter, he was drunk, his sewer breath splattered me with a wave of rottenness and memories, I almost fell backward and the loss of balance set me moving off my bar stool, I fled in silence like a coward, shot out of the bar without looking back, couldn't keep from hearing phrases like, Don't go so fast, little boy, with a few obscenities that overwhelmed me with impotent rage, like when you take punches without being able to return them.

Outside a freezing wind from the ocean was sweeping down the avenue, the city was deserted; even in front of the Cannons there were hardly any people, a few tourists returning to their fashionable hotels. I ran down the street toward the Grand Zoco, mechanically made the rounds of the square, bought a pack of cigarettes without

thinking about it, two guys I had already seen were warming themselves around a brazier, I traded them one of my remaining bills
for a stub of kif, went to smoke it discreetly on a bench set a little
apart. Everything became quiet. The drug calmed me down. The
city was covered with a calm, dark veil, I was far away all of a sudden, behind a wall between my body and the world, I thought again
about the bookseller, about the parking lot guard, about Sheikh
Nureddin, about Bassam, as if they were completely foreign to me,
as if all that had no importance whatsoever. Tangier was a black
dead end, a corridor blocked by the sea; the Strait of Gibraltar a
fissure, an abyss that barred our dreams; the North was a mirage. I
saw myself lost once again, and the only firm ground under my feet
and behind me was the expanse of Africa down to the Cape on one
side, and to my east all those countries in flames, Algeria, Tunisia,
Libya, Egypt, Palestine, Syria. I rolled myself another well-loaded
joint thinking that this hash came from the Rif, that Meryem might
have seen the plants growing from her windows, that she herself
might have pressed the stuff on large drying racks, before shaping
the paste darkened by oxidation, wrapping it in a transparent film;
she'd keep the crumbs in her pocket that she scraped off the plastic
of her gloves, to eat them in solitude, and laugh all alone or fall
asleep, dream, maybe, and remember the few hours we had spent
together, how I had undressed her almost without wanting to, shyly,
after she had kissed me on the mouth holding my hand, and there
was a simple, beautiful tenderness in these memories resurrected by
the hash, I gleaned a little joy from them. The dance of the lights
of Tangier accelerated my thoughts, I needed a plan, no question
this time of ditching everything without a cent, of going back to
the mud and the humiliation. I thought again of my parents, my
mother especially, of my little brothers, what could they know, what
did they think of me, the Sura of Joseph came to mind, *My father,
I saw eleven stars prostrate before me, and the sun and the moon*, I had
forgotten that I knew these verses by heart, Joseph sold for less than

nothing to a merchant from Egypt, Joseph whom God instructed in the interpretation of dreams, Joseph whom Zuleykha tempted. The lights from the ferries streaked across the Strait, a maritime caravan. Maybe I could find work in the new port in Tangier Med or in the Free Zone, then after a while manage to emigrate, after all it was Bassam who was right, you had to leave, you had to leave, the harbors burn our hearts. Solitude became a mass of fog, a thick cloud, of Evil or fear; I was slightly nauseous. I began to shiver from cold on my bench and all of a sudden I was hungry, very hungry.

After devouring a sandwich in two mouthfuls on the way, I went back to my room at the Propagation; everything was deserted, silent, a silence that beat at my eardrums; I fell asleep like a rock.

THE next morning my mouth tasted like an ashtray and my eyes were red, but otherwise I was in pretty good shape. I shelved a few books, breakfasted, read the commentary on the Sura of Joseph in the *Kashshaaf* as the sun spread over the rugs. At times, the faces from the day before came back to me, the bookseller in tears, the moustache on the parking lot bastard, like an upwelling of sewage that I kept trying to check by concentrating on my reading. I tried to convince myself that what was done was done. What's done is done. The future is what counts.

Sheikh Nureddin reappeared in the early afternoon, dressed in civilian clothes, that is in a dark blue, rather elegant suit. He greeted me politely, I might even say warmly. He asked me if I had prepared the books (it was Thursday) and I answered yes. He said perfect. Tonight we have a meeting in town, I'll be back tomorrow morning. And he went out. No remark, no allusion to the previous day's punitive excursion.

Finally I found solitude. I looked at a few Internet sites, sent some Facebook messages to girls I didn't know, all French, like throwing bottles into the sea. *I am a young Moroccan from Tangier, I'm looking for your friendship to share my passion: books.*

I'll show you ladies how cultivated I am, I thought, hence the note about the books, slightly exaggerated perhaps, but sober and precise. I should add that I chose girls who definitely were pretty, but who wore glasses and who came from cities I knew nothing about, but imagined were cold, boring, and thus propitious for reading. (It goes without saying that I never received a reply; in their defense, I have to admit that if these girls ever glanced at my profile, which I had taken care to make public, they would have seen among my friends not only Bassam's convict's face, but also the Group for the Propagation of Koranic Thought and Al-Jazeera, which, seen from Bourges or Troyes, had very little chance of inspiring tenderness.)

I napped a little, dreaming about the above-mentioned young women. Then I reread the beginning of *Total Chaos*, one of my favorite thrillers; I imagined that Tangier suddenly became Marseille, which wasn't very likely, as I snacked on a bag of chips; night fell gently; the smell of the sea was all around me.

I lay on the floor without a light until it was dark out.

BASSAM rushed in and almost trampled me.

"What are you doing in the dark? Were you sleeping?"

"Not really," I said.

He was overexcited, as usual. He kept pacing in circles like a puppy around its mother's basket.

"What's happened to you now?" I asked. "One more guy to beat up?"

"No, this time it's bigger than that."

"Is it the Prophet's sword?"

"Stop your blasphemies, you degenerate. It's time for revenge."

I thought for a minute that he was joking, but after I turned on the light I could see that his weasely eyes shone with a strange madness, in the center of his thick peasant's head.

"What kind of shit are you talking about?"

He fed me some vague paranoid theory according to which only an attack that would shock people's sensibilities would get things underway by precipitating the West, the population, and the Palace into confrontation. It was all Sheikh Nureddin, with hardly any Bassam. He had a tiny pea in place of a brain.

"You have a pea instead of a brain," I said.

What's more, I knew very well that, in truth, he couldn't care less about political Islam. After all, we had fallen into religion when we were little, we'd had enough of it.

"Drop these stories about an attack, come on, we'll go out. The Sheikh won't come back before tomorrow."

I saw Bassam stare at me as if I were the one who was completely crazy.

"I have to pray to purify myself."

I sighed. I wondered what Sheikh Nureddin had done to him, or what he had promised him. Houris in Paradise, maybe. Bassam had a weakness for stories about houris, who were always virgins you could fuck for eternity on the shores of Kawthar, the Lake of Abundance in the hereafter.

But I too had my houris.

"You know what, I met two great girls last night, two Spanish students. They're staying till tomorrow. We smoked a joint together, and I'm supposed to meet up with them soon."

"Stop joking around."

But his eyes had lit up.

That made a big impression, in his head.

"I don't believe you."

"That doesn't matter. I need you to come with me, to take care of the second one. I won't lie to you, she's not as pretty as the first, but she's still nice. Come on, do this for me."

"So, what're their names?"

That was it, I had him hooked.

"Yours is Inez and mine is Carmen."

I could have thought of something more original, but that had come out point-blank, without a second's hesitation.

"And how old are they?"

"I don't know, twenty-four, twenty-five," I said.

"Oh man, it sucks, but I promised the Sheikh I'd stay here and wait for his orders. And spend the night praying."

"We can stay for a little bit with them, and then you can come back and pray, what's the difference?"

I thought: if all of Sheikh Nureddin's recruits were as easy to manipulate as Bassam, the victory of Islam won't happen very soon.

He suddenly took on the relieved look of someone who'd made a difficult decision.

"Okay, but just for a little bit, alright? Afterward I'll come back."

"Whatever you want."

Now I'm committed, I thought. I'll be mincemeat when he finds out that the fat Inez and the beautiful Carmen stood us up.

No matter, I'll improvise.

And it will still be something that Sheikh Nureddin won't have, those few hours of prayer. A tiny victory.

Bassam combed some of my hair gel into his hair, breathed into his hand to check his breath; he was trembling with eagerness.

"Let's speak Spanish on the way, to practice a little," he said.

"*Con mucho gusto, hijo de puta,*" I replied.

And we were off; a warm light rain was beginning to fall.

THE shower didn't last, but the weather could provide me with an excuse for the absence of our imaginary friends; everyone knows that Spaniards never go out when it rains. We walked for half an hour to reach the center of town. Bassam kept bombarding me with questions in an Iberian mixed with French and Arabic, pretty incomprehensible but delightful; he wanted to know everything, precisely where I had met these young women, what we had said to each other, where they came from, etc. I improvised these details, hoping to remember them so I wouldn't betray myself later on— Valencia (Madrid or Seville seemed too obvious to me), students, on vacation between semesters, and so on. I wondered if Bassam was really tricked or if the game let him dream, like me. I talked about it so much I was almost disappointed myself not to find them at the meeting place, supposedly in a tearoom near the Place des Nations. I bought a cake for Bassam, who devoured it in a few minutes, nervousness no doubt. We looked sort of foolish, us two, in this pastry shop; all around guys were on dates with their fiancées, they all wore pretty, colorful veils, and were stuffing themselves with lemon tarts or rosewater milkshakes while their men, mustachioed, no doubt dreamed of groping their breasts, thinking it was a pretty good deal, a few sweets in return for a session of heavy petting afterward in the nice warmth of a car or on a sofa. I think I was a little jealous of these fellows just slightly older than us, they had acquired the right to slip their hands into the panties of their cousins in exchange for an official engagement and a little cash for rings and necklaces. As for us, we were waiting for our phantom Spanish girls, looking like out-of-town yokels slathered in hair gel.

Bassam was fidgeting next to the crumbs of his black forest cake, whose candied cherry sat prominently, abandoned, in the middle of the plate.

I pretended to get impatient too, what the hell are they up to, what the hell are they doing, five more minutes and I'll tell Bassam we should go drown our sorrows in beer somewhere—it was raining again.

It's well known, Spanish girls don't go out in the rain.

Suddenly I saw Bassam leap out of his chair; he craned his neck like a giraffe and gave me a few kicks under the table. I turned around; two young European girls had just come in; brunettes, with long hair worn down, bangs over their eyes, they wore harem pants, dozens of bracelets on their forearms, leather handbags and clogs made from the same material: Spaniards without a doubt, incredible. Actually no, it wasn't all that incredible, but it placed me in a delicate position.

"No, it's not them," I said to Bassam.

He looked at me disconcertedly, sighing.

The two girls must have entered the bakery for shelter from the rain.

Bassam was irritated, he began wondering if I hadn't been taking him for a ride; the fact that two Spanish girls came in as we were waiting for two other ones gave him the feeling that something wasn't right. Young Iberians strolling in pairs in Tangier in this season weren't as common as all that.

An idea came into his head:

"Go ask them if they maybe know Inez and Carmen."

I almost replied Who?, but remembered the names of my two ghosts just in time.

"Maybe they're in the same group."

He wore a challenging look on his face, a dangerous look; he was trying, above all, to test me, to find out whether or not I had lied to him.

I sighed; I could tell him I was too chicken, he wouldn't have understood. I saw him again the way he was the day before, cudgel in hand, beating the bookseller; I wondered what the hell I was doing there, in a tearoom with my pal the madman with the pickaxe.

"Okay. I'll go."

Bassam was literally licking his chops, his fat tongue slid over his upper lip to gather the last bits of chocolate shavings; he picked up the candied cherry and popped it into his mouth, I turned my eyes away before seeing if he chewed it.

"Okay. I'm going."

Never had I dared to approach a foreign girl directly; I had talked about it a lot, we'd talked about it a lot, Bassam and I, during those hours we spent looking at the Strait; we had lied a lot, dreamed a lot, rather. He was looking at me with his naïve, brotherly look, I remember having thought about my family, my family is Bassam and Meryem and no one else.

"Okay. I'm going."

I went over to the girls' table, I'm sure of that; I know I said something to them; I have no idea in what gibberish, in what babble I managed to make myself understood; I just know—I had all the time in the world to think it over later—that I looked so sincere, so little interested in them with my story of Carmen and Inez, I so hoped they knew this Carmen and this Inez, that they didn't suspect a thing, they answered me frankly, and it all happened in the most natural way in the world, and then they saw clearly, as they heard Bassam, as they saw Bassam's face, that it wasn't a trap but that there was indeed, in Tangier, a Carmen and an Inez, floating in the air like phantoms, and they were sorry for us, but it's raining, you know, they said, it's raining, and I laughed internally, I had a good laugh thinking that the rain, to which we never pay any attention, the rain can change a fate as easily as God himself, may Allah forgive me.

LOOKING at them carefully, they weren't all that alike, our two Spaniards; they came from Barcelona, their names were Judit and Elena, one was darker, the other rounder; both were students and were coming—a miracle—to spend a week in Morocco, on vacation, exactly as I had imagined, on their winter break, or spring break, I don't remember anymore, but for me it was the Arab Spring arriving, let them send us nice students, that's what all revolutions were for, girls you could picture wearing extraordinarily refined lingerie and who were inclined to show it, without annoying you with questions of family, religion, propriety, or good manners, rich girls who, if they took a liking to you, could allow you to cross the gleaming Straits with a single signature, introduce you to their parents absentmindedly, this is my friend, and the father would rightly think you looked suspiciously dark-skinned but would nod his head as if to say well, my girl, you're the one who decides, and we'd end up happy as God in Spain, home of black ham and the gateway to Europe.

Bassam's eyes said all this, all of it except for the pork, of course; he was looking at the girl in front of him like a passport with photos of naked girls instead of visas, so much so that Elena took her time arranging her T-shirt over her shoulders to hide her chest, a gesture that Bassam interpreted not as modesty but as provocation—she also pulled up her bra, annoyed by his looks, without realizing that her action called attention to these objects concealed from Bassam, that her slender hands on her own skin, grasping the strap, pushing aside the cloth to place her fingers on it, and then effecting a slight upward movement accentuated by the involuntary sound of elastic, was making sweat bead across Bassam's forehead, who couldn't tear his eyes away from her décolleté, those salt or rather pepper shakers blocked by the whiteness of the secret and yet so-visible cloth, and Bassam licked his index finger, unconsciously licked the tip of his index finger before crushing the crumbs of black forest cake scattered over his plate so they would stick better, without saying anything, devoted to his contemplation; Elena was trying to defuse this visual trap with language, she was gesticulating and articulating words to make the boy's gaze rise twenty-five degrees and pass from her chest to her face, as is the custom with people who don't know each other, but his desire, those breasts and that hand that got caught in the cloth inspired so much shame in Bassam that he was unable to look Elena in the eyes, since that would have been like looking his own thoughts, his being, and his whole education in the face, and all this kept him from both lifting his head and from truly enjoying, sneakily the way the Europeans do, the extraordinary spectacle, the excitation provoked by chastity when, despite herself, she contradicts herself, denies herself by unveiling, to the imagination of the one contemplating her, what she is trying to hide.

Bassam was just more sincere than I, simpler perhaps; it's a question of temperament, or of patience; I talked a lot with Judit; from time to time I even had a question for Elena; I was trying, I struggled, me too, to make out what she might be hiding under her blouse, discreetly, without insisting, I managed to keep my eyes meeting hers, but when she turned her head to address her friend or stare annoyedly at poor Bassam I indulged to my heart's content, while still sadly acknowledging that the girl whom fate had placed opposite me was not the better endowed of the two, no matter, since from the start Judit seemed closer, more open, and more smiling.

Very soon my three words of Spanish were not enough for conversation, so we switched to French; it was, I think, the first time I actually spoke with foreigners, and I had to search for my words. Fortunately Judit's Catalan accent made it easier for me to understand. Bassam said nothing, or almost nothing; from time to time he would mutter something in an impenetrable idiom; when he found out that these two angels fallen from the sky were studying Arabic in Barcelona, he began speaking in classical Arabic, just like one of Sheikh Nureddin's sermons, not counting the grammatical mistakes. He began asking Judit and Elena if they knew the Koran, if they had already read it in Arabic, and what they thought of Islam. He had to repeat each question two or three times, because he spoke quickly and articulated poorly, his eyes lowered.

The night before we were taking part in a punitive expedition, with our cudgels, and tonight we were converting two foreign girls to the religion of the Prophet. Sheikh Nureddin would be proud of us.

I found it hard to believe that they really were studying Arabic, that is, that they were interested in my country, my language, my culture; this was a second miracle, a strange miracle, which might make you wonder if it could be diabolic—how could two young women from Barcelona be so interested in this language that they wanted to learn it? Why? Judit said her Arabic was very bad, and that she was ashamed to speak it; Elena launched into it more easily, but her pronunciation was like Bassam's in Spanish or French: incomprehensible. I was a little ashamed; around us the guys who were watching their fiancées drink milkshakes and inhale deeply, eyes closed over their straws, weren't missing a scrap of our conversation. They were definitely thinking to themselves: look at those two idiots, they've unearthed a pair of tourists and they're talking to them about the Prophet, what assholes.

I suggested we go somewhere else. Bassam whispered something to me in Moroccan, very quickly, very softly.

It was nine o'clock, Elena suggested we get something to eat; I thought about the few dirhams that remained in my pocket, they could get me a sandwich, but not much else. Elena suggested we go to a little restaurant she had spotted in the old city. I must have made a funny face, Judit no doubt understood my embarrassment, she said we could go to a café instead, claiming she wasn't very hungry, the tea had cut her appetite. Her friend seemed a little annoyed, Judit said a few sentences in Catalan. Bassam whispered something in my ear, with a conspiratorial air, why not take them to the Propagation for an Arabic lesson? I had to keep from breaking out laughing; I could picture Sheikh Nureddin finding two female Infidels in his mosque and Bassam half naked, explaining the exploits of Hamza to Judit and Elena. Not today, not now, I said.

For my part, I could invite them to smoke a joint on the ramparts, I still had a little kif left from the night before, not very romantic—and what's more they might get scared, refuse, turn against us, especially Elena, who didn't seem very adventurous.

We stood in front of the bakery for a good five minutes.

Let's go to a café, I said.

Judit answered great, where should we go? Where are you taking us?

Bassam hovered round us, shifting from foot to foot.

Never had I thought so quickly.

And the idea came to me:

To Mehdi's. We'll go to Mehdi's.

Bassam opened his eyes wide, clapped his hands, of course, to Mehdi's, you're the best. He was overflowing with cheerfulness.

Judit smiled, a wide, dazzling smile, and I felt like a hero.

MEHDI'S was the only place in Tangier where two nineteen-year-old North African darkies like us could appear with foreigners without shocking anyone or bankrupting themselves, one of the only mixed places, neither poor nor rich, neither European nor Arabic, in town. During the day, especially in summer, it was a cafeteria where college and high school students guzzled sodas under trellises and creeping vines, and at night, in winter or when it was raining, there was a small room that was welcoming enough, with benches and cushions, where young guys, Moroccans and foreigners, drank tea. As I remember it, the decor was a mélange of touristy orientalism and utilitarian modernity, a few black and white photos in aluminum frames between the Berber rugs and fake ancient musical instruments. The place had no name, just the battered plastic sign of a brand of carbonated drink, everyone knew it by the owner's first name, Mehdi—a very tall guy, thin as a reed, not very pleasant, but discreet and not meddlesome—who spent most of his time sitting on his own terrace, a Parisian-type cap on his head, smoking Gitanes. Bassam and I had gone there like everyone else, and had even once or twice bought a Pepsi for Meryem there in the summer.

It was a bit far, we had to climb up the hill west of the old city, but it had stopped raining; Judit and Elena were happy to walk a little. I walked beside Judit and Bassam just behind with the other; I heard him speaking in Arabic and as soon as Elena said she didn't understand, which was most of the time, he would repeat exactly the same phrase, but louder; Elena would reiterate her incomprehension, apologetically; Bassam would raise his volume bit by bit, until he was bellowing like an ox, as if the louder he repeated the words, the more chance the poor Catalan had to understand him. He no doubt thought that a foreign language was a kind of nail you had to drive into the reticent ear, with big blows from a vocal hammer: just as he had taught miscreants respect for religion with a cudgel, but this time with a smile.

Life seemed beautiful to me, even with Bassam shouting in the night, and walking through these neighborhoods around the market I'd haunted a year and a half ago, this time accompanied by a girl, erased—at least for a little while—the whole series of ordeals and curses of the last two years and especially, so close and painful, the memories of last night, the faces of the bookseller and the loathsome parking lot attendant, by whom I would have liked not to be disturbed at that precise moment, I remember, I clenched my teeth, overcome by a real feeling of sickness, the power of shame, an echo almost as powerful as the previous night, the aftershock of an earthquake, so much so that my companion asked me, seeing my sudden shivering, if I was cold or if something was bothering me.

Judit was observant and attentive; we had spoken of Revolution, of the Arab Spring, of hope and democracy, and also of the crisis in Spain, where everything can't all be sweetness and light—no work, no money, beatings for anyone who had the gall to be "Indignant." Indignation (which I had read vaguely about online) seemed a sentiment that wasn't very revolutionary, the sentiment of a proper old lady and one that was sure to get you beat, seemed a little as if a Gandhi without plans or determination had sat down one fine day on the sidewalk because he was indignant about the British occupation, outraged. That would no doubt have made the English chuckle softly. The Tunisians had set themselves on fire, the Egyptians had gotten themselves shot at on Tahrir Square, and even if there were real chances of it ending up in the arms of Sheikh Nureddin and his friends, it still made you dream a little. I forget if we had mentioned, a few weeks later, the evacuation of the Indignant Ones who had occupied Catalonia Square in Barcelona, chased away like a flight of pigeons by a few vans of cops and their truncheons, supposedly to make room to celebrate Barça's championship win: that's what was indignant, that soccer would take precedence over politics, but apparently no one really protested, the population realizing, deep down inside, that the success of its team was, in itself, a beautiful celebration of democracy and of Catalonia, a Great Night that reduced Indignation to a negligible quantity.

Judit also asked me about Morocco, about Tangier, about the ripples of protest; my answers remained evasive. When she asked me if I was a student, I replied that I was working, I was a bookseller, but that I planned on going to school. The profession of bookseller seemed to inspire respect in her. After all it wasn't a lie. I was dying to ask one question, but kept it for later, out of shyness no doubt, or maybe more simply because I had heard Bassam asking it to Elena right behind me, in a slightly different form, however: Why had she chosen to learn Arabic, was it to convert to Islam? Fortunately, Elena hadn't understood Bassam's Koranic style, which could be translated as "do you want to come forward in Islam?," I almost broke out laughing, but it was better not to hurt his feelings; after all, he should have been at prayers, and because of me here he was flirting with a Spanish girl; he could be forgiven his prophetic Arabic.

Once we were at Mehdi's, sitting on cushions around four teas, with no one else there except Mehdi himself, immersed in his newspaper, Bassam withdrew a little from the conversation, mainly for linguistic reasons: he was tired of shouting himself hoarse and we were speaking French, or at least something not far from it. I was showing off a little, saying I had learned the language all by myself from detective novels; Judit seemed to admire that. I'd like to be able to do that in Arabic, she said. There must be Arabic thrillers,

Egyptian probably (I don't know why, I imagined Cairo more propitious for weird stories of the lower depths). I thought maybe I could buy her a few, which reminded me of the previous night's expedition to the bookseller's; I said to myself that if I had met these girls twenty-four hours earlier I'd have found the courage not to take part in that cowardly, useless expedition. But that was probably not true.

Bassam was visibly impatient, he was tapping his feet and no longer smiled. He wanted to go back and I could sense, despite all the desire I had, that this tea couldn't last forever; Elena yawned from time to time. Judit explained to me that they were planning on staying one more day in Tangier before going on to Marrakesh. One day, that wasn't much. There are lots of things to see here, I said, before immediately regretting my sentence; I'd have had a lot of trouble making up a list.

Fortunately, neither of them demanded to know what these marvels were, and ten minutes later, when it was Bassam's turn to yawn so wide it could've dislocated his jaw, and when he seemed to have been hypnotized by the swaying of Elena's breasts to the point of closing his eyelids, Judit gave the signal for departure. I didn't insist on holding them back, I even agreed it's time, yes, I have to work tomorrow morning. I explained that the next day I was setting up a table of books in front of the neighborhood mosque, I repeated the name of the mosque and of the neighborhood twice, à la Bassam, to be sure they had understood. Come see me if you're in the neighborhood, I added for more clarity. It wasn't very likely that they'd be "in the neighborhood" given the immense touristic interest of our suburb, and when all was said and done I wasn't so sure I really wanted them to see close up the contents of my piles of books, but you have to understand that it was terribly frustrating to let them go like that, without suggesting anything to them, even indirectly. Judit and Elena were staying in a little hotel in the old city, we walked them back; I'd have liked to tell them the history of Tangier, of the citadel, the little streets, but I was absolutely incapable.

There is always a certain embarrassment in saying goodbye, especially on a silent, deserted street, next to the trashcans of an inn whose tired neon lights, on the balcony, under the sign, from time to time electrified the thin lines of rain that were beginning to fall again. It's one moment too many, when you don't know if you should draw it out or, on the contrary, shorten it and disappear. You'll get wet, Judit said. Thank you for tonight, I whispered. Bassam held out his hand to Elena without lifting his eyes to her face; better stop there, the gleaming city and the Propagation of Koranic Thought was waiting for us; the stroboscopic light that fell intermittently on Judit's face froze her eyebrows, lips, and chin. See you soon then, maybe, I said. *Ilâ-l-liqâ*, she replied, those were the first Arabic words I heard from her mouth, *Ilâ-l-liqâ*, her pronunciation was so perfect, so Arabic, that, surprised, I mechanically responded *Ilâ-l-liqâ*, and we started on our way back.

I don't know if it was the rain that reawakened Bassam, but a hundred meters after we left the girls, he couldn't stop talking. Oh wow, oh wow, what a night, hey pal, did you see that, man, they're crazy about us, I should have pushed for giving them Arabic lessons, they definitely would have followed us, did you see how she was showing me her tits, still it's incredible, I thought your story about Carmen and Inez was a load of crap, what an amazing stroke of luck. Oh wow.

The strangest thing was that he didn't seem frustrated or disappointed about bringing them back to their hotel, he was just happy and couldn't care less about the rain. Me on the contrary, half soaked—and we still had a good forty-five minute walk to go—I felt a terrible void, a weariness, as if, by showing me Judit before taking her back, Fate had only increased my loneliness tenfold. Now, walking toward our neighborhood, it was Meryem who came back to me painfully, her tenderness and her body; the arrival of the Spanish girl revived her absence, showed me the path of my true love, I thought, and the more the reality of that single physical contact grew distant—almost two years—the more I thought I was realizing how important she was to me since Judit's presence, instead of immediately arousing new desires, had reminded me of details (smells, textures, moistures) that were manifesting in the rain: the incurable melancholy of hormones. Bassam was wound up like a clock, going on with his oh wows which were overwhelming me. Bassam, shut it, I shouted. Just shut up, please. He stopped short, standing stock still in the middle of the boulevard without understanding. I yelled, you're right, you know what? We've got to go, leave Tangier, leave Morocco, we can't stay here anymore.

He looked at me as if I were a halfwit, a retard who has to be spoken to gently.

Be patient then, he said, because God is on the side of the patient.

He was quoting the Prophet, with irony, maybe. If Bassam was capable of irony. I felt as if I were completely drunk, all of a sudden, immensely, hugely intoxicated, with no reason whatsoever. Yesterday the expedition with the Group, tonight Judit. If all that had a meaning, it was completely obscure.

It was raining harder and harder, we ended up flagging down a passing taxi that cost me my last dirhams.

After we reached the Propagation of Koranic Thought, Bassam started praying. I smoked a joint while he stared at me wide-eyed. Sheikh Nureddin doesn't like that, you know. We have to be pure.

I held up a fragrant middle finger, which made him laugh.

The kif calmed me down a little—Judit on loop in my thoughts, I kept reliving the evening, her smiles, her thoughts about Morocco, about the Arab Spring, about Spain, I could see her hazel eyes, her lips, and teeth, up close. I rushed to the computer, looked for her on Facebook, there were lots of Judits in Catalonia, some without photos, others with, not one who looked like her.

I ended up landing on pages devoted to Barcelona, I traveled through the city, from the harbor to the hills, walked up La Rambla looked for the university, the Barça stadium, contemplated the Gaudi façades; I suddenly discovered a modern, strange skyscraper right in the middle of the city, a huge iridescent penis, a brightly colored phallus full of offices that stood facing the sea, a disproportionate organ that made me wonder for an instant if it was the obscene farce of a mad hacker or the excessive fantasy of a porn director, how could they have built that tower in the center of such a beautiful city, an insult, a provocation, a game, and this building seemed there for me, to remind me painfully of what I had in place of a brain, an omen, perhaps, an obscure mark of Fate, Barcelona was under the sign of the penis, I turned off the computer. Bassam had fallen asleep on the rug; he was snoring a little, on his back, a half-smile on his face, calm.

I went to bed; the night was spinning a little, there were shooting stars on the ceiling, I fell asleep.

FRIDAYS were always exhausting days, I had to make two or three trips with a hand cart to bring the books and CDs, stack them first inside the mosque, then move the trestles, then the big boards with someone's help, all of which took a good two hours. Then I had to set up the books in nice piles, after having covered the tables with paper, and be more or less ready when they made the call to prayer; Sheikh Nureddin would lend me a hand, then bring me the cashbox and the rolls of brand-new ten-cent pieces on which a bee calmly gathered nectar from a saffron flower.

Of course, I always had to renew my supply, the clients were usually the same. That morning I had brought one box of *Sexuality* and another of *Heroines*, of course, the mainstays of my sales, but also some beautiful Korans with commentaries in the margins, a few brochures by Sayyid Qutb, *The Life of the Prophet* in two large volumes, three illustrated books for children (*Prayer, Pilgrimage, The Fast*) and a pretty book I liked a lot, *Stories of the Prophets*, tales from Noah up to Mohammed. Plus some chanted versions of the Koran on CD and DVD.

Usually, clients would glance quickly over the offerings as they went into the mosque and would linger when they came out; during prayer and the sermon, aside from a few passersby, there was no one, and in any case according to Nureddin I wasn't supposed to sell anything during prayers, Muslims are supposed to stop all commerce.

The weather was ominous; I had taken care to bring along the big plastic tarp to protect the books in case of a shower even though, according to the weather reports, it wasn't supposed to rain.

There weren't many people on the esplanade, a teenager was staring at me, it was my little brother Yassin, this day was off to a great start. He was carrying a bag with some bread, it had been almost two years since I'd seen him. He realized I'd seen him, turned his head away, hesitated, walked away a few steps, then came back, I was waiting for him with a big smile, I held out my hand over the books, he didn't take it, just spat:

"You should be ashamed to show yourself here again."

Enough was enough, all this because I had been found naked with Meryem.

"What the hell business is it of yours, you little shit?"

Hearing the curses, a few onlookers turned to look. Sheikh Nureddin, who was a few feet away, did too.

Yassin's attitude suddenly changed 180 degrees.

"You know, despite the unhappiness you caused, Mom misses you terribly."

He looked quite moved all of a sudden.

I didn't really know what to say.

"Tell her I miss her too."

We weren't about to start bawling over *The Life of the Prophet*, or *Sexuality in Islam*. We looked at each other for a little while without saying anything, I wanted to hate him, I wanted to take him in my arms, like when he was a kid, he was fourteen now, I just held out my hand a second time, he took it sadly, simply said, see you sometime, yes, till next time, I felt like that meant never, good riddance idiot, you have Mom and even Dad, Nour who just turned twelve, and Sarah, the last one, who's two years younger, you have all those people around you and even a grocery store that's waiting for you with open arms, a bright future thanks to me so don't go busting my balls, I wanted to offer him a book as a souvenir, but he was gone, the people you want to insult always leave too quickly, or I'm the one who's not prompt to insults and violence, that's possible.

For the time being I trembled as I stacked and unstacked the piles of books, a pure rage in my heart, without understanding a thing, as usual, I didn't understand the excessiveness of their hatred; I didn't see that I was missing pieces of the puzzle; I naively imagined that it all had to do with our two naked bodies, mine and Meryem's, and nothing else, for men are dogs, blind and mean, like my brother Yassin, like me, ready to bite but, above all, not to talk, Friday noon on the esplanade of a suburban mosque, in Tangier or anywhere else. And everything I didn't know, Sheikh Nureddin knew, he who, as soon as Yassin had left, came over to me, asked me if that was indeed my brother with whom I was speaking and offered me a compassionate look, a tap on the back, and a few verses to comfort me. My chest tight and my eyes burning, I felt like a child again, a child ready to call for his mother, that mother whom I missed while a crowd of faithful hurried into the mosque, and only at that instant did I realize that I no longer had a family, that I could shout till I was dead and no one would come, never, nevermore, and that even if my father or mother were in that crowd they would ignore me, and I was so focused on myself, a wounded brat, that I was absolutely unable to see the waves of unhappiness that had billowed up around me.

I sold *Heroines of Islam* to a guy who bought it for his wife, I remember, he asked me if I could wrap it for him, he made a face when I said no: for five meager dirhams he wanted a book *and* wrapping paper, I had a burning desire to tell him he could go fuck their asses, his heroines, his money, and even his wife, if he wanted, but I didn't dare. The revolution wasn't happening anytime soon.

I listened to the sermon that was retransmitted over the loud-speakers, it was about the Sura of the People of the Cave and Alex-ander's trips to the land of Gog and Magog; the Imam was scholarly and pious, a wise man not much schooled in politics; he annoyed the hell out of Sheikh Nureddin and our friends.

I waited for Judit to appear, I was convinced she'd come, she had to come. I hoped she had remembered the place, the name of the neighborhood. It was for her I had chosen to lug a pile of *Stories of the Prophets*, I was planning on offering her one, it was a handsome book for someone studying classical Arabic, and not too difficult, I thought.

Everyone came out of the mosque, Bassam first; I sold a few books, as usual, time passed slowly, I kept looking in all directions to see if she was coming, not too focused on my work. Bassam kept teasing me, he knew very well what I was hoping for.

At two o'clock, the time to put things away, I had to face the obvious: she wasn't coming. Life's a bitch, I thought. My sole visitor was my idiot of a little brother.

I started putting things away, death in my soul. Bassam kept gently teasing me. I wasn't in a good mood. Sheikh Nureddin in-vited us to lunch at a little neighborhood restaurant, like every Friday, with the rest of the "active members" of the Group; I lis-tened to them talk politics, Arab Revolutions, etc. It was amusing to see these bearded conspirators licking their fingers; the Sheikh had spread his napkin over his chest, one corner tucked into his shirt collar, so as not to get stains on himself—saffron sauce doesn't come out easily. Another man held his spoon with his fist like a cudgel and shoveled food in a few inches away from his plate, to have the least distance possible to travel: he stuffed semolina into his wide-open mouth like gravel into a cement mixer. Bassam had already finished, his cheeks streaked with yellow, and was now passionately sucking a last chicken bone. The beards of these prophets glistened with semolina grains, were spotted with a shower of golden snow, and they needed to be brushed off like rugs.

I vaguely followed the conversation from afar, without taking part in it: I knew that, like every Friday, they were going to go over the sermon of the detested Imam, whom they would end up calling a *mystique*, in French. For Sheikh Nureddin, *mystic* was an insult even worse than *miscreant*; I don't know why, but he always said *mystique* like that, in the language of Voltaire, perhaps because of its resemblance to *moustique*, mosquito, or *mastic*, gum; Sufis or those who were suspected of being so were his bête noire, almost as bad as Marxists. Right now, the conversation was centered on the Cave, and on its commentary; one was asking why the Imam hadn't insisted on the first verses, that attack against the Christians, and the fact that God had no son; the other was worried about the emphasis placed on the dog, the guardian of the Seven Sleepers, who watched over them during their sleep; a third found that there really were more pressing matters to concern oneself with than the land of Gog and Magog and Two-Horned Alexander. Sheikh Nureddin brought the discussion to an end, spitting out *Mistik! Mistik! Kullo dhalik mistik!* which delighted everyone.

I couldn't manage to take an interest in anything except Judit. She hadn't come. How could I see her again? If the two girls were following their itinerary as planned, at least the one I thought I had understood last night, then a priori they were leaving Tangier tomorrow for Marrakesh. An idea: I could still go by their hotel. Leave a note, who knows, with my email and phone number; I had cellphone credit that was eternally exhausted, but I could still receive calls. Even better: bring her the book (or even several books, too bad for the weight in her backpack—I pictured her with a backpack, the symbol of European youth, instead of with a rolling suitcase) with the above-mentioned note inside it. Until now I had never taken anything from the stock, I read the books that interested me, but that's it. I didn't think Sheikh Nureddin would get upset over a few missing copies, after all the goal of the association was to propagate Koranic thought, so I was working in the right direction.

I didn't want to lower myself to the point of waiting all night in front of their hotel for them to appear. I had to be firm on that point, even if the temptation was great. Lunch seemed endless to me.

And then finally the Sheikh got up, and everyone took his lead; I thanked him, he smiled at me warmly, I took advantage of the moment to ask him if he could advance me two hundred dirhams against my next month's salary, he answered even five hundred if you need it, what's it for? I didn't want to lie to him, I told him it's to buy a gift for a friend, and invite her out for ice cream, I felt as if I were a child, a teenager asking his parents for the cost of a movie ticket to buy some cigarettes, he looked very happy with my frankness, he said no problem, if it's for a noble cause, and handed me five 100-dirham notes, I hadn't asked for so much, it was a fortune, half my salary. You're doing your work well, you're one of us, you study a lot, you have a right to have fun too. I liked this almost brotherly friendship, all of a sudden I was ashamed of deceiving him, in one way or another. Bassam was watching me with envy, Sheikh Nureddin had taken out the bills without hiding anything, Bassam had the right to another kind of pay: violence and danger.

From Friday night till Sunday, I had the weekend off; I didn't have to answer for my use of time to anyone. My gratitude to Sheikh Nureddin said a lot about my naivety, not to mention my stupidity. My thinking had become bogged down in rose jam. As the Spanish proverb says: *An idiot's skin is thicker than cast iron.* I went back to the Group at the same time as everyone else, they were getting ready for a meeting from which I was excused, so much the better; just the once won't hurt, instead of settling down quietly on the rugs, they locked themselves up in the Sheikh's little office, with a conspiratorial air. I supposed it had to do with the attack that Bassam mentioned to me yesterday, but I was incapable of imagining that it concerned a real action, even less one of the most cynical and paranoid violence. The fact that the Group for the Propagation of Koranic Thought was a respectable institution guaranteed, I thought, that it would keep its activities within the (cowardly, it's true) limits of the law.

I took three books that I wrapped rather pathetically in newspaper (still, the paper was in Arabic, so it went with the theme) and headed out. I had taken care to put a thriller in my pocket; if the girls didn't appear, I'd drown my disappointment by blowing the Sheikh's dough reading and knocking back some beers.

And I set off, my mind finally made up to cool my heels in front of their hotel until they appeared. Which just goes to show I had no moral strength whatsoever.

THAT night, after having spent the afternoon and evening with Judit, when I was indeed sad to have left her again but above all happy to have seen her again, I had my first nightmare, at least my first real nightmare as an adult. Not an erotic dream that would have allowed me to rediscover the woman I had just left but a horrible dream, where my little brother appeared, the one I'd seen just that morning, infernal visions that were going to go on repeating themselves pretty much identically until today. The subject matter of the dream varies little, its form is more shifting—the violence, the color, the images of fear persist, you never get used to them, despite how often it comes: there's hanging, either I myself am hanged or I come across a hanged body still in convulsions; or the sea is suddenly streaked with an increasingly dense red current that ends up drowning me as I'm swimming; or rape, skeletal old men rape me, laughing, while I can't move or cry out—all these scenes are interrupted at their climax by a breathless awakening or, on the contrary, they go on endlessly, the long agony of watching a familiar corpse floating in the air, frantic, swimming in waves of blood. The women who have witnessed me sleep tell me I can groan for a long time, huddled with my arms over my head, or I'll keep tossing this way and that, letting out stifled cries. The sequence of scenes can vary, some can go away for a while and then come back, without warning, without my ever managing to understand the reason for their reappearance.

I woke up in the middle of the night with these images and for an instant, in the darkness, I mentally prayed, my first reflex against fear was prayer, to implore God, and I would have given anything for there to be someone by my side, until I chased away the mental representations by turning on the light, replacing them with the familiar objects of my tiny room. I spent a long time calming myself down. I clung to the vision of Judit's face. She had promised that she'd return to Tangier on her way back, in five days, that she'd email me about her trip. The terrifying dream slowly disappeared as I remembered her. I would have happily gone with them to Marrakesh, I'd never been there. It was strange to think they would know my country better than me. But was it really my country? My country was Tangier, at least that's what I thought; but in truth, I had realized that afternoon, Judit's Tangier did not coincide with mine. She saw the international city, Spanish, French, American; she knew Paul Bowles, Tennessee Williams, and William Burroughs, so many authors whose remote names vaguely reminded me of something, but about whom I knew nothing. Even Mohamed Choukri, icon of Tangier, I knew who he was, but of course I had never read a word by him. I was very surprised to learn that they studied his novels in modern Arabic literature at the University of Barcelona. Speaking with Judit about Tangier, I had the feeling we were discussing a different city, two images, two foreign territories linked by the same name, a homophonic mistake. No doubt Tangier was neither one nor the other, not the memories of the old days of the international city, not my suburb, not Tanger-Med or the Free Zone. But the fact remains that with Judit and Elena, strolling about with them all afternoon and a good part of the evening, after having practically run into them by chance two hundred meters away from their hotel, my package under my arm, I had the strange sensation of being dispossessed. Finally it was Judit who told me about the history of the old city, for instance; it was she who knew, who looked for places, traces, memories; it was she, finally, who offered me a copy in Arabic of *For Bread Alone*, found at a random bookstore along the way. I tried to show that I knew things too; I tried to be funny, at least, to seem intelligent, but the awkwardness of my spoken French and her complete ignorance of Moroccan made me clumsy, a little coarse, without nuances; sometimes I felt as if I were being regarded frankly as an idiot. So I struggled to try communicating in classical Arabic, where I could shine, but even if she didn't understand well but had good pronunciation, I felt a little as if I sounded like a radio announcer or a Friday sermonizer, which took any naturalness and spontaneity away from my jokes. You try acting funny and charming in literary Arabic, it's no piece of cake, believe me; people will always think you're about to announce another catastrophe in Palestine or comment on a verse of the Koran. But Judit seemed interested in me; she asked me questions about my family, I told her my father was from the Rif, that he came from a village next to Nador and that my mother was Arabic, from Tangier, that she had grown up in Casa Barata. I had no desire to expand on the subject, but it had to be covered. Number of brothers and sisters. Studies, high school. Tastes, hobbies. Religion. Obviously, a problem; how could I tell her I was a practicing Muslim, without coming off as an enemy of Western women, more or less reactionary. There was the Bassam method, which consisted of singing the praises of Islam for hours until he achieved the conversion or death from boredom of the Infidel. I brought out a cliché like "Faith is in every person's heart" or "All things sing the praises of their Creator," which sounded fine and less pompous in Arabic, and changed the subject. Judit acquiesced. Elena must still have had her endless conversation with Bassam from the night before in her head and was grateful to me. She didn't speak much in any case, and I had to be careful that my passion for her friend didn't exclude her from the conversation. Fiancée, girlfriend? At least as difficult as the previous subject; I thought of Meryem for an instant, I said not at the moment, which let on that I had a certain experience of women while still being available. Clever.

It was my turn to ask questions, especially the one I was most interested in: Why Arabic? Why Arabic studies? Aside from the fact that professionally such a specialty seemed to offer few job opportunities, I wondered why on earth young Catalonians from Barcelona were on a path that was indeed fertile, but that was exactly opposite from the yearning of most inhabitants of the Arabic world: to get rid of this unfair curse and emigrate north. Judit easily explained her choice to me: she had always loved traveling and literature; she had begun studying English, and had taken advantage of the possibility to take a few courses in Arabic as an elective, just to see; finally, the language had fascinated her and she had made it her major. Simple as that. As for Elena, she didn't really know how to answer; she said I don't really know, just like that, by chance.

I didn't dare ask the other question that I was dying to ask, to find out whether or not they had boyfriends.

Then the conversation returned to literature; Ibn Battuta, the medieval traveler from Tangier who had been practically all over the known world, as far as China (that one I knew, without having read him of course—thirty years on the road only to end up in Fez again, what was the point).

"It's surprising that Tangier is famous chiefly for the people who have left it," I said in my finest literary Arabic.

"Good Lord, that *is* strange," Judit added, laughing, in the same language.

"Ibn Battuta began his travels at twenty-two, so I don't have much time left to win renown."

And so on, for hours. And when I had to leave her, at around midnight, after having eaten dinner, a tea at Mehdi's, then another, knowing that the next day they were leaving for Marrakesh, that it wasn't very likely we'd ever see each other again, despite her promise to stop in Tangier on her way back, when we had to confront that same embarrassing farewell moment as the night before, trying not to say goodbye, when I had been wondering all afternoon if I'd try to kiss Judit, casually, to place my lips on hers and when we were there, Elena a little withdrawn, a little erased in the shadow of the overhanging balcony where that revolting neon light was still blinking, at that precise instant when people look at each other with tenderness since they're headed toward absence and memory, when desire is all the keener since it guesses its vanity is faced with the departure of its object, we were facing each other in silence, and I was incapable of doing anything except leaving, all caught up in the stream of my half-baked romantic thoughts, it was time to be a man, to move toward her like a man and kiss her on the mouth since that's what I wanted, what I dreamed about, and if we don't make an effort toward our dreams they disappear, nothing changes the world except hope or despair, in equal proportions, those who set themselves on fire in Sidi Bouzid, those who get beatings and bullets on Tahrir Square, and those who dare French-kiss a Spanish student in the street, obviously that has nothing to do with the others but for me, in that silence, that instant lost between two worlds, I needed as much courage to kiss Judit as to shout Qadafi! Bastard! in front of a jeep of Libyan soldiers or to yell Long Live the Republic of Morocco! alone smack in the middle of the Dar-el-Makhzen in Rabat, and this moment stretched out, we'd just said goodbye and it was she of course who ended up bringing her face close to mine and placing an ambiguous, disconcerting kiss on the corner of my mouth, a kiss that could pass either for clumsiness or a pledge, but I could still feel her breath so close, and the softness of her lips, and I turned around like a tin soldier after squeezing both her hands for an instant in mine, and then left at almost a run back to the world of nightmares.

Doubt in my heart. Certainty in my heart.

The Propagation of Thought was deserted, no trace of Bassam.

I immediately sat down in front of the computer, got out the piece of newspaper where she had copied out her email address, wrote her a long impassioned letter that I erased little by little, piece by piece, ending up with nothing but *"Bon voyage! Je t'embrasse et à très bientôt j'espère!"* I sent her the same message via Facebook, Judit Foix; unfortunately there was no photo on her profile page.

They were taking the 7:30 train the next morning for Marrakesh, which they'd reach after ten hours and one changeover in Casa; I supposed they'd get to their hotel around seven at night, Judit might not go online right away, she'd need time to find an Internet café or Wi-Fi, so I couldn't expect a reply before, at best, nine o'clock. If she replied. I almost decided to take the train myself to accompany them to Marrakesh; the ticket cost 200 dirhams, maybe a little less by bus, but then I'd have to pay for the hotel, eat, I didn't know anyone there, Sheikh Nureddin's advance would have lasted two days. And above all I was afraid of putting on too much pressure and spoiling the little I had been able to win. I just had to be patient. Write to her, and again, not too much.

The next day, after a hideous night interrupted by nightmares, hanged men and waves of blood, I went down to the sea; I spent most of the day reading a thriller, sitting on a rock; a bright April sun warmed the seawall. I managed to concentrate on my reading; at times I would lift my eyes from the page to observe the ferries, in the distance, between the new harbor, Tarifa, or Algeciras.

At night I watched Spanish TV, switching between the Andalusian and the national channels, trying to pay attention to the language, to soak it in; no one from the Group reappeared, neither Bassam nor Sheikh Nureddin. I checked my messages God knows how many times, no news of Judit; I ended up going to bed and even managed to fall asleep.

RESTLESS night; nightmares; still that image of the hanged man. After waking, a note from Judit; she tells me that Marrakesh is wonderful, humming, mysterious and animated. The train journey was very pleasant, Morocco is a magnificent country. She sends hugs and kisses too, see you soon.

I replied immediately.

I don't remember my actions or movements that day, as if the too-luminous, too-noisy event of the night before left all others in shadow, against the light. I must have done the usual, read, walked a little, surfed the web.

At seven-thirty that night, I was in front of the TV; I had seen photographs of a destroyed, ripped-apart café, tables overturned, chairs scattered; images of the half-deserted Jamaa el-Fna Square, except in one corner, where onlookers were gathered outside a police cordon; ambulances and fire trucks were coming and going with their sirens blaring and on the upper floor there was a terrace and a ruined roof, a sign half-torn off that read, in French and Arabic, *Café Argan*. The subtitles of the Spanish news channel kept saying *Atentado en Marrakech: al menos 16 muertos.* I spent the night between the TV and the computer, trying to find out more—by ten o'clock I was reassured, there were no Spanish people among the victims, most of them were French. It was indeed a bomb attack, not a suicide bomber as they'd thought at first, said the online news sites. In one particularly horrible photo, the corpse of a man was stretched out among the rubble; the photo was on all the websites. The terrorists hadn't yet been arrested; French and Spanish policemen would come lend a hand to their Moroccan colleagues. President Sarkozy offered his condolences to the families; the King did as well.

Even if I was reassured about Judit, I was terrified by these images. The numbers came through at night, sixteen dead, including eight French citizens. A catastrophe for Morocco, according to the papers. There were fewer tourists already because of the political unrest, this massacre wasn't going to encourage them to return. It seemed pretty indecent to me to talk about the economy when all these people were dead.

Confusedly, I hoped Bassam had nothing to do with any of it. He still hadn't come back to the Group; neither he nor the Sheikh, no one. I remembered his phrases from the day before yesterday, an attack, something people would remember, push things to confrontation—impossible.

I wrote another email to Judit, asking for news about her; she replied almost immediately, to tell me they were fine, they were in the square when the explosion occurred, but far enough away, they were very afraid, pretty shocked, and wondered if they should come back right away. Elena's parents are very worried, they think there might be other attacks and they're begging her to leave Morocco immediately. So they might not come back to Tangier after all to take the plane as planned.

Small compensation: the message ended with *kisses, I'm thinking of you*. My heart leapt when I read those words.

That Sunday, I went to the terrace of a café on the Place de France; everyone was talking about the attack, thinking, no doubt, that there was a chance we might be blown up as well. I wondered if that man lying dead on the café terrace had felt anything, if he had understood what was happening before everything darkened in the detonation.

"That's the first time I've seen someone reading a *Série Noire* in a café in Tangier."

The voice came from behind me and spoke French. I turned around, a bald man in his early fifties was smiling at me.

"That's a funny coincidence, I collect thrillers," he added.

For a second I thought he wanted to pick me up or buy the book I was holding, *The Prone Gunman*, but no, he just wanted to know where I'd found it. I hesitated before answering, for a number of reasons. We chatted for five minutes; I enjoyed talking about my favorite authors, Pronzini, McBain, Manchette, Izzo, it was nice to forget the images of the outstretched body and the overturned tables at the Café Argan. The guy was flabbergasted to discover that a young Moroccan could know these books.

"It's one of my passions," I explained. "I learned French reading them."

Jean-François had been living in Tangier for a few months; he was the branch head of a French business in the Free Zone. He liked the city: if in addition there were a bookseller able to provide him with old detective novels, he'd be overjoyed.

I gave him the address of the bookseller, explaining that I wasn't sure if he was open, but if he was, he'd find what he was looking for. He thanked me, then asked me if I knew how to use a computer. I replied of course.

"And can you type fast?"

"Of course."

"With how many fingers, two?"

"More like four."

He said Listen, I might have something to offer you. My business works for French publishing houses. We're digitizing some of their catalogues. We're always looking for students who know French well and like books.

Yesterday the attack, the day before yesterday Judit, and today a job in the Free Zone. I thought of the first sentences of Mahfouz's

Chatter on the Nile: "It was April, the month of dust and lies." The idea of being able to take a break from the Propagation for Koranic Thought was more than tempting. I explained to Jean-François that I worked in a religious bookstore, but that I had some free time. He seemed impressed.

"How old are you?"

"Almost twenty," I replied.

"You look older."

"It's the gray hair."

In recent months I'd had some graying at my temples. At the same time, if I did actually look older, he wouldn't have asked me the question; there must have been something childlike in my face still, contradicted by my appearance and the traces of gray.

"Come see me at the office on Monday between four and five, we'll talk."

He gave me the address and left the café. I looked at *The Prone Gunman* in front of me. Thrillers were powerful things. I wondered how one would translate الله أعلم into French. God knows more than we? God alone knows Fate?

I didn't know that I had only four months left here; I didn't know that I would soon leave for Spain, but I could glimpse the hand of Fate, the power of the interconnectedness of invisible causal series called Fate. Going back to the Group, at nightfall, the world seemed as if it was on fire; Morocco, Tunisia, Libya, Syria, Greece, all of Europe, everything was burning; everything looked like those images of Marrakesh that the TV was broadcasting over and over, a decimated café, overturned chairs, corpses. And in the middle of all that, the astonishing irony of a lover of thrillers who was offering me work without even knowing me, just because he had seen I was reading Manchette. And Meryem. And Judit. And Bassam, with his cudgel. And the worst, which is always yet to come.

Monday noon, there was no one at the Group, and by now I was almost sure they had something to do with the Marrakesh attack.

Make fun of me, say I was particularly naive, but imagine for a second that your next door neighbors, your boss, and your best friend were found complicit in a terrorist act; you wouldn't believe it at first; you'd look around you, raise your arms as a sign of powerlessness, shake your head no, no, I know those people, they're not involved. In my head there was a world between beating up neighborhood drunks and organizing, seven hundred kilometers away, the death of sixteen people in a café. Why Marrakesh? To safeguard their positions in Tangier? To strike the most touristic city in Morocco? Where had they found the explosives? Had Bassam known about it, for weeks possibly? An action like that isn't put together overnight, I thought. And I thought Bassam was too open, too direct to hide such a big thing from me for long. He must have learned about it the night he had spoken to me.

They might have killed strangers; they'd almost even killed Judit, who knows. They'd beaten up my favorite bookseller; they had offered me shelter, food, and an education. My room was too little; the commentaries on the Koran, the grammar books, the treatises on rhetoric, the Sayings of the Prophet, his Lives, my shelf of thrillers: these magnificent books were obstructing my view. Where were they, all the members of the Group? At noon, I called Sheikh Nureddin and Bassam on their cellphones from our telephone: no answer. I had the feeling that no one would come back, that this office had served its purpose, that they had left me, the naive one, to get the beatings and deal with the police. That's why the Sheikh had so easily given me five hundred dirhams. I wasn't going to see anyone ever again. Not a single one of them. Stay with my books until the cops arrived. No, I was paranoid; impossible. I had read so many thrillers where the narrator realizes he had been used, manipulated by the crooks or the forces of law and order that I saw myself, sole representative of the abandoned Group for the Propagation of Koranic Thought, waiting calmly for the cops and ending up being tortured in place of the beards.

Sheikh Nureddin's office wasn't locked. I told myself I was imag-ining things on my own, that they would come back momentarily, expose me, and make fun of me till the end of my days.

The bookstore's cash box was there, on the table, no one had emptied it for weeks, there were about two thousand dirhams in it.

I found other bills in a leather bag, euros and dollars, ten or fif-teen thousand dirhams in all, I couldn't believe my eyes.

Otherwise everything was empty, the desk diaries had disap-peared, the contacts, the notebooks full of orders, the account books, the activities, the business affairs of Sheikh Nureddin, all gone. Even his personal computer wasn't there. Just the monitor.

I was all alone in the midst of dozens, hundreds of shrink-wrapped books.

I took a walk around the neighborhood, to see if I might come across a familiar face that belonged to the Group; no one. I went to Bassam's house, a few feet away from my parents', I met his mother and asked if she knew where he was; she gave me the kind of look you reserve for contagious beggars, muttered a curse and slammed the door, then reopened it to hand me a dirty old envelope with my name on it—Bassam's handwriting. I glanced at it, it wasn't dated today; apparently some old thing he had never mailed, since he hadn't known where to send it. His mother closed the door again abruptly, with no explanation.

At four o'clock I had a meeting in the Free Zone with Jean-François for the new job; I wanted to change, to make myself as handsome as possible, I felt as if the world were crumbling into pieces. Going back to the Group, I thought I saw two shady look-ing characters hanging around our premises; cops in civilian clothes, who knows. I checked my email, there was a message from Judit, she wrote that she was finally coming back to Tangier as planned, but alone; she didn't have enough money to get a new ticket for Barcelona; she'd be there a little before the set date, the day after tomorrow, she said, after having seen Elena off at the airport.

This news warmed my heart, even if I was a little wounded that she wasn't doing it to see me again sooner and for longer, but for unfortunate financial reasons.

I made my decision, without waiting for the outcome of the afternoon interview. I gathered together all the cash that there could be in Sheikh Nureddin's office, even the ten-cent pieces. I had almost fifteen or twenty thousand dirhams in bills and coins. More cash than anyone had ever seen, I could have taken a taxi to the suburb of Nador to find Meryem, say I'm taking this young woman away, here's ten thousand dirhams for your trouble, no one would have objected.

It was April, the month of dust and lies.

I gathered my things together, the hundred or so thrillers took up so much space you wouldn't believe, I emptied the boxes we had just gotten from Saudi Arabia to put them in: in all, with the *Kash-shaaf*, *The Stories of the Prophets*, the dictionary, the books I liked, there were three big boxes; even some clothes had gone into each of the boxes; plus I took the Group's laptop, the screen, the keyboard and two or three things I had to keep.

A real house moving, and nowhere to go.

When everything was ready, I left for the Free Zone in a bus; I left all my things at the Group, took only the cash and the laptop, that made me look important, a laptop. I thought Jean-François wouldn't remember me, or else that the secretaries (very dark Moroccans, short skirts, black pantyhose, nice legs, disdain in their looks and voices) wouldn't let me get to their boss, but no, ten minutes after I reached the office I was shaking hands with Jean-François; he addressed me formally with *vous* now, saying, aha, here's Mr. Friend of the *Série Noire*, and all of a sudden the women in black stockings and miniskirts began regarding the young yokel who had just arrived as a human being; the boss disappeared very quickly, I was placed in a tiny room that adjoined the director's office, a Frenchman appeared, handed me a book; there you are, he said, our business is to make these things into digital files, copy two pages of this on this computer for me. I took the book, put it on a stand, and copied it while the Frenchman looked at his watch, a big shiny timepiece, after two pages I said, okay that's it, he replied, hey not bad, you've got something, let me look it over, my word it's pretty good, wait a second. Jean-François reappeared, the other man called him Mr. Bourrelier, it looks good to me Mr. Bourrelier, he said, no problem, Jean-François looked at me smiling, and said I know a good thing when I see it, you go over the details together, Frédéric.

Frédéric called in the secretary, she took my papers, which she photocopied; Frédéric asked me when I could begin, and I thought a second: if Judit was arriving in Tangier tomorrow I'd want to spend some time with her. Next Monday? That's fine with me, Frédéric replied. You're paid by the page, 2,000 characters, 50 cents. That means about 100 euros for an average book. Then we deduct corrections, at 2 cents each. If you copy out 20 books a month, you get 2,000 euros, more or less, if the work is done well.

I made a quick calculation: to reach 20 books per month, let's say 200 pages per day, you had to copy out 25 pages in 60 minutes. One page every two minutes, more or less. This Frédéric was an optimist. Or a slave driver, depending.

"Wouldn't it be simpler to scan the books?"

"For some of them, no. For the ones with slightly transparent paper, it's almost impossible, the results are erratic. The OCR doesn't understand anything, and then you have to take the book apart, lay out the page, correct things, it ends up costing more."

To me he sounded like he was speaking Chinese, but fine, he must have known what he was doing.

"Can I take the work home?"

"Yes, of course. But you have to work here at least five hours a day, for tax reasons."

"Okay."

The secretary had me sign a contract, the first one in my life.

"Good, see you Monday. And welcome."

"Till Monday, yes. And thanks."

"Thank you."

I went to say good-bye to Jean-François, he shook my hand, saying, see you next week, then.

And I went back to Tangier. On the way, the sea shone.

Judit was arriving tomorrow. In fifteen days I'd be twenty. The world was a strange mixture of uncertainty and hope.

In the paper, still no news of who was responsible for the attack in Marrakesh.

So it was almost seven o'clock when I got back to the neighborhood; night was falling. I had had time to make a plan. First I wanted to clarify a few things; I felt full of energy. I went back to see the bookseller.

My heart dropped when I reached his shop; the display wasn't out, but the metal shutters were raised. I had a lump in my throat, I gathered all my courage and pushed open the door; after all I had been coming to this place since I was fifteen or sixteen, I wasn't going to let Sheikh Nureddin take it away from me.

The bookseller was sitting behind his desk, he lifted his head; on his face I saw surprise, then hatred, scorn, or pity. I had expected insults; I had imagined myself asking his forgiveness, he would have forgiven me, and we'd have resumed our conversations like before. He remained silent, staring at me, his brow knit; he said nothing; he was contemplating my stupidity, was drowning me in my own cowardliness; I was shrinking, crushed with shame; I couldn't manage to speak, or to take out the envelope with the dirhams that I had naively prepared for him, I muttered a few words, hello, sorry, I choked and turned tail, fled once again, fled faced with myself; I left at a run; there are things that can't be fixed. Actually, nothing can be fixed. As I left the store I imagined he'd run after me saying "Come back, boy, come back," but of course not, and when I think about it today it's entirely logical that he had only scorn and no pity for a lost kid who had chosen the cudgel and Sheikh Nureddin. I walked quickly to the Group's premises, my guilt was changing into aggression, I was mentally insulting the poor guy, what came over me, good Lord, to go back there, and two small tears of rage emerged from the corner of my eyes, there was smoke in the night, a thick, whitish smoke mixed with ashes scattered by the wind; a vapor of anger was weighing down the springtime, a burnt smell was invading my throat and it was only when I reached the corner of the street, seeing the crowd and the fire trucks, that I realized that the Group for the Propagation of Koranic Thought was burning; tall flames leapt from the windows and licked the upper floor of the building; from outside, with their hoses, firemen sprayed water on the openings, mouths with tongues of fire that spat tons of half-consumed paper debris, while a squad of policemen were trying their best to keep the crowd away from the catastrophe. Hundreds of books were going up in the breeze, invading the air as far as Larache or Tarifa; I pictured the blister packs melting, the heat attacking the compact pages of stacked books that ended up catching and transmitting the destruction to their neighbors, I knew my stock well, near that window was the supply of *Heroines*, *Sexuality*, and all the little manuals, over there were the cubic yards of commentaries on the Koran, and right in the middle, on the synthetic rugs that must have been liquefied, my boxes, the *Série Noire* were flying away too, the Manchettes, the Pronzinis, the McBains, the Izzos and all my nice shirts, my fabulous shoes, my patent leather; the polish must have been burning, the hair gel would fuel all of it and soon, if the firemen didn't manage to get the fire under control, it would be the gas canister in the kitchen and the one in the bathroom that would explode, sending into the air once and for all what remained of Sheikh Nureddin's institution.

The neighbors were there, I recognized them; one was in his bathrobe, he had thrown a bright silver survival blanket over his

wife's shoulders, who must have been in a nightgown; some were
silent and downcast, others on the contrary were bellowing and gesticulating like mad. The firemen seemed to be having trouble gain-
ing control of the literature-fed flames.

After three minutes of morbid, dumbfounded contemplation, I
was suddenly overcome with fear; I rushed down the hill toward
the center of Tangier. The whole neighborhood knew that I was
the bookseller at the Group for Propagation of Koranic Thought.
The police were no doubt going to look for me, especially if, as I
imagined, the Group was linked closely or remotely to the Marrakesh attack. I didn't have anywhere to go. Sole possessions: a bag
containing a laptop, some cash, and the copy of Choukri's *For Bread
Alone* that Judit had given me and that I had taken with me to read
on the bus.

At least I didn't have to worry about the boxes, every cloud has
its silver lining. When you leave on a journey, said the Prophet, you
have to settle your affairs as if you were going to die. I had seen
the bookseller again; the Group was burning, and all my possessions
with it; all I had left were my parents. For a few days, and despite
the argument with my brother, I had very much wanted to see my
mother again. Not today. Not enough strength. Little by little my
adrenaline was ebbing, I fell asleep in the bus that took me downtown. Suddenly I was exhausted. I couldn't manage to think. Finding out what or who had provoked the fire was all the same to me. I
got out by the Grand Zoco, a little haggard. Strange day. Now I had
to find a place to sleep; I almost took a room in the same hotel as
Judit, but that might be a little too much, if she found me set up in
the room next door when she arrived in Tangier. Plus I wasn't sure
if she was staying in the same place, it was likely but not certain.
I chose another inn, not far, a little lower down near the harbor;
the owner looked at me as if I were a leper, young, Moroccan, and
without a suitcase; he demanded I pay three nights in advance and
repeated ten times that his hovel was a respectable place.

The digs weren't bad, with a little wrought-iron balcony, a pretty view of the harbor, the roofs of the old city and above all, Wi-Fi. I searched for news of the fire online, it must not have been a major event, no one was talking about it yet.

I sent a message to Judit, then I went out to buy some clothes and have a bite to eat.

I was ready to leave. I'd had no family for two years, no friends for two days, no luggage for two hours. The unconscious doesn't exist; there are just crumbs of information, scraps of memory not important enough to be dealt with, tatters like those old keypunch strips you used to feed computers; my memories are those scraps of paper, cut up and thrown into the air, mixed together, patched up—I had no idea if they would soon settle down in order to make new sense. Life is a machine to tear out your being; it strips us, from childhood on, in order to repopulate us by plunging us into a bath of contacts, voices, messages that change us endlessly, we are always in motion; a Polaroid just gives an empty portrait, names, a single yet complex name they project onto us and that's what makes us, so you can call me Moroccan, Moor, Arabic, immigrant or by my first name, call me Ishmael, for example, or whatever you like—I was about to be smashed by part of the truth, and look at me running around Tangier, ignorant, not knowing what had just burned down along with the Group for the Propagation of Koranic Thought, clinging to the hope of Judit and my new job as if they were my life raft. At times I think I can relive the schemings and thoughts of the person I was at that time, but of course this is an illusion; that young man who bought himself two black shirts, two pairs of jeans, some T-shirts, and a suitcase is an imitation, just like the clothes he gets; I thought that the violence that surrounded me had no hold over me, no more than the violence in Tripoli, Cairo, or Damascus. Blinded, all I thought about was Judit's arrival, about those super-sentimental verses by Nizar Qabbani that we used to copy out, in high school, in secret messages for girls who were moved by them, the lines I had already recited to Meryem, عيناك آخر مركبين يسافران فهل هنالك من مكان؟, when we were gazing at the Strait, not daring to hold hands, and especially the next line, إنني تعبت من التسكع في محطات الجنون، ظلي معي, wandering among the stations of madness—Judit's eyes were then, as this poet-for-the-ladies said, the last boats setting out. I remember, Meryem was worried; she was afraid of our relationship, afraid of the consequences, afraid, afraid of what I could make her do; she didn't know what solution to find for this adolescent love, she was hesitant to confide in her mother, after all hadn't she herself married her first cousin, and I remember that one day, when I had sent Bassam to find her, far from the neighborhood, she told me she was afraid I would abandon her to emigrate, so then I tried to reassure her with Qabbani's verses, when the truth, if it exists, is that I couldn't have cared less about her, about her, I mean I cared less about her than about satisfying my desire, my pleasure, managing to undress her, to caress her, and when I finally understood, after reading her last letter, in that old envelope picked up at Bassam's house, when I finally understood that I was responsible for her death, out there in that lost village, for her hemorrhaging during a furtive, amateur abortion, because I hadn't responded to her despair, any more than I had to the despair of her mother, who died of sorrow a few weeks later, in this paradise of modern Morocco where in theory no woman bleeds to death or ever kills herself or even ever suffers under the blows of any male, for God and family and tradition watch over them and nothing can hurt them, if they are decent, if they are merely decent, as Sheikh Nureddin said so well, Sheikh Nureddin who knew the truth, just as the whole neighborhood had learned it, Bassam in the lead; when I knew I could no longer escape that reality since it was as sordid and tangible as the number on a banknote, as precise and real as the bee gleaning nectar from the saffron flower on the new ten-cent coin I returned with each of the books I sold; when death, fixed and immutable as those coins, caught me by the ear to tell me O my boy, you skipped a step, for eighteen months now you've been living in ignorance of me, the world, my world, had to be well and truly destroyed so I didn't destroy myself further, after this deflagration; Judit had to be by my side so that I didn't give in to tears, once the shock was over: all of it confirmed an intuition; of course I knew too, my body knew, my dreams knew even if at that moment, at the moment of Meryem's death at the far end of the Rif, I was in the process of getting myself beaten up in a police station in Casa or begging for an apple at a market—my nightmares, clearer, became only more painful, more vivid, even more unbearable; my conscience, more confused and even less sure of itself, riddled with regrets and with that terrible sensation, which could draw tears of shameful sorrow from me, because, in my dreams, for months, I had been sleeping with a dead girl: with Meryem who was disappearing in the flesh-eating coffin while I was seeing her alive and well, as the seasons passed; she was accompanying me when she was no more and that was so mysterious, so incomprehensible in my still-young heart that I saw a disgusting betrayal in it, a piece of filth even greater than my responsibility for her death, a hatred that turned against Bassam, against my family, against everyone who had prevented me from mourning for Meryem and had forced me to lust for her dead body—just as you slowly withdraw the shroud from a corpse to observe its breasts. On the marble table, I had dreamed of her cold belly and pubis. It was there, the shame, there, in this slippage of time; time is a woman from the graveyard, a woman in white, who washes the bodies of children.

I bought some shirts with my back tensed, sensing a catastrophe, without knowing it had already taken place. I attributed my feverishness to the fire, to Judit's arrival, to the attack and to Bassam's disappearance, without sensing that the worst was already there;

I hesitated for a long time in front of a pair of pajamas, hoping Judit would see me in them; I had a fleeting thought, a little sad all the same, about the only woman who had ever seen me naked, not knowing that she no longer existed.

That evening was one of the longest ever.

Solitude and waiting.

I lingered online to find news, news of anything, of Bassam, of Sheikh Nureddin, of Judit, of the world, of Libya, of Syria. The flames were taller than ever. I went out for a walk; the night was warm, the town was crowded, Tangier could, in the spring, be thrilling and dangerous. Everything had turned against me; the burnt smell lingered in my nostrils and blocked the smell of the sea. Young people were walking in threes, in fours, restlessly, swaying their shoulders; at a bend in the street, I saw a guy my age, half-mad, violently attacking a potted tree, flinging it on the ground and shouting insults, for no reason, before being pummeled in turn by the shop owner, who had burst out of his store—blood splattered onto his white T-shirt, he lifted his hand to his face, seeming stunned, before running away, screaming. I remember, the tree was an orange or lemon tree, it had little white flowers, the owner of the store set it back upright in its pot, stroking it if as it were a woman or a child, I think he even spoke to it.

I was a few yards away from the French bookstore, so I went in; I looked at the shelves a little, those serious books were intimidating, expensive and intimidating, you hesitated to open them for fear of staining the cream-colored covers or damaging the bindings. There was a section on Tangierian literature, and they were all there, the authors Judit had mentioned: Bowles, Burroughs, Choukri of course, but also a Spaniard by the name of Ángel Vázquez, who had written a novel called *The Wretched Life of Juanita Narboni*—what I was looking for in books was more to forget my own messed-up life, to forget Tangier; I found the "detective novel" section, there were

mostly huge books whose size seemed gigantic to me, disproportionate to my old *Série Noires* gone up in smoke, just as intimidating as
the serious novels. I left a little sad at not having found company, an
unknown book that had the power to change the course of things,
put the world back in order; I felt tiny when faced with real literature. I went down to the sea and thought of Bassam; if he really was
an accomplice in the Marrakesh attack, I wondered if I'd ever see
him again.

Neon bars winked at me, guys were lounging in deck chairs
and basking in the spring weather; they all looked like smugglers.
I could never have been so far from my home, even in Barcelona,
Paris, or New York; these streets breathed something forbidden in
the dangerous night, so far from the neighborhoods of my childhood, so far from that childhood from which I was barely emerging
and that the steep alleys reminded me of with their radical difference. I wondered if I would ever dare go into one of those joints
with red lights, smelling of cigarettes, desire, and dereliction, if I'd
ever be old enough for those places. After all I had some money
now, and soon I'd want to have a drink, maybe even talk to someone. I appreciated alcohol for the image it gave me, of a hard, adult
male, who fears neither his mother's anger nor God's, a character,
like the ones I wanted to resemble, the Montales, the nameless
detectives, the Marlowes, the private eyes and cops in noir novels.
Why do we cling to these images that form us, these examples that
shape us and can break us, while at the same time building us up,
identity always in motion, forever being shaped, and my loneliness
must have been so great that night because I went into a tiny bar
called El Pirata, whose brownish sign must have known the glorious era of Tangier's international status, and the Occupation as well,
the boss with straightened hair dyed platinum blonde was watching
me and no doubt wondering if I was even old enough to be there.
I said hello, sat down at the bar on a stool, ordered a beer. She

looked at me as if to scold me, but served me. I wondered what she was thinking, how a young hick like me got there, all alone; maybe she wasn't imagining anything at all. Barely five minutes later, a girl came out from behind a curtain, she was thin as a whip, bony legs in black stockings, pale cheeks despite her makeup, she hoisted herself up onto the seat next to me, I had entered this joint, you had to follow through; or maybe I had entered precisely for this, to speak with someone, hostess or whore, unlike the characters in my novels I averted my eyes, a little ashamed, her name was Zahra, at least that's what she said; she had scars on her face, very thin lips, she smelled of jasmine, and beneath the perfume her clothes exhaled the incense of cedar from the room where I let myself be led by the hand ten minutes later, a greenish sofa shiny from use beneath a halogen lamp set to low, Zahra sat down and undid the buttons on her shirt, she wore a white bra whose lace gaped open, revealing her tiny breasts with very dark areolas, she said give me two hundred dirhams, searching through my pocket let me not look at her for an instant, I handed her the money, she put it under one of the couch cushions, she spread her legs and lifted her skirt to show me her sex shaved to its almost black skin, matching the edges of the stockings that covered her bony thighs, I was torn between shame and desire, she motioned me to approach, I didn't move, she whispered come on, don't be afraid, she caught my hand to place it on her chest while caressing my crotch, her breath moved up along my belly, she began undoing my belt, I stepped back and pushed her away; she gave me a funny look, finally shame got the upper hand, I went out. The lady behind the bar sniggered "Already?," I didn't even turn around.

The street was deserted, I was a little disoriented, my heart was pounding. Today was vile. I thought for an instant of Meryem, then of Judit, as I walked to my hotel.

Tomorrow will be another day.

I tried to read *For Bread Alone* a little, without managing to, the images of Zahra's sex inserted themselves between the book and me. They remained for a long time in the darkness, long after I had put out the light.

WHEN Ibn Battuta began his journey, as he was leaving Tangier headed east, in 1335, I wonder if he hoped to return to Morocco one day or if he thought his exile would be absolute. He spent some years in India and the Maldives, in the service of a Sultan who appointed him a Cadi, a judge, no doubt because he was learned and knew Arabic; he even married the Vizier's daughter. When he left the archipelago, after traveling through a city where women had only one breast, he met a man living alone with his family on a small island, and envied him; he owned, Battuta said, *a few coconut palms and a boat he uses to fish and to visit the neighboring islands when he wishes. By God, he says, I envied this man, and if that island had belonged to me, I would have settled on it till the end of my life.* He ends up returning to Morocco, and I picture him ending his days in a little monastery for dervishes where he found peace, as he wrote the narrative of his travels, perhaps, or as he recounted to whoever was willing to listen his adventures beyond the seas. I don't remember any mention of prostitutes in his memoirs as they have reached us; Ibn Battuta had female slaves, singers, and a few legitimate wives he married in the course of his travels. But I confess that later on, in Barcelona, in the midst of whores and thieves, among the smoke of trashcans on fire, amid the truncheons of helmeted police, Zahra's thin face and her cunt often returned to me like a regret, like one more sadness to add to the list, an ambiguous remorse, what sort of man was I then, my youth thought, if I was incapable of enjoying a woman I had paid for and who was offering me, between her black stockings, her stubbly private parts; more than once I was tempted to slip twenty or thirty euros to the prostitute forever seated on the stoop of the building next to mine, in the Raval, and go upstairs with her just to rediscover a self-respect, a confidence in me that had mostly stayed behind with skinny Zahra and the laughter of her Madam.

Fortunately I was alone, that night in Tangier; I wouldn't have liked Bassam laughing at seeing me flee from the alcove with the green sofa after exactly two minutes. Men are dogs who rub against each other in solitude, only the hope of Judit gleamed in my misery even if, shy as I was, assailed by memories of Meryem, I would no doubt tremble before kissing her, shiver before going to bed with her, if the occasion presented itself, and the closer this mirage got— just a few hours separated me from her return to Tangier, as I stood in the early morning on my balcony—the more terrified I became. The events of the last few days whirled in my head, the debris of nightmares reddened the dawn mist over the Strait.

The fire at the Group worried me, I wondered how long I had left before the cops arrested me.

I felt a little like a fugitive.

Despite my new job, the money I had as advance, I was at a loss, anxious, just as powerless as when I'd been faced with Zahra the night before; the suit of age was too big for me. I missed a mother, a father, a Sheikh Nureddin, a Bassam.

Judit's arrival was a real disaster.

Maybe I shouldn't have waited for her at the train station as a surprise; I shouldn't have made her dizzy with talk, I shouldn't have acted as if we had an intimate, close relationship which didn't exist—I went too fast; I had formed my plans alone and quickly, à la Bassam, without caring about what she might have experienced in Marrakesh, a story that didn't exist. Judit saw me as I was, a young stranger who was holding her too tight. Maybe she was scared. She told me it was horrible, the way it felt, after the attack, the square that had been so bustling where everyone acted as if nothing had happened without believing it, where all of a sudden the huge machinery for enchanting tourists had ground to a stop.

She said actually, you know, in Marrakesh I saw your friend, Bassam, the one who was with us the other night.

As she said that she looked me in the eyes. I wasn't sure if she really had an intuition about what that meant. It was unimaginable, in any case. Unimaginable to think that she could have come across, a few hours later, one of the people who had made the bomb explode in that café. Despite all the clues I had had, I couldn't bring myself to realize it. That this attack actually existed, beyond the images on TV, was unthinkable. That Bassam could have participated in it without talking about it to me was, essentially, almost impossible.

Judit didn't say it's strange he was in Marrakesh, when we had seen him the day before without him mentioning his trip.

I walked her back to her hotel. Judit was distant, she barely opened her mouth the whole way, I tried to fill in the silence by speaking the whole time, which was probably not a good idea. My chatter seemed to force her even further into a disturbed silence.

Sometimes we sense the situation is escaping us, that things are getting out of hand; we become afraid and instead of calmly looking, trying to understand, we react like a dog caught in barbed wire, thrashing about madly until it slices open its throat.

My anger was a panic, it had no other object than to conquer Judit's coldness. I used her gift as a target, the book by Choukri of which I'd read five pages.

"It's a disgrace," I said, "how a Moroccan Muslim could write such things, it's an insult."

Judit said nothing, we were arriving at the Grand Zoco just before the gate to the old city. She just looked at me civilly; to me it felt like a slap.

I sank into an idiotic diatribe on this novel that I hadn't read and its author, a poor specimen, an illiterate beggar, a degenerate, I said, and the more absurdities I emitted, the more I felt as if I were drowning, floundering in a sea of stupidity while Judit, still so beautiful, was walking on water. I was sweating as I dragged the wheeled suitcase, in the end she didn't have a backpack but a bitch of a wheeled suitcase and as a good escort I had insisted on pulling it myself. I was out of breath, I couldn't continue my speech, which was becoming sporadic, there were too many thoughts in my head: the agitated swirling of my confused movements was pushing away my life raft. I sensed she had just one desire, to reach her hotel and get rid of me, to forget the long train trip, to forget Marrakesh, to forget me and catch her flight, and deep inside, in my innermost depths, I knew she was right. I wanted to seem literary and interesting, I continued my speech, holding forth as only a good male chauvinist can, I said, you should read Mutanabbi or Jahiz instead, that's real Arabic literature, Choukri isn't for girls. I had just shot a bullet—not in my foot, but smack in my head. This time Judit's look contained complete scorn. She said, yes yes, perfunctorily, and if I'd been the least bit courageous I'd have chucked the suitcase, stopped, let out a long string of curses and said sorry, let's stop everything, let's rewind, let's act as if I hadn't said anything since the start, as if I weren't obsessed with you, as if nothing had happened these last two days, as if nothing had exploded in Marrakesh, as if the fires weren't reaching us.

"My house burned down yesterday," I said all of a sudden.

She turned her face to me without pausing.

"Oh really?"

And I didn't know what to say; I could have added "yesterday I also went to the whorehouse without managing to fuck"; my eyes were burning, from sweat no doubt. I was a lost child who was asking for help from an unknown foreigner.

"What happened?"

"I don't know, everything burned. I took a room at an inn."

Her eyes told me she had trouble believing me; suddenly I saw the unlikelihood of my situation, no more family, no more friends, no more house, alone in Tangier, the drifting city.

"It's a long story."

"No doubt."

She looked straight ahead; it seemed to me she was quickening her pace.

Of course all this had begun with original sin, undressing Meryem, but it seemed to me it had become an international conspiracy, an enormity, an aberration, like the monstrous offspring of couples too closely related.

"We're here."

There was relief in these words uttered in unison; Judit's hand was clutching the suitcase I was holding the other end of, as if she were afraid I'd leave with it.

"Thank you for coming to get me at the station, it was nice of you."

She seemed sincere. Sincere and exhausted.

"It's nothing, it's normal."

"*Ilâ-l-liqâ,* then. Till the next time."

I said goodbye in turn, I didn't hold out my hand, or my cheek, or anything, and I left.

I must have been completely exhausted myself, washed up, psychologically destroyed, since I began to cry. It started in the street; the burning in my eyes got stronger; I felt a wetness on my cheeks, just like when you're little and you're bleeding from your nose and you suddenly discover your hand is red with blood. This wasn't blood. This was water, tears streaming down, and my vain attempts to wipe them away with my shirtsleeve were useless, they kept coming, more than before, I was so ashamed to be bawling like that in the street, I ran up the stairs of my hotel four at a time, slammed the door behind me, locked it, splashed water on my face, nothing helped, I was still sobbing like a kid; I collapsed on the bed, buried my face in the pillow to stifle these sobs, and let myself give in to sorrow. I must have dozed off. An hour or two later I had the mug of a boxer after an unequal fight—swollen eyelids, red eyes—but I felt better. A shower and nothing would show.

The opened envelope lay on the floor next to my bed; the old note from Bassam, which his mother had slipped me probably by mistake, was written on a piece of lined notebook paper; it began with باسم الله الرحمن الرحيم، هذه رسالة لك يا أخي، إنا لله وإنا إليه راجعون؛ folded inside was Meryem's letter for me, which he had kept all this time. I realized why he hadn't given it to me; he must have thought about destroying it, so I wouldn't find out, so I'd never know till the end of time what my heart had guessed, that she no longer existed, I couldn't even manage to say that she was dead, there, I had the truth in front of my eyes, there was nothing else, I had broken the Universe, the wrath of God was upon me, his rage, his powerful, blind, but just rage was destroying everything around me, I felt infinitesimal in my hotel room, lost in the heart of the world, I began crying again, on the balcony watching those idiotic boats crossing the Strait.

YOU never remember entirely, never really; you reconstruct, with time, the memories in your mind. I am so far, now, from the person I was at the time that it is impossible for me to once again exactly locate the power of sensations, the violence of emotions; today, it seems to me I would not be able to withstand such blows, that I would shatter into a thousand pieces. No one would survive such powerful shocks.

If I was certain about Meryem's death, though, she had never been so alive, since I was discovering her voice in her writing; her letter was a call for help that resounded in the midst of the darkness, in the desert. A cry straight out of the caves of Hercules, by which you enter the Underworld; a dirty joke of fate. She said she loved me, called me her love, she said we had to get married, otherwise she would have to abandon the child to an orphanage; her despair was too much for me, I burned the letter in the hotel bathroom, إنا لله وإنا إليه راجعون along with Bassam's letter. I will never know what happened over there between Al-Hoceima and Nador, no one will ever know. Bassam explained the details to me with strange, medical words, in his childlike scrawl. He said nothing of himself, but surely, to write such a letter, he must have made up his mind to disappear as well; otherwise, why tell me now what he could have explained to me the day before face-to-face.

I paced in circles in my room; night fell slowly. I rolled myself a joint, smoked it on the balcony; turned on the computer; looked online for updates about the attack, about the Group for the Propagation of Koranic Thought; nothing new. Details, clarifications about the bomb, the type of explosives, but no arrest. I found a short, two-line piece, arson in a religious bookstore, hundreds of books destroyed. Arson. The police must be wondering why none of the members of that association had reappeared.

The muezzin had just made the call to evening prayer.

I had a note from Judit apologizing for not having been more talkative earlier, she was exhausted. If I wanted to go out for tea that night, I could come by her hotel.

Strangely, I no longer wanted to. I didn't want anything.

I went to the bathroom, showered for a long time, washing my feet, my hands, my forearms, my face. I put my blanket on the rug, turned to the east, and prayed. I made four prostrations thinking of nothing but God.

The night was there, it was gazing at the lights of the ferries going to Tarifa.

As I recited the Fatiha, as I breathed out the verses without any thought troubling them, as I repeated the holy words, I became calm again.

There was an intimate strength in silence, a precious song.

It lingered in me.

The Spanish coast shone, to the left of my improvised Kiblah.

I wondered if I had enough cash to pay for an illegal passage to Spain. I was more and more convinced that Sheikh Nureddin had left this money for me. It was inexplicable otherwise; he must have had pity on me. He knew the horrible story of Meryem and my aunt. With me, he had always been fair and kind. Deep down I hoped they had nothing to do with Marrakesh, neither the Sheikh, nor Bassam; unfortunately what I had been able to see for myself, the cudgels and the sermons, left me little hope.

What the hell would I do in Spain? There was my uncle who was working in the Almeria province, but it was no use going to see him. Also they had a crisis there. No work. In any case I didn't have any papers. Go off in search of adventure?

I thought Paris would be more lenient. Paris or Marseille, the cities of books and detective novels. I pictured them as somewhat alike, populated with sons of grouchy Italians, fighting Algerians, gangsters who spoke slang. I was fifty years behind the times, but still, there must be something left, after all Izzo had written *Total Chaos* not long ago, I thought. I imagined visiting him, sending him a note saying *Dear Sir, I am a young Moroccan fan and I would very much like to meet you.* I looked at Wikipedia and found out he was dead. Manchette, too, had died a long time ago. Aside from a few remote and idiotic cousins I didn't know anyone else in France.

The main thing was to get ready as fast as possible: find lodging that didn't cost an arm and a leg like this dive, buy some clothes, start working. This business of copying out texts intrigued me. Ask for a passport, just in case. Wait for news from the police, which would certainly end up coming; read everything I could to train myself. Forget Meryem, Bassam, and Sheikh Nureddin.

Put a plan into action.

Have a program.

Work for the future.

After all, twenty is the finest age in life.

I got another email from Judit on Facebook, posted four minutes earlier, it said You're not coming by, then? I replied—I'll be right there.

LAKHDAR, Judit said to me in the middle of the night. Lakhdar, and I liked the way she said my name, her slight Spanish accent, her stress on the *dad*, that letter that exists only in Arabic.

"Lakhdar, that's not very common, is it?"

My head was on her shoulder.

"No, it's pretty rare in Morocco. But common in Algeria. My father liked the name, I don't really know why."

"What does it mean, other than 'green'?"

"Actually Lakhdar has two meanings, 'green,' but also 'prosperous.' Green's the color of Islam. Maybe that's why my father chose it. There's also a prophet who was important to mystics. Khidr the Green. He appears in the Cave Sura."

"Lakhdar. I'll call you the Green Hornet."

"You're more beautiful than Cameron Diaz."

She gently caught my hand and guided it downward.

THE weeks and months that followed, before November and my start as a waiter on the Comarit ferries, went by so quickly that my memories are like them, brief and quick. Work for Jean-François was hard, dull, and mind-numbing; my room, halfway between the center of town and the Free Zone, cold and inhospitable; I shared the apartment with three workers slightly older than me but I felt they had never been my age. They seemed to be a bottomless fountain of stupidity. As soon as they got a few dirhams they'd blow them on a new tracksuit, sneakers, hash; they dreamed about a nice life, the high point of which would be the purchase of a double bed from the corner furniture store and a car from the Nissan or Toyota dealer; every day they surfed on *voitureaumaroc.com* and dreamed of luxury sedans they could never buy, look, here's a 1992 Jaguar for a hundred thousand dirhams; they wore huge sunglasses that rounded out their faces and their Bluetooth earbuds were always in place. They were smooth, interchangeable, and noisy. But they were company, human activity next to me; they hit on garment factory girls, whose small soft hands ached from the throb of sewing machines, or if they couldn't get them, then on the fish girls in the frozen-food plant, who smelled of grouper or shrimp from chin to innermost cunt, and all these girls were responsive to the vulgar advances of my fake-Ray-Ban-toting roommates who brought them in great ceremony, like princesses, to eat hamburgers in those big American chains that somehow gave them the impression of living life, real life, not the life of nerds, of hicks who didn't have the luck to work in the Free Zone, and thus not only earned less, much less, but above all were much less distinguished, having neither sunglasses nor fancy phones; the whole performance made for a huge waste, far, far different from the neighborhoods where I had grown up, true, but also and especially from the ones where I wanted to live.

In any case I didn't have much time off, not much time to interact with my housemates, work was terribly time-consuming and resembled the work of the sewing-machine slaves or the prawn-shellers, but without the smell: I spent twelve to sixteen hours in front of the screen, back bent like a string bean picker, faithfully copying out, with my four or six fingers, books, culinary encyclopedias, handwritten letters, archives, anything that Mr. Bourrelier handed me. The job was well-named: *saisie kilométrique*, typing by the kilometer; more precisely "double typing," since this mind-numbing work was done twice, by two different mind-numbed idiots, and then the results were cross-checked, which gave a reliable file that could be sent to the sponsor. Mr. Bourrelier's customers were extremely diverse: publishing houses that wanted to make digital use of or reprint an old backlist, government officials who had tons and tons of written stuff to go through, cities, town halls with overflowing archives, universities that sent old tapes of lectures and teachings to transcribe—you felt that all of France, all the verbiage of France, was landing here, in Africa; the whole country was vomiting language onto Mr. Bourrelier and his slaves. You had to type quickly, of course, but not too quickly, since you had to pay for corrections out of your pocket: every time a crosscheck of the two samples revealed a mistake, the word or phrase in question was verified and the misprint deducted from my salary. The first book I copied was a travel book about the African coasts at the end of the eighteenth century; pirates, slaves, that sort of thing. There must have been a goldmine in this genre of literature, because after that I was off to Russia, typing out *A Frenchman in Siberia*, written in 1872; and you might have thought this work was interesting, but more than anything it was exhausting, you had to pay attention to spelling and to proper nouns; you got lost in the flesh of words, in letters, sentences, as close as possible to the text, and sometimes I'd have been quite incapable of summarizing what such or such a page that I had just copied out was talking about. At least, I said to myself plausibly, after a few months of this treatment my French might be impeccable, but above it was all frustrating—I of course didn't have the time to look up unknown words in the dictionary; I copied them out as is, without understanding them, and the number of typos stemmed from my incomprehension, from my lack of knowledge of one term or another.

Mr. Bourrelier was nice enough to me; he often said to me Ah, sorry, still no thrillers on the horizon, but if there ever are any, I swear they'll be yours. I was a good worker, I think, I tried to be serious and didn't have much else to do.

One day, my zeal got me a poisoned gift: when I arrived at work one morning, Mr. Bourrelier called me into his office. He was cheerful, he was laughing like a child, I've just gotten some excellent news, he told me. Magnificent news. A very big order from the Ministry of Former Combatants. It involves digitalizing the individual files of all combatants in the First World War. It's a very fat contract. We replied to their call for bids, and we were chosen. They're handwritten files, impossible to deal with them automatically, we'll have to copy them out by hand. We're beginning with the dead.

"Aren't they all dead yet?" I asked naively.

"Yes yes, of course they're all dead, there aren't any more French fighters from the First World War alive. I mean we're going to begin with the 'Dead for France,' a separate batch of files."

"And how many are there?"

"One million three hundred thousand files, total. Then there're the wounded and the ones who got out alive, that'll be more cheerful."

One million three hundred fucking thousand dead, you don't really realize what that represents, but I can assure you that makes quite a bit of work for typing by the kilometer. Gigabytes and gigabytes of scanned files, a special program to enter the data, last name, first name, date and place of birth, serial number, date, place, and type of death, sic, *type of death*, they didn't weigh themselves down with fancy phrases, at the time, do you think, they had hundreds of thousands of files to fill out. All of it handwritten, in a beautiful fountain-pen calligraphy: Achille Brun, soldier, 138th Infantry Division, Died for France on December 3, 1914, in the hospital at Châlons-sur-Marne, Type of death: war wound (crossed out) typhoid fever (added), born January 25, 1891, in Montbron in Charente; Ben Moulloub, Belkacem ben Bohammad ben Oumar, second class, 2nd Regiment of Algerian Infantrymen, Died for France on November 6, 1914, in Soupir, in Aisne, Type of death: killed by the enemy, born in 1884 in (illegible), *département* of Constantine, and so on a million three hundred thousand times, even with the special program you needed one or two minutes per file, especially to decipher the names of unknown holes in the wall, Algerian douars, Senegalese villages, French hamlets I knew nothing about; some of the soldiers stayed in my memory, like that Achille Brun or that Belkacem ben Moulloub, and it was strange to think that these ghosts of poilus were making a posthumous trip to Morocco, to Tangier, in my computer.

We divided up the work, my colleagues (French literature students or young typists, mostly) and I: one hundred fifty or two hundred files in the morning, and sixty pages of books, minimum, in the afternoon. The problem was that you couldn't give up one project for another; everything had to be done at the same time: copying out the memoirs of Casanova for a Quebec publishing house was at least as urgent as the "Killed by the Enemy." The volumes of *History of My Life* were immense, endless. I confess having taken great pleasure, despite the sleepless nights, in typing them out by the kilometer. This Casanova was funny and likeable, courtly, crafty; he spent his time running around with his sex on fire, hence on running around taking care of his venereal diseases, which didn't seem to cause him any shame; for him, the body, women, youth had nothing shameful about them. There was an ironic intelligence in him that reminded me of Isa ibn Hisham and Abu al-Fath al-Iskandari, the heroes of Hamadani — but in a longer version, of course. The Casanova was one of the rare books I actually *read* as I was copying it out: over three months' work, without any slacking.

I always wondered how much Jean-François Bourrelier billed for our services, and what his cut was; I never dared ask him. One thing was for certain, the Killed by the Enemy and Mr. Casanova didn't touch a penny of it, and as for myself, after the accounts were audited (money withheld for corrections, etc.), I rarely managed to get more than five hundred euros a month, for a minimum of sixty hours' work a week, which was an extraordinary salary for a young yokel like me, but far from the tens of thousands of dirhams promised. When payday arrived, Mr. Frédéric always looked slightly apologetic, he'd say Ah, there were a lot of corrections, or else Good, this month isn't too bad, but you'll do better next month, you have to get used to these dead-soldier files and accelerate your pace.

I told all my stories to Judit in interminable letters, that was my recreation, every night, when I should have hated the computer and above all its keyboard I would write at great length to Judit to explain what we had done that day, Casanova, the poilus and I; I told her about Achille Brun the typhoid-stricken and about Belkacem ben Moulloub dead in Soupir, about Casanova and Tireta watching an execution on the Place de Grève from a window, in the company of two ladies, without going so far as to dare tell her the obscene but hilarious details of Tireta's mistaken shot.

I began writing her poems as well, mostly in French and stolen from Nizar Qabbani; French or Spanish poetry seemed dry to
me, not flowery enough. I always ended my missives with a verse,
الحب يا حبيبتي قصيدة جميلة منقوشة على القمر *Love, my love, is a*
beautiful poem embellished on the moon, and so on. Judit was more
discreet about her feelings, but I sensed, in her emails which were
sometimes in French, sometimes in Arabic, that she appreciated our
correspondence; she told me about her life in Barcelona, her everyday routine, her annoyance with the stupidity of her classes, her
boredom at the university, where the professors themselves seemed
to scorn the texts they taught as if they were a dead language like
Latin. Through her, I began to hate these puny Arabic scholars in
colonial shorts who every day regretted the fact that Spain had for
a few centuries been Arabic, sighing over Andalusian texts in which
they saw nothing but lexical difficulty. She told me look, we're
studying such-or-such a poem by Ibn Zaydún, such-or-such a frag-
ment by Ibn Hazm whom they called Abenhazam, and I would rush
to a bookstore to find the book in question; most of the time it was
a wonder to me, a jewel from another time whose Arabic filled my
mouth and eardrums with unprecedented pleasure. Despite the dead
poilus and Casanova, I felt very Arabic thanks to Judit; I followed
her studies from day to day: she would ask me grammar questions, I
would open the grammar books and classical commentators to find
an answer for her; she heard of an author and the next day I would
send her an annotated file with extracts and summaries.

Of course, these activities were incompatible with my co-renters' way of life, who had been unearthed by a kind of syndicate
of French companies, which tried as much as possible to facilitate
lodging for their personnel; Adel, Yacine, and Walid all came from
Casablanca, they were "skilled technicians" and worked in an auto-
mobile parts factory, on the assembly line. Every night they saw me
immersed in my files of dead soldiers or in my books, and took
me for a madman. Sometimes they'd shout Lakhdar *khouya*, you're

going to make yourself deaf and blind, it's worse than masturbation, all that, come out for a spin in the open air, you'll see some girls! No no, he'll just see the sea, but that can't hurt him! *Moulay* Lakhdar, you're pale as prepubescent underwear, come inhale the exhaust from our car! And they'd end up leaving, earpiece in place, for Tangier and its delights, cruising with the music at full blast for hours till they ended up stuffing their faces with hamburgers around midnight, coming home brimming with excitement, and sprawling in front of the TV smoking joint after joint before returning to the factory the next day.

I hadn't heard anything about Sheikh Nureddin or Bassam since the attack, they hadn't reappeared; little by little my fears of seeing the police turn up had lessened and the Group for the Propagation of Koranic Thought seemed far away, over there, in those endless suburbs peopled by hundreds of hicks like me, but yet very close; of course I had followed the news on TV; they ended up arresting three suspects, I didn't know any of them: they had odd-looking faces that didn't exude intelligence, but photos of criminals are rarely flattering. Every day I expected news of Sheikh Nureddin and Bassam being arrested, but it never came.

Just a few days after Judit left, there was another horrible attack, which profoundly affected me, as if I myself had been present, maybe because we had been at the place not long before. The Café Hafa is situated on the cliff top, suspended above the Mediterranean, lost among the bougainvillea and jasmine of the neighborhood's luxury villas; it may well be the most famous place in Tangier and one of the most pleasant on nice days (a table set a little apart, where Judit had taken my hand before kissing me, I remember, I've thought about it often since, I was ashamed, very ashamed, I was afraid we'd be seen, kissing in public is a misdemeanor) especially when there aren't many people, late morning for instance, and you feel as if you have the sea and all the Strait to yourself. I learned from the paper that a man had entered the café, taken out a long dagger or sword and attacked a group of young people sitting at a table, no doubt because there were foreigners among them; a young Moroccan my age died, and another was wounded in the thigh, a French boy; there were two Spanish girls with them: they were all students of translation at the university in Tangier. The suspect fled down the cliff, pursued by the café's customers and waiters, and managed to escape. An artist's rendering of his face was attached to the article; he had the same round head and childlike face as Bassam, it could have been him. Maybe he had suddenly gone mad. First Judit sees him in Marrakesh just after the explosion and then a face that resembles his appears in *Le Journal de Tanger*. I couldn't picture him stabbing young students calmly sitting in the sun; it wasn't possible that he'd changed so quickly, and yet I couldn't help but remember how readily he had beaten up the bookseller. It seemed to me that the question *Why?* would remain forever without an answer, even if it was indeed Bassam who had helped place the bomb in the Café Argan and stabbed a Moroccan our age, even if I had him in front of me, if I had asked him why? why do it? he would have shrugged his shoulders; he would have answered For God, out of hatred of Christians, for Islam, for Sheikh Nureddin, what do I know, but he would lie, I knew he would lie and that he certainly didn't know the reason for his actions which, in fact, had none, no more than there was a reason for beating up the bookseller, it was like that, it was in the air, violence was in the air, the wind was blowing that way; it was blowing pretty much everywhere and had swept Bassam up in idiocy. I thought about what I'd brought about despite myself, unhappiness and death; Bassam held the club and maybe the sword, but the ideological causes I could see from the height of my twenty years didn't convince me: I knew Bassam, I knew that his hatred of the West or his passion for Islam were all relative, that a few months before meeting Sheikh Nureddin going to the mosque with his father annoyed him more than anything, he never bothered getting up one single time at dawn for the *fajr* prayer, he dreamed of going to live in Spain or France. But when I thought about it carefully I was also aware that, *a contrario*, just because he liked girls or dreamed of Germany and America didn't prevent anything whatsoever. I knew that Sheikh Nureddin had grown up in France, and when I had spoken with him about it he appreciated some aspects of the country and he acknowledged that, if not for living in the midst of *kuffar*, infidels, it was better to live in France than in Spain or Italy, where, he said, Islam was scorned, crushed, reduced to poverty.

All those months spent with the Group for the Propagation of Koranic Thought had brought me closer to Nureddin; he was good to me and I knew (or liked to believe) that he had taken me in without any ulterior motives; he gave me lessons on morality, true, but no more than a father or a big brother. He would often repeat, laughing, that my detective novels were rotting my mind, that they were diabolical books that were driving me to perdition, but he never did anything to stop me from reading them, for example, and if I hadn't seen him with my own eyes leading the group of fighters at night I would have been incapable of imagining for a single second that he could be connected, closely or remotely, with a violent action.

Apparently, the three brutes of the Marrakesh attack had acted alone, at least that's what the police said; they had learned on the Internet how to create a bomb and make it explode. But Bassam's presence there, then, affirmed by Judit, led me to envision networks, connections, paranoid conspiracies; I even thought for an instant that Sheikh Nureddin was actually in the service of the Palace, an agitator, a double agent, whose mission was to make all reforms and progress toward democracy fail, which would explain the fire at the Group's headquarters, to wipe out all traces, and also the fact that I had never been bothered.

The attack at the Café Hafa seemed to me particularly cowardly and worrisome, maybe because the victim could have been me, Judit and me, maybe because it was on my territory, here and now, and no longer a rumor—a tremendous one, true, but far away. I have to confess, for a long time I was afraid, when I'd sit down at a café in Tangier, of seeing Bassam appear, sword in hand.

I had to stop thinking about these things too much if I didn't want to become completely paranoid.

Fortunately the dead soldiers, Casanova and my poems for Judit left me little free time. عيناك آخر مركبين يسافران فهل هنالك من مكان؟ *Your eyes are the last boat leaving, can you make room for me?* إنني تعبت من التسكع في محطات الجنون، ظلي معي *For I am tired of wandering through the harbors of madness. Stay with me! So that the sea will keep its color*, and so on, always Nizar Qabbani. My idea was, of course, to end up composing my own verses without the help of my prestigious elders, but that was a lot of work. My Poem Number One, the first that was really mine, was the following:

> *Start of the warm season*
> *Here I am*
> *Explorer lost beneath his ceiling fan*
> *A telephone*
> *A computer*
> *A love made of wax I watch its drops fall*
> *To seal my letters*
> *Tonight I will read Casanova*
> *Thinking of you*
> *I will bathe in your eyes on every page there is a woman*
> *Who will look like you*
> *Every night*
> *I hold a masked ball at the end of the world*
> *For naughty ghosts like you*

Judit would have preferred me to write her poems in Arabic, after all that's your language, she said, it's the one you know best,

and she was right of course, but I couldn't manage it: Arabic poetry
is infinitely more beautiful and complex than French; in Arabic,
I felt as if I were writing sub-Qabbani, sub-Sayyab, sub-sub-Ibn
Zaydún; whereas in French, since I hadn't read anything, any poet,
or very little, aside from Maurice Carême and Jacques Prévert at
school, I felt much freer. The ideal thing would have been to write
in Spanish, that's for sure: I could see myself composing a collection
entitled *El Libro de Judit*, The Book of Judit, but that wasn't going
to happen anytime soon.

For a little change of air, every Saturday I'd go into town, in the
morning to the library of the Cervantes Center, and in the afternoon to that of the Institut Français, or vice-versa, and between the
two, I'd hang out in cafés, people-watching. I didn't feel lonely, I
just felt as if I no longer belonged to the city, that Tangier was leaving me, going away. It was ready to go. Judit gave me hope. I sensed
I was about to leave Morocco, that I was about to become someone
else, leave behind me a part of the past unhappiness and misery,
forget bombs, swords, my dead; forget the ghosts of soldiers killed
by the enemy, the hours and hours spent copying out, ad infinitum,
fleshless names so I could finally set foot, I thought, in a country
not eaten away by resentment, or poverty, or fear.

On May 2nd, the day after May Day, Osama bin Laden was
killed at night by American commandos and his body thrown out
of a plane into the Indian Ocean. The news was in all the papers:
the thin man with the long beard and spellbinding stare had been
crushed like an insect, in the midst of his wives and medications,
trapped in his own strange villa, with fortified walls like a fortress—
at least that's what the journalists told us. The most sought-after
terrorist in the world was thirty miles away from Islamabad, and
had been for years, the article said. People wondered why they had
unearthed him today, and not yesterday or tomorrow; why they
hadn't arrested him, why they had thrown his remains to the fish.
It didn't matter much, you sensed that Bin Laden had lost his body,

his physical presence, a long time ago—he had become a voice who spoke from time to time from an imaginary cave, hidden in the depths of the centuries; the very reality of his existence seemed increasingly doubtful and his submersion completed his transformation into a character, a demon or a saint: someone who for me, in the confusion of childhood, inspired both horror and admiration, hope and terror, someone who had victoriously defied the United States of America by spreading destruction now became a slightly disturbing myth, a lame symbol, who limped between greatness and wretchedness. I remembered that at school, he was one of Bassam's heroes; we used to play in the schoolyard at being Afghan fighters; today Bassam had disappeared and Bin Laden had met his fate in the form of black-hooded Navy Seals, 'seals,' who had dragged him down into the depths of the abyss. In itself, it made no sense, aside from one more farewell to the world of yesterday.

When Judit told me she was going to enroll in an Arabic course at the Institut Bourguiba in Tunis for all of July and when she suggested I join her there, I said to myself that would be a first journey, just as Ibn Battuta, leaving Tangier for the East, paused in Tunisia. I very much wanted to see with my own eyes what a revolution in progress was like; I felt as if I were living in the age of Revolt and actually felt much closer to a young twenty-year-old Tunisian than to anyone else—I imagined that Tunis must be a little like Tangier, that I wouldn't feel out of place there, the Tunisians were Maghrebs, Arabs, and Muslims, and what's more all those young people, my brothers, or rather my cousins, had managed to get rid of their dictator—the prospect of seeing all that close up delighted me. So I ran to negotiate my vacation with Mr. Bourrelier—I naively imagined that one must have a right to days off, and in fact, that was the case, but it was not possible to take them (except in precise cases linked to the registry office, marriage, births, deaths to which I could not lay claim) except after a year of work. Jean-François was very annoyed. He told me he couldn't make an exception that would risk creating a precedent, but on the other hand, he said, and just for a week, we can arrange something; you set your mind to doing your files and pages, and we'll close our eyes to your obligation to be present at the office for five days. If ever any of your colleagues ask, we'll say you're sick and working from home, and that's it. But above all don't let anything happen to you over there and don't miss the plane back, okay, we'd have to fire you.

So I was going to have to travel with the dead poilus and Casanova, funny company, but fine, Judit was in class all day, I'd work at the same time as she was working, that was all. And a week was better than nothing. Plus, to go to Tunis, thanks to the Maghreb fraternity, I didn't need a visa, just a passport, and on Friday July 15, 2011, in the late afternoon, after having made a semi-definitive hole in my savings, I took a plane for the first time. The Ibn Battuta Airport is adjacent to the Free Zone, so I went there on foot after work; I was well dressed, I had put on a jacket and shirt despite the heat; hair combed, shoes polished, a little emotional, I must have broadcast my airplane-novicehood from miles away. I tried to pass myself off as a regular, as if the airport were a nightclub or a bar where you could be refused entry, displaying a weary scorn faced with the formalities, the obligatory stripping, all the while my heart was gripped with anxiety—I was afraid something bad would happen, that the customs officer, typing my name into his computer, would learn that I was wanted by the police, his screen would start blinking, a siren would wail, and a squad of fat cops with grey hats would lay into me, but no, nothing happened, they returned my passport almost without looking at me and after a wait that seemed very long to me, opposite the huge windows looking out on the runway, I boarded the plane, not scared stiff, let's not exaggerate, but not exactly reassured; through the porthole I saw a guy wearing a headset walking next to our plane as it backed up, as if he were leading a dog by the leash, it was very strange; I was very surprised by the noise of the engines and the power of the acceleration when the Airbus rolled onto the runway, and I thought this thing would never take off, I felt slightly nauseous when it finally lifted off, and felt a great exaltation when, looking over the wing, pressed against the porthole by the angle of takeoff, Tangier and the Strait appeared beneath me, as I had never seen them before.

Judit had returned for three days in early June, three days of happiness, complete harmony, and pleasure that had left me sad and more solitary than ever when they had finally come to an end and I had gone home back to my roommates—I hadn't wanted to invite her to my place, first of all because I just had a single bed, and secondly because I was jealous, I didn't want any other Moroccan to approach her, especially not the three specimens who shared my daily life. Just imagining them seeing Judit in pajamas, spying on her in the bathroom perhaps, gave me murderous thoughts. The idea of not being Judit's sole, unique Arab made me crazy. I knew she had already had "fiancés," as she called them, that she'd had boyfriends at the university, friends, of course, but those Catalans were a category apart in my head. I was something different. I was her Arab. I wanted to be the only Arab in Judit's life. (So I was worried about her stay in Tunisia, I have to admit; I pictured her being the target of incessant advances of hordes of young frustrated Tunisians; I was well-placed to understand how they might feel.)

So I went out of my way to find two rooms next to each other in a small hotel—Moroccan law, champion of good morals, forbade us from taking a single room without being married. Our balconies communicated, and we didn't even have to go out into the hallway to visit each other. It was sort of amusing, it had its adventuresome side. But still I was a little ashamed, when Judit asked me why we couldn't share a double, to reply it was because I was Moroccan: If I had been foreign, no one would have bothered us.

We hadn't left the hotel much during those three days, aside from a few excursions, Cape Spartel, the caves of Hercules, the Kasbah Museum and the Marshan Cemetery to see Choukri's grave;

the remarks of the café waiters, the museum employees or even the passersby, when they saw me alone with Judit, didn't encourage me to go out: it was as pleasant as a kick in the ass, that mixture of scorn, jealousy, and crass vulgarity that made me want to give them the finger with a heartfelt phrase about the sisters or mothers of the parties concerned. Walking with Judit was to receive, at every street corner, a serious quantity of symbolic gobs of spit, because I was a young Moroccan, and strolling in the company of a European girl without, seemingly, belonging to the social class that visited the private beaches or bars of luxury hotels, a class that could allow itself anything. Judit herself realized it, and I felt she was sorry for me, which made me even sadder. Even at Choukri's grave, a moron my age came over to bother us; he asked me in Arabic what we were doing there, which is a funny question to ask in a cemetery— I replied, we're coming to get ourselves buried, of course, when I wanted to say "We're coming to your funeral, ass," but I didn't dare. After all, he might have been sincere, maybe he wanted to help us.

I'd become a little savage, in fact, I think. Locked up with my books, in my solitude, alone with Judit, I no longer had any contact with the outside world, aside from my three co-renters, who couldn't really be called the "outside world."

In the meantime, I had read *For Bread Alone*, and even the next one, *The Time of Errors*; I had to apologize to Judit: this Choukri was something else. His Arabic was dry as the sticks his father beat him with, hard as famine. A new language, a way of writing that seemed revolutionary to me. He wasn't afraid, he told his story without hiding anything—sex, violence, or poverty. His wanderings reminded me of my months of vagabondage, at times; the feeling was so strong that I had to close the book, the way you walk away from a mirror when its reflection doesn't suit you. Judit was happy I had seen the light; she told me about the unique history of the text of *For Bread Alone*: published first in translation, banned in Morocco in Arabic for almost twenty years. It wasn't hard to see why: poverty, sex, and drugs must not have been the taste of the censors of the time. The advantage is that today the books have so little weight, are so little sold, so little read that it's not even worth banning them anymore. And Choukri was buried in great ceremony, with ministers and representatives from the Palace, in Tangier about twenty years ago—as if all those higher-ups were celebrating the fact of his death by accompanying him to the grave.

Judit's departure, after our three days and three nights, had plunged me into sadness and solitude; I fought them as usual, by work, reading until my eyes were burning with fever, and love poetry. I thought about the forty-five days that separated me from my trip. I looked at pages and pages of information about Tunisia, about the Revolution. Ibn Battuta just devoted a few lines to Tunis, where there were, he said, many important ulemas; he was there at the end of Ramadan, and took part in the celebration. I myself would be there just before the start of the fast, which meant I was barely a month behind my illustrious predecessor.

AS if on purpose, a new blow of fate, I received the first email from Bassam two days before my flight. I confess I was thinking a little less often about him and Sheikh Nureddin, that I hadn't returned to the neighborhood since the fire at the Group for the Propagation of Koranic Thought, that I was living a little like an exile, and one morning, glancing over my inbox as always just after getting up, to see if I'd already gotten a reply from Judit to my missive from the day before, I noticed a bizarre message, which I took at first for one of those emails offering to effortlessly lengthen your virility by five centimeters, or to buy Viagra at a discount price to strengthen it, with the sender's name as "Cheryl Bang" or something like that. What intrigued me was the subject line: *News*, and I opened it—the note had just three lines:

My very dear brother, how are things with you? I'm far away here and it's hard but Inshallah we'll find each other again on this earth or in Paradise. Take care of yourself khouya, think of me and all will be well.

It wasn't signed, and I wondered for an instant if it was spam, but I don't know, I felt as if I could hear Bassam in these lines, I was sure it was him. Why such a message? To reassure me? He was far away, it was hard, where the hell could he be hiding? In Afghanistan? Mali? No, there couldn't be any Internet over there. Who knows, maybe the fighters of Al-Qaeda in the Islamic Maghreb had Wi-Fi in their tents. Or else he was writing to me from a secret prison. Or maybe these few words were not from him, but just automatically generated by a machine, and I was completely wrong.

I confess I hesitated to reply to this Cheryl; I ended up not doing so. I was afraid; after all, if he had written to me from that strange address without signing off, there was definitely a reason. I pictured him in his Land of Shadows, with the Khidr who carried his messages to me, that Land of Shadows where he wielded the sword, gun, or bomb, emboldened by prayer, with other fighters, strips of cloth tied around their heads, as they appear in videos online. But no doubt it was far different, the deserted mountains of Afghanistan or the most distant corners of the Sahara.

Take care of yourself, khouya, *think about me and all will be well,* it's with that phrase in my head that I left for Tunis.

I didn't mention it to Judit.

I told her about everything, though, at night, during those first nights—Meryem, Bassam, Sheikh Nureddin, my months of wandering, the beating of booksellers, and she was sorry for me, she had caressed me in the darkness the way you apply the magic balm of a kiss to the hurts of a crying child; I had confided to her my fears about the Marrakesh attack, she had confessed that she had thought about it, too, when she had found herself face to face with Bassam as she was leaving her hotel. At first, she said, I thought he was with you, that you had prepared that as a surprise for me, coming to Marrakesh with him. And then I was a little afraid, he made me afraid, he seemed extraordinarily nervous, she said, feverish, as if he were ill. He kept looking around him. For a long time, she added, I wondered if we had mentioned the name of that hotel during our conversations in Tangier. It's possible, but I don't remember. It's all pretty scary.

I agreed, it was all frightening; I had told her by email about the attack on the Café Hafa, and had shown her the artist's rendering when she returned to Tangier. She simply said, It's him, it's horrible, we have to do something.

It's him, it's terrible, it's Bassam, he's gone mad, you have to go to the police and tell them.

I tried to convince her it wasn't him, if he was in Tangier I'd know it, he'd have gotten back in touch with me one way or another, so she had calmed down a little.

We're playing at scaring ourselves, I said.

I didn't want to worry her more by telling her that I had received that enigmatic email. I wanted Tunis to be perfect, magical, as Tangier had been six weeks before; I wanted to be there for her, help her with her classes, talk to her for hours about Arabic grammar and literature, fuck a lot, fuck as often as possible and see what had become of the Revolution.

Nothing less.

Judit came to pick me up at the airport; the Tunisian customs officers looked like the Moroccan ones, gray and hefty; they yelled at me because I hadn't filled out the immigration papers, the existence of which I was entirely ignorant, but they took pity on me and let me through without having to go to the end of the line.

Judit was waiting for me at the exit, I hesitated just for a second about embracing her—but after all we were in the airport of a revolutionary country. I set down my little suitcase, caught Judit by the waist, she threw her hands around my neck and we kissed—finally she was the one, a little embarrassed, who put an end to our show of affection.

I had just taken a plane for the first time, and for the first time, I was in a foreign country. Judit spoke a lot, very fast, about Tunis, her classes, the city, her apartment, her friends; I looked at her, her long hair lightened by the summer, her fine, precise features, a certain roundness to her cheekbones; her lips, with all those sounds continuously coming out of them.

Night was falling.

Judit had decided to treat me to a taxi to ride into town; on our left we could see the lagoon, the lake of Tunis; the sky was still reddening a little in the west.

She lived in a tiny, rather charming apartment ten minutes by foot from the institute where she had her classes; on the ground floor, next door to an office building, two white rooms looked out onto a little patio, also white, its floor made of blue tile: one bedroom with a large mattress on the floor and a little desk, and a kitchen-living-dining room; all of it couldn't have measured more than thirty square meters, but the proportions were perfect; I confess I took a lot of pleasure in typing out my dead poilus every morning, watching the shadows grow shorter in the courtyard, then the summer sun exploding on the bluish tiles; in the evening, when Judit returned, we would spray water on the tiles and lie down on them, naked in the false cool of the humidity, until night fell.

On Saturday, Judit showed me around the center of Tunis and the old city; the heat was less stifling than you'd have thought: a little bit like Tangier, a light breeze blew in from the sea. But the glare was so great that the lagoon looked like an immense expanse of salt, dazzling white. The Tunisian dialect was amusing, more singsong than Moroccan or Algerian, with something oriental about it, I thought. The Medina was a vast labyrinth for devouring tourists and you had to lose yourself in its winding streets to escape from them calling out to you every two minutes, *my friend, my friend, a tea my friend? A rug, a souvenir?* I was quite proud that they usually talked to me in French because I was with Judit.

The day before, the day of my arrival, there had been violent clashes between demonstrators and police in front of the government palace, on the Kasbah square; the whole neighborhood had been blocked off, and the sit-in of young people demanding among, other things, the resignation of the Minister of the Interior, had been dispersed with batons and teargas. The Internet was calling on people to revive the Revolution, which one sensed was in the process of dying, or coming to an end, depending, and the elections, in October, had returned power to the hands of Ennahda's Islamists, as everyone must have expected. The young people sensed that the fruits of their revolt were being stolen from them, and that the rioting would give birth to an extremely conservative, if not reactionary, government—democratic indeed, but they weren't going to laugh as much as under Ben Ali. As we arrived at the still-barricaded Kasbah square, full of vans of cops and helmeted men, I thought I could smell the sharp stench of teargas—the acid tears of the revolutionaries. The fighting the day before had spread to a large part of the country and to Sidi Bouzid, bastion of the opposition; the police had even used real bullets—to frighten the crowd, they said, but a fourteen-year-old kid had still been killed by a ricochet. According to what I read online, a lot of activists thought the Friday gathering had been organized by Islamists.

In the summer heat, the Tunisians were complaining more about the (relative) absence of tourists than about the provisional government. They all clung to the date of October 23, which would put a democratic end, they thought, to the gas and the police brutality.

For me, maybe because I was foreign, there was a certain sadness in this transition, this post-Revolution, and Tunis seemed paralyzed, petrified in the grenade smoke and the whiteness of the summer.

I was not Ibn Battuta: I was not about to meet important ulemas, or listen to sermons in mosques, even if that wouldn't have displeased me, but I would have had to be alone there: In Tunisia, as in Morocco, mosques are forbidden to non-Muslims. Since Judit found this measure rather discriminatory—she assured me that was not at all the case in Cairo or Damascus—I searched for the cause, and it was the French, more precisely the first Resident-General in Morocco, Lyautey, who established this law, which then extended to all Maghreb under French rule, to ensure respect among the different religious communities. I don't know if it's good or bad; it seemed strange to me that groups of tourists could freely enter the mosque of the Umayyad or of Al-Azhar and not the ones in Kairouan or Zitouna, not to mention Judit who, while not a Muslim, knew many passages from the Koran by heart and was entirely respectful of the religion. Out of solidarity, then, I didn't go into the famous courtyard with ancient columns or the prayer hall of the most famous mosque in the Maghreb, but no matter. I was only there to be with her, and the week passed quickly; I found that our connection grew stronger every day, closer, so much so that soon it would be very hard to part ways. We spoke a language that belonged only to us, a mixture of literary Arabic, Moroccan dialect, and French; Judit was making huge progress in Arabic daily. And in fact, when I had to leave Tunis, after seven days of dead soldiers, of Casanova—Judit watched me work, over my shoulder, laughing at my poilus and finding the Venetian's language rather hard to understand—of poor-man's pool sessions on the patio, of strolls to the Goulette, to Carthage and to La Marsa, the closer the time for departure came, the more depressed I felt about going back to Tangier, all the more so since this time we had no prospect, no plan of getting back together again anytime soon. Judit promised me she would return in the fall, but she didn't know when or how, no doubt she wouldn't have the money.

And then we had to bring ourselves to say good-bye.

"It's my turn to visit," I said, taking her in my arms in the Tunis airport.

"That would be good . . ."

"I'll find a way to get to Barcelona. *Allah karim.*"

"*Sahih.* I'll wait for you, then."

"*Inshallah.*"

"*Inshallah.*"

And I left, my heart in my shoes.

COMING back was very hard, I had to work twice as hard because I hadn't managed to keep up my crazy pace from before; I had run out of money; I was fed up with my co-renters, their stupidity was exhausting; I was counting on Ramadan to boost my morale, but fasting, in the heat and the long summer days, was tough and, beyond everything else, I found it hard, in solitude, to rediscover the festive and spiritual side that should have made the hunger and thirst bearable; I kept thinking about the previous Ramadan, with Bassam, Sheikh Nureddin, and the companions of the Koranic Thought, our *iftar* in the little neighborhood restaurant, the readings from the Koran till late at night, and the taste of childhood, the familiar and familial taste that the month of fasting had and that did come back to me now, but only to plunge me into sudden melancholy. Alone, the *iftar* was just a moment of sadness, and even if we made an effort, my terrible companions and I, to be together, the freeze-dried soups, the cans of sardines, or the noodles (not to mention their remarks) added to the sadness. Then I delved alone into my Koran and my Ibn Kathir, but without managing to concentrate, the names of the poilus and Casanova's memoirs kept dancing in front of my eyes—even when I tried to break the fast in a restaurant and go to the mosque to listen to the readings, it was in vain, I took nothing from it.

After two weeks, I stopped fasting, angry with myself, but what the hell, it was better not to pretend. I spent more time at the office, because the air-conditioning made working more pleasant: at my place, even with no shirt on, I was sweating onto my keyboard. I pictured my combatants suffering from thirst in the summer, in the trenches, the mud must have dried and crusted, the number of men killed was alarming, each one had a name, a place, sometimes I would consult the database to find all the ones who'd died in the same place, as I typed I could glimpse the extent of the catastrophe, Verdun, the Somme and the Chemin des Dames led the list of massacres, and after work I would look at documentaries about World War I on the Internet: the hell of the bombs, the life of the trenches, the terrifyingly cynical military decisions. I reconstructed, with the documents we were digitalizing, the campaign of Belkacem ben Moulloub and many others: *Journal of marching and operations of the 3rd Regiment of Algerian Infantry Corps, November 1914. November 5, '14: At 1 o'clock German attack on the front at the most advanced sections. This attack was stopped by our fire. At 6 o'clock violent German attack on the entire front of the 2nd battalion. The undersigned used almost all his ammunition, he withdrew but stuck to the old trenches along the route occupied by him on the 3rd. The 3rd Battalion set up in its connecting trenches facing north. The 12th Company is sent as reinforcement but cannot completely verify the momentum of retreat. Heated battle all day. The reinforcements arrive too late: the enemy saw the weak point and attacked with very superior forces. But the Germans couldn't cross the Yser Canal. 6 November '14: At 5 o'clock violent gunfire on the entire line accompanied by violent cannon fire. No troop movements. The 9th Company has three killed by raking fire,* among them Belkacem, he won't see the end of the war, he won't return to Constantine.

I received a second message from Bassam, this time I was absolutely sure it was him:

Ramadan karim, Lakhdar *khouya*! Here we're suffering, but we're holding strong.

The email was sent from an equally strange, but different, address, a Robert Smith or something like that.

Still mysterious.

Sometimes, to clear my head, late at night, I'd go swimming at one of the beaches on the other side of the airport; the Atlantic was cold and turbulent, it was pleasant, I thought hard about Judit and dreamed she was coming to join me on the spur of the moment, or that I was leaving to visit her. She was on vacation somewhere in Spain with her parents, and didn't write much, just a text from time to time, from her cellphone. I was afraid she'd dump me, that she'd get tired of me or meet someone else.

I had to leave. I was fed up with Tangier.

I had decided to talk to Mr. Bourrelier about it, he might have an idea—after all, thriller-seekers have to help each other out. I asked him if by any chance he might be able to get me a job in his business in France. He opened his eyes wide: in France! Really, if we're set up here it's because it costs less, it's not to send our workers to France! Anyway, isn't she in Spain, your girlfriend? (He had gone back to *tutoyer*-ing me when we were alone.) I agreed, saying I didn't speak Spanish very well, and in any case, with a Schengen visa, you could go anywhere.

"No luck," he said, "if you had done the Revolution in Morocco, you could have landed by the thousands in Ceuta or Tarifa like the Tunisians in Lampedusa. Then Zapatero would have slipped you papers to send you north, as a gift to Sarkozy, like Berlusconi . . . It's too bad . . ."

That made him crack up, the bastard.

"Actually, that would have been a good solution. But the Revolution is over here. The Constitutional reform has been adopted, and the elections are about to take place to elect a new government."

"And you're happy?"

"I don't know. All I want is to be free to travel, to earn money, to walk around quietly with my girlfriend, to fuck if I want to, to pray if I want to, to sin if I want to, and to read detective novels if I feel like it without anyone finding anything to object to aside from God Himself. And that's not going to change right away," I said.

He looked at me gravely; I suddenly felt as if he were taking me seriously.

"Yes, that fight isn't won yet."

"All young people are like me," I added. I suddenly felt emboldened. "The Islamists are old conservatives who steal our religion from us when it should belong to everyone. All they offer are prohibitions and repression. The Arab Left are old union members who are always too late for a strike. Who's going to represent me?"

Jean-François suddenly seemed to be concentrating on something.

"You know, in France, I'm not sure they're any better off on the political front. Plus, with the crisis . . ."

He seemed to be thinking.

"Listen, for your travel plans, I might have an idea. I'm not promising anything, but I'm good friends with one of the directors at Comarit. They have lines for Spain, but also for France. At least you could see the country. I'd hate to lose you, but if you have your heart set on seeing the sights, here, outside of books, you're not going to travel much."

All Tangier natives knew about Comarit, a shipping company, because its name was written in big letters on the ferries entering the port from Tarifa or Algeciras. I didn't quite see what I could do on a ferry, I had no knowledge of the sea, but this conversation gave me hope. Speaking frankly with Mr. Bourrelier had made me realize who I was: a young Moroccan of twenty from Tangier who wanted nothing but freedom. I wrote a long letter to Judit telling her this story and the possibilities that went with it, she replied almost immediately with *Siiiiiiiiiiiiiiiiiiiiiiiiiiiiiiiiiiiiiiiiiiiiiiiiiiii!* I felt my heart glowing.

THAT night I was again captive to my nightmares. I dreamed I was slapping Judit, very hard, I was beating her because she was jealous of Meryem; I was hitting her with all my strength, and she was shouting, she was screaming and struggling between blows, but she wasn't running away—after a while I rejoined Meryem in her bedroom, began to caress her, undress her, I put my hand between her legs, it was warm, then I turned toward an old Sheikh who was there, next to the bed. That's normal Lakhdar, he said, death warms corpses up after a certain amount of time, it's like that, and I said it's annoying, all this blood coming out from there, and he replied but it's from you, this blood, and I looked at my penis, a red liquid was streaming from the urethra, continuously: the more excited I got from Meryem's burning body, at the contact of her remains, made incandescent by being long dead, the more blood spurted out; I penetrated Meryem, my sex was consumed by hers; her eyes were still closed. Judit had replaced the Sheikh by the side of the bed: she said yes, yes, like that, that's good, you see, you're filling her, that's good, look, and in fact the blood was coming out of Meryem's motionless lips, overflowing from her nostrils onto her white teeth, I was terrified but I couldn't stop, I moved in and out of her in a clinging warmth.

I woke up with my belly sticky from semen, my heart pounding.

I told myself I was crazy, that I had come down with some terrible mental illness; I curled up in the night like a dog, moaning with anguish.

II

BARZAKH

THE sole material trace of my childhood still left is two photos I've always kept in my wallet: one of Meryem when she was little, on vacation in a village, sitting against a tree, and another of my mother with my little sister Nour in her arms. Nothing else. I've often wondered what would have happened if, instead of always running farther away, instead of trying to escape the consequences of my actions, I had returned home, if I had insisted, if I had tried to impose myself on them at all costs, to repent, accept all the punishments, all the humiliations; I've often wondered if they would have ended up taking me back, if I could have found a place with them. Of course the question shouldn't be asked, I have to accept my travels, which are another name for Fate.

Like those soldiers in 1914, who left their villages or douars without knowing what was awaiting them, on September 21, 2011, I boarded the *Ibn Battuta*, a ferry belonging to the Comanav-Comarit Company, at the port of Mediterranean Tangier for my first crossing of the Strait, headed for Algeciras as a bar waiter and general dogsbody, or rather, mostly as a dogsbody. A cabin boy. The ship's name, *Ibn Battuta*, seemed to me a sign, a good omen. The crew looked askance at this teacher's pet who'd never set foot on ship, but fine, I thought, the main thing would be to make myself accepted little by little. I tried to be obliging and to answer the scornful looks with kindness, which might have made me seem weak or an idiot but no matter, I was on the sea, en route to Spain. Obviously, I had no visa to leave the Algeciras port; for the time being I'd do round trips, circles in the Strait, but someday they'd end up letting me disembark.

I had no plan.

Jean-François's friend had agreed to hire me for a pitiful salary, which just barely paid for my rent in Tangier. But don't worry, he said, there are tips, bonuses, extras. Mr. Bourrelier had been sorry to let me go, there were still miles of dead men to whom a digital existence had to be given and books that awaited a new electronic life, but deep down he was happy for me, I think. So, bon voyage, he said to me as he held out his hand, and above all don't forget, if you want to come back you'll always be welcome.

The *Ibn Battuta* was not the *Pequod*, not a single mast, no whale oil: it was an old British vessel 130 meters long, built in 1981, and could transport a thousand passengers and two-hundred-fifty cars at nineteen knots, despite at least a meter's thickness of several layers of paint that had to have weighed it down a little. It took between an hour and a half and two hours to reach Andalusia, and we did two trips a day; I was beginning to help unload the trucks and cars either at six in the morning and getting home at six at night, or at eleven in the morning, in which case I was back by eleven at night.

I remember my first crossing. I had seen the sea every day since I was born: I had watched for hours as these ferries crossed the Strait, and now I was on board one of them. It was September, the season for migrating north wasn't over yet, the boat was full of Moroccans who were going home, to Spain, France, or Germany. Crates packed full, trailers, entire families (grandfather, grandmother, father, mother, son, daughter, and sometimes uncle, aunt, cousins) often piled into two or even three cars, in a convoy, and their desire to go back seemed inversely proportionate to their age: the young ones were impatient while the old ones sighed. For all these people the crossing was a little recreation before the long road that awaited them, twelve, twenty, even thirty hours of driving.

It was my first day and I didn't know how to do anything; I was supposed to help with maneuvering the vehicles, but since I didn't know how to guide the drivers to park, the guy in charge of loading quickly told me to get lost, actually more vulgar than that, so I climbed onto the upper deck, where the cafeteria was, and helped the bartender put away some crates of Pepsi in the fridges, until he in turn told me to fuck off because I broke a bottle out of clumsiness. I went over to lean on the railing and wait for the ship to dock. The deck smelled of a mixture of sea and diesel, the metal vibrated gently under my arms, to the rhythm of the engines; the line of cars and trucks diminished, they disappeared into the belly of the ferry, it was a wonder to see so much inert, living matter that could be transported by the giant creature we were on. The officer who had hired me was in his forties, he had welcomed me on board, he was the vessel's second-in-command—I knew absolutely nothing about boats, it was comical. Especially the names of things. Seamanship is, above all, vocabulary. Bow, stern, port, starboard. I got more kicks in the ass, literally and figuratively, during those four months than all my life. But I ended up learning, a little at least; I learned how to park the vehicles like sardines in a can; I learned how to orient myself in the immense tub, from the engine room to the gangplank, and above all I learned little by little to make myself, if not appreciated, at least accepted by the crew.

There weren't many young people on board the *Ibn Battuta*. Most of the crew were over forty. It should be said there weren't many of us for a ship of this size; the absence of cabin service, like restaurant service (aside from the sandwiches and chips I sold at the cafeteria) allowed for a pretty reduced staff: the crossing was much too short to worry about details.

I wasn't Sinbad, that's for sure. Despite the calm of the sea, the boat's movements caused a strange sensation inside me, as if I had smoked too many joints—not really sick, but not entirely in form either. My body, my legs especially, no longer seemed to obey the same laws as on terra firma, and were overcome by a slight undulation, or rather oscillation, a new rhythm that made even the most ordinary movements—like climbing a staircase, or walking across a deck—require a different acuity than normal: all of a sudden, moving from one place to another was no longer such a natural phenomenon that you could do it without thinking about it; on the contrary, everything reminded you that you had to be terribly aware of it, under pain of zigzagging, slipping slightly, or even, in November, finding yourself flat on your ass, thrown unceremoniously onto the deck by a judder of the boat.

But still, it was magnificent to be there: the view was intoxicating. In the morning, when the sun was still low, the hills of Morocco grew distant, glimmering, until they became green and white spots, promontories for giants, for Hercules, and the light seemed to play with its columns, on the side of Cape Spartel; then the Andalusian coast grew nearer, and then you thought of the expedition of Tariq ibn Ziyad, the conqueror of Spain, and of those Berbers who had defeated the Visigoths: I was commanding my own army of trucks, of old Renaults and Mercedes; together we would retake Grenada, and the Guardia Civil of Algeciras port wasn't going to stop us. First the entire country had to be anaesthetized with a few tons of good Rif hash, parachuted in for free over the big cities, our aerial offensive; regiments of Gnawas would make the walls of the last hostile cities tremble with their instruments, and finally my tractor-trailers and my cars of emigrants would leave the belly of the *Ibn Battuta* in a glorious procession, headed for the Alhambra: Spain would become Moroccan again, something it should never have stopped being.

The cops of the Algeciras port must have shared my way of seeing things, since they mistrusted us like the plague; they suspected us of trying to swindle them, of smuggling contraband, of letting in illegal immigrants. At least, I say "us," but I should speak rather of the old sailors on the boat: as for me, they were content to despise me. When we reached the quay, we began unloading; I was then on European soil, and this sensation was strange, in the beginning— until the fences and sheds of Customs at my back made me realize I was actually nowhere.

At the end of October, when the Tunisians had just democratically brought Ennahda's Islamists into power and when the Spaniards were getting ready to elect the Catholics of the People's Party, just as the Moroccans, almost simultaneously, were on the point of going to the voting booths themselves, I began to get tired of these sterile round trips on the Strait. My salary was late in coming, they weren't paying me, my savings were reduced to not much; the work was pretty tiring and monotonous. I had made a friend among the crew, Saadi, an old sailor in his sixties who had sailed all the seas of the globe, and who was in pre-retirement on the Strait. He told me strange stories, tales worthy of adventure novels, and I pretended to believe them; in any case, it helped pass the time.

I no longer had much of a chance to pursue my career as a poet: I came home too beat to write, and even reading became an activity for Sunday, when I didn't work. But my apartment was very far from the port of Mediterranean Tangier and it took me a good forty-five minutes by bus to get to work or come home. In short, I wondered if I hadn't made a huge mistake in leaving Mr. Bourrelier and the dead soldiers. Even my correspondence with Judit wasn't kept up much. I thought of her, a lot even; in the beginning, I would take advantage of the Algeciras stop to send a handwritten letter to Barcelona—*I'm writing to you from Andalusia*—but very soon, we realized these missives and postcards took at least as long to reach her as if I had sent them from Tangier. Judit was getting more and more involved in anti-system opposition, as she called it; she had joined a discussion group connected to the Movement of Indignants, they were getting ready for some major actions post-elections. What she described of the situation in Catalonia was rather frightening; the nationalist right in power was systematically destroying, she said, all public services, with the University in the lead: they were reducing supplies, the teachers saw their salaries waning from one semester to the next. She was worried: the quality isn't great as it is, we're wondering what's going to become of it all, she said. She was at a crossroads, in the last year before her diploma, and she had to choose her path, a master's probably, or a long stay in the Arabic world; she wasn't sure about trying to become an interpreter—in short, she felt a little lost, and so grew more and more indignant.

I had received one or two emails from Bassam, still just as enigmatic, each time sent from different addresses. He didn't ask me for news; he didn't give me any of his own; he just complained about the difficulty of existence and quoted Koranic verses. One day, the Sura of Victory: *When the victory of God and the Conquest will arrive,* etc.; another, the Sura of Butin: *And your Lord revealed to the Angels: "I am with you: strengthen the believers. I will strew terror in the hearts of the impious. Strike above the neck."*

No one had claimed responsibility for the attack on the Café Hafa, and the papers no longer mentioned it. Only the elections held the media's attention, the elections in Tunisia, Morocco, Spain—you felt as if a wave of democracy were unfurling onto our corner of the world.

I was suspended, I was living in the Strait; I was no longer here and not yet there, eternally leaving, in the *barzakh*, between life and death.

My nightmares were recurrent and were spoiling my life; either I dreamt of Meryem and rivers of blood, or of Bassam and Sheikh Nureddin; I kept seeing attacks, explosions, fights, massacres with knives. I remember one particularly horrible night I dreamed that Bassam, his eyes empty, a band of cloth around his forehead, was slitting Judit's throat like a sheep's, holding her by the hair. This atrocious scene haunted me for many days.

When I had the time, I tried to pray at regular hours, to rest my mind; I regained a little calm in the ritual prostrations and the recitation. God was merciful, he consoled me a little.

I had to find a way to rebuild my stock of thrillers, the only one that was left was Jean-François's going-away present: a copy of Manchette's *Full Morgue*, which he had given me because he had two. It was a good book, very good even, written in the first person, the story of an ex-cop named Eugène Tarpon who had become a private detective without any work, a drinker of Ricard whose sole prospect was to go back to live with his mother in the French sticks. Kind of despairingly funny, it took my mind off things.

Judit didn't have enough money to come visit me; I didn't have a visa to take the bus in Algeciras and go see her. I could only look at Spain from behind the Customs fences, just as hundreds of guys in my situation were looking at the barbed wire around Ceuta or Melilla; the sole difference being that I was on the continent. For a long time I thought about stashing myself in a truck or trying to sneak through in the line of cars, and I could've probably managed it, but to what purpose. Energy was starting to fail me. The strength that Judit's presence, Judit's body, had given me in Tunis was getting sapped away little by little. I was content to let the days go by, to sail, without much hope, ready to spend eternity between the two shores of the Mediterranean.

IT happened in January. A blow of Fate, once more; at a point when we hadn't seen a penny of our wages since September, when I had ended up in despair, very seriously contemplating signing up again for the dead poilus, when Judit had almost completely stopped sending me news, replying very laconically to my messages, and when I was beginning to suspect she had met someone else, one night, when we had arrived at Algeciras early that morning as usual and had waited all day for the order to cast off without understanding why we weren't leaving, the captain called us all together. There were thirty-two of us in the cafeteria. He wore a funny expression, surprised, maybe, or defeated, or both at once. He didn't beat about the bush. He said, well boys, the boats have been seized by the Spanish court. We can't move from here until we receive word. The company owes millions of euros in gas and harbor rights. There you are. He raised his eyes to the room. Everyone began talking at the same time. He answered the nearest questioners. Yes, you can return to Tangier on a ferry belonging to one of our competitors, they'll take you, of course. But that will be regarded as abandoning your post, a breech of your contract, and you'll lose all your rights over your unpaid wages in case the ships are sold. At least that's what I thought I understood.

It seemed completely absurd. We were stuck in the port of

Algeciras. Fine, me, I'm going back, I thought. Back to Mr. Bour-relier and the War of '14, which I never should've left.

The captain kept answering questions.

"Luckily the tanks are full, we have enough oil for electricity and heat for a good while. And we should be able to get by and not die of hunger. Worst case we could get our colleagues to send in sup-plies from Tangier."

"I have to stay here, yes. But you . . . It's your choice."

"Two weeks, possibly. Perhaps less. The company has to pay part of the bill for the seizure to be lifted."

"At least we have enough room—we have all the cabins . . . There should even be some spare sheets and blankets."

"I don't know, we could play charades. If we were in the navy, we'd take the opportunity to repaint the hull."

He began cracking up. A lot of guys were laughing. But there were others who found it much less amusing. The ones who had wives and children in Tangier, for example. It was a strange feeling to be stuck here, ten miles from home: less than an hour by bike on solid ground.

The next day, we were news in the local paper, which the Span-ish dockworkers brought us:

> *Un nuevo drama laboral en el sector maritime recala en el Puerto de Algeciras. Un total de 104 marineros, los que componen la tripulacíon de los buques* Ibn Battuta, Banasa, Al-Mansour *y* Bouhaz, *afrontan una situación muy precaria, abandonados a su suerte por la naviera marroquí Comarit, que se encuentra en graves problemas económicos que están motivando un drama social que salpica también a otros purtos del Mediterráneo.*

There was a photo of the *Ibn Battuta*; you could see some of the crew on board, including me. It was the first time I had been in the paper, I'd have liked to email the link to Judit, but obviously we had no Internet. I sent her a text to tell her, she replied almost immediately *Wow! Incredible! Keep me posted!*

For a bit I thought she might take a bus and come see me, after all she could enter the customs zone without any problem. I dreamed of being the last crew member on the *Ibn Battuta*—we'd have the whole boat to ourselves, I'd have gotten hold of the nicest cabin and we'd have spent a dream vacation together, a magnificent motionless cruise, looking at the containers waltzing on the cranes and the to and fro of the transporters.

But there were still a good thirty or so crewmembers between me and my dreams. I couldn't quite see myself telling the Captain or Saadi "I need a double cabin, I invited my girlfriend to spend a few days with us," as if our ferry were a country house. We received a few visits—journalists or dockworkers, mainly—but no one stayed overnight, of course.

The time passed very slowly. In the morning I would walk around a little on the port, in the Zone; I would greet the Spaniards working there, often they'd offer me a coffee and we'd chat for a few minutes; they would ask me, So, what's new, and I'd invariably reply, Nothing new for now. They told me it was funny, *qué locuna*, they could at least give you a visa to go look around town. I would always reply, oh yes, *no estaría mal*, hoping but not believing that one of them would one day take the initiative of going to negotiate with the cops from the *Policía nacional*. They should send you oranges from your place, they're in season, one of them said, who had just unloaded a bulk carrier of citrus fruit, and he laughed, and was immediately scolded by another, showing more solidarity, who said it must not be much fun, still, put yourself in their place, if we were stuck in the port of Tangier, it definitely wouldn't be very funny.

After the coffee I would continue my tour of the docks, mentally take note of the movements of the ships, there were boats for everything, different shapes according to what they contained; poultry boats that transported thousands of clucking chickens in cages; vessels loaded with bananas and pineapples that smelled so strong you felt as if you were plunging your head into some fruit juice; refrigerated ones overflowing with frozen products in special containers; immense barges laden with train tracks, sand, or cement; grain boats like floating silos and modern container ships, real multi-colored vessels with ten floors. Some of them came from very far away via the Suez or the Atlantic, others from Marseille, Le Havre, or northern Europe; they rarely stayed docked more than a few hours. A few were new or freshly repainted, others were carting, along with their cargo, tons of rust, and you wondered by what miracle they didn't break apart at the first wave.

Then I would return to the *Ibn Battuta*, there was always a chore to do, cleaning, swabbing the deck, laundry, peeling potatoes; we weren't repainting the hull yet, as the captain said, but we were so bored out of our minds that if some good soul had given us some paint, I think we would have set about it. I was discovering life on board ship—docked, that is.

The bane of sea life is the cockroaches. They are the real owners of the boat. They're everywhere, by the thousands, on all floors; they come out at night, so much that you'd better not wake up at three in the morning and turn on the light: you'll always find three or four, one or two on your blanket, one on the wall and one calmly settled on your neighbor's forehead, on the cot opposite, and you imagine that they act the same with you when you're sleeping, that they gently stroll about on your closed eyelids, which terrified me at first, made me tremble with horror—after a while you get used to it. The roaches come from the lower decks, from the heat of the engine rooms; that's where their numbers are highest, and the engine workers live with them. I don't know what they could feed on, I suppose they treat themselves to our supplies and eat from our plates. All attempts to exterminate them were seemingly doomed to fail: as soon as a boat is contaminated with cockroaches, that's it, nothing can be done. No matter how hard the deck and gangways are scrubbed with bleach and no matter how many traps are set in our cabins, they still appear. Saadi told me you could tame them, a little like birds. He confessed that before, at night, on his freighter, during the long hours of his watch, he would talk to them.

Saadi had adopted me, so to speak: we shared a cabin, and in the long boredom of evenings on board, his company was magical. He worked in the engine room; he was the one who pampered the ship's two Crossley motors. Listening to him was like skimming through an endless book you never got tired of, since its contents were vast and slightly different every time. He told me about the Southern seas, the Leeward Islands, which are, God forgive me, he said, the earthly version of Paradise—men who have seen them always keep that wound in their heart and find no rest until they can return to them. He also knew the big seaports of China, Hong Kong, Macao, Manila. Singapore is the cleanest city in the world; Bangkok the noisiest, and the most disturbing. He told me about the interminable line of brothels and strip clubs in Patpong, where Americans flock by the hundreds; a lot of them make the trip just for that, you'd think there weren't any whores in the United States.

He had seen the cat-shaped Celebes, Java and Borneo, long Malaysia and the strait of Malacca, where there are so many ships they have to line up like cars in a traffic jam.

He spoke to me of the cows of Bombay—anyone can milk them in the street, directly into his cup of tea—and about the port of Karachi, the most dangerous on the planet, he said, you wouldn't last a day there. It's the realm of contraband, drugs, weapons. Custom inspectors don't exist over there, he said. Everything is paid for in bottles of whiskey. The whores of Karachi are so badly treated they all have scars, bruises, cigarette burns.

Saadi had been through the Suez Canal I don't know how many times, crossed the equator to go to Brazil, Argentina, South Africa.

He had seen such violent storms that an immense freighter could dance like a fishing boat and where everyone was sick, everyone, even the pilot who steered with a bucket within mouth's reach so he could puke without letting go of the controls; he had seen sailors die at sea, fall into the water and disappear in the turbulent immensity or else drop dead of fever or of sudden sadness, without enough time to reach terra firma to take care of them: then they'd throw the body into the waves, or the corpse would be folded up and piled into a freezer, according to the captain's wishes; he had seen drunk sailors who could only sail with bottle in hand, sailors in knife fights over a girl or a wrong word, and even pirates, in the Gulf of Aden, boarding his ship and then abandoning it after a pitched battle with a military frigate, when the entire crew was locked up in the bottom of the hold. But strangely, the places he talked about with the most emotion were Anvers, Rotterdam and Hamburg, he loved the ports of the North, immense, bustling, serious, which adjoined big cities that had all the modern comforts—subways, luxury brothels, display windows, supermarkets, all kinds of bars, where the beer was cheap and where you could walk around without the fear of taking a knife in to the back like in Karachi.

Imagine dozens of kilometers of docks, he said, harbors over ten fathoms deep where the biggest boats in the world can moor—boats of the high seas, which normally never see any port: with our containers, we looked like small craft, pleasure boats next to those colossi when we passed each other in the channels. And the cities, ah my son, unfortunately we never stayed very long, but you've never seen so many skyscrapers, buildings of all kinds, in all colors like in Rotterdam, for instance. You've never seen so many immigrants, of all possible nationalities. As a matter of fact, I don't think I saw more than one or two Dutchmen. There was a brothel full of just Thai girls, for instance. I even learned recently that the mayor of Rotterdam is Moroccan. That tells you how they respect foreigners, up there. A little like in the Gulf, I said. That made him crack up. You idiot, Rotterdam and Doha, they're not the least alike, fool! And Hamburg! In Hamburg there are supermarkets for choosing whores and lakes in the middle of the city. In Anvers, in the center, you feel like you're in the Middle Ages. But not a filthy Middle Ages like the Medina in Marrakesh or Tangier, no, an elegant, well-ordered Middle Ages, with magnificent squares and buildings that take your breath away.

"Then it would be more like the Renaissance," I said, to appear clever, to show I knew some things, too.

"What the hell difference does it make? I guarantee you've never seen ports like Anvers, Rotterdam, or Hamburg. Rotterdam was completely destroyed during the war, and look it at today. In our country it takes two years to fill a pothole in a street, imagine the number of centuries it'd take to rebuild Tangier if it was ever bombed, God forbid."

Saadi had spent thirty years at sea, on a dozen different vessels, and for four years, he had been crisscrossing the Strait on board the *Ibn Battuta*. Saadi was divorced and had married a very young woman who had just given him a son, of whom he was very proud.

"Is that why you didn't stay in Europe somewhere? Because of your family?"

"No, my son, no. It's because when you spend months and months on a steel tub, you yearn for nothing except to go back to your armchair, your home. Europe is fine, it's beautiful, it's pleasant to be there on a stopover. But there's nothing like Tangier, it's my city."

My experience of sea life had resulted only in this shipwreck in the depths of the Algeciras port, not very glorious—I asked Saadi if he had ever seen anything like it, boats stuck in a port. He told me in Barcelona, a Ukrainian freighter had been abandoned by its owner, who was unable to pay for the hull and the repairs: the entire crew had left except one sailor, who stayed to collect the results of the sale of the ship and bring the money back to his comrades. The Ukrainian stayed for over two years alone on his old tub, said Saadi, living off charity and a little cash the former crew sent him from Odessa. Everyone knew him in the port; he was a real hero. At that time we were doing a Piraeus–Beirut–Larnaca–Alexandria–Tunis–Genoa–Barcelona line, we called that the bus trip. I would see the Ukrainian every two weeks. He was an incredible man, with amazing drive. Every day he'd go annoy the offices of the ship owners and port authorities to find a buyer for his pile of rust and avoid its being auctioned off, where he would have lost everything—and believe me, Lakhdar, an old freighter, even more or less repaired, isn't sold like a used car. I would give him a hand to make his engines run; I remember, they were magnificent Soviet models, real clockwork, even with their tens of thousands of hours on the meter, they could have gone round the world. The tub was in bad shape, that's true, the propeller shaft needed replacing, and part of its electrical system had to be rewired, but someone would end up buying it, it was just a matter of time. So the Ukrainian waited. He had a whole series of tricks to survive. Since he was there full time, he knew all the dock workers, all the guys in the harbor master's office, he'd play cards with them, organize little trades with passing boats, cigarettes, alcohol, even cans of Russian caviar which he'd resell to a high-end grocer uptown. A great guy. He always went to the same brothel and ended up marrying a Colombian prostitute—one day when we landed in Barcelona as usual, the boat wasn't there. He had sold it to a Greek company. It's still sailing, the old tub, I passed it not too long ago. The guy organized a hell of a party to celebrate his departure; he invited dozens of acquaintances into a filthy club and it was a party to remember, believe me, legendary, the bride's friends danced half naked, everyone ended up dead drunk—at the end of the night, completely hammered, he solemnly announced he was leaving to settle with his wife in Bogotá, thanks to the few millions of pesetas the sale of the boat had brought him; he was abandoning fiancée back home and comrades to Odessa; he was going to America, far inland, with his beautiful mulatto.

Wicked tongues added that he planned on getting into contraband with the cash.

Later on we learned he'd been killed by a bullet to the head in the middle of the street in Barranquilla, but the rumors didn't say if the Odessa sailors' revenge had caught up with him, if a Colombian drug dealer had settled his account, or if he had simply been the victim of bad luck.

That's the only story I know about someone who stayed very long in a port, aside from us, my son.

That was reassuring.

Saadi's stories always had a dark, tragic side, but I never managed to find out if it was the somber aspect of his personality or if, actually, the life of sailors brought this dark side with it—we were a hundred sailors stuck in Algeciras, on four ferries; I doubted any of us would manage to flee to Colombia or Venezuela with the least penny: the news was bad; the shipping company had a huge debt, in Spain, in France, in Morocco; we would probably never see our missing salaries. After a month of waiting, demoralized, half-dead of cold and boredom, when no one seemed to be interested in our fate as economic shipwreck victims, we had the idea of addressing the media, to attract the public's attention. The dockworkers' union gave us a hand. There were several articles in the papers:

> Like their colleagues stuck in Sète, the crew of Comanav-Comarit in Algeciras are familiar with hard times. The Tangier-Algeciras line has not been in operation since the beginning of January. Stuck in Algeciras, the sailors are seeing their situation worsen day by day. Lack of food and fuel, no salaries for several months, non-payment of health insurance . . .

However, unlike the seamen presently in the French port, the sailors in Algeciras are addressing the media. They recently held a press conference with the support of the Spanish. They have had enough and they want to go home. Many of these men left wives and children in Morocco, some of whom are living in deplorable conditions.

One hundred sailors are at the Algeciras port where a total of four ferries are docked: the *Banasa*, the *Boughaz*, the *Al-Mansour*, and the *Ibn Battuta*, placed in sequestration last January for reasons of outstanding debt.

Nothing came of it. All we managed to get was one more visit from Mme. Consul.

What made me despair above all was the absence of Internet. I'd left my computer back in Tangier; there was a "visitor's room" in the port with telephone booths and two computers, but you had to pay, and we had no money. I couldn't withdraw cash abroad from my account in Tangier. My phone credit had been used up in texts to Judit. It was horrible. A Spanish charity organization had brought us some clothes; I had gotten two pairs of patched-up jeans, some oversized shirts, a striped sweater, and an old khaki parka lined with synthetic wool.

Judit seemed to have completely lost interest in me. Thinking back on it, the last six months had strained our relationship; we were writing to each other less often, we spoke less on the phone, and now, shut up in the port of Algeciras, I had almost no news from her, which threw me into melancholy. I recounted my tribulations to Saadi, who sympathized, but encouraged me to forget her; you're twenty, he said, you'll fall in love with other girls. He told me about whores, about brothels all over the world, where he had found pleasure and company, an immense family scattered over the four corners of the earth. He remembers the first names of all the girls he'd visited. He said you know, when you follow the same route, you regularly go through the same ports, so you find the same groups of friends, the same whores, the same customers. You get news about so-and-so who passed through the week before; you have drinks, play cards—it's not just shooting your load. It's leisure time.

I confess that in my wretched solitude, I'd listen to him and dream about being a regular at a friendly whorehouse, where the girls would like me and a large-hearted Madam would take care of me—then I thought of Zahra, the little whore in Tangier I hadn't dared touch, and those dreams vanished, like all the others. There can't be any more love in brothels than hairs on the cunt of a Moroccan whore.

Saadi was a little like a big brother or a father, he was worried about me, would ask me questions; I told him about my life, and he would exclaim oh la la, listen, Lakhdar my son, you've had some hard knocks; he blamed my father, he said, for having so hard a heart; he shared my doubts about Bassam and Sheikh Nureddin. He said in a low voice if you want my opinion, all that's the fault of religion, may God forgive me. If there weren't any religion, people would be much happier.

He understood I wanted to emigrate, to leave Tangier—he just said that, with this old tub, you didn't really choose the best way.

The more days went by, the more I said to myself, all right, I'll leave for Barcelona, I'll find a way to leave the port, come what may. And a few hours later I'd think, all right, I'll go back to Tangier and find Mr. Bourrelier again.

The worst thing was having nothing to read, aside from the paper in the port cafeteria; I couldn't keep rereading *Full Morgue* over and over again. I had recovered a tiny Koran that a kind soul have given me, I squinted my eyes over it to learn a few suras by heart, the one of Joseph, and of the People of the Cave, it was a good exercise.

A prison exercise.

We hadn't committed any crime, the ship owner had committed it for us, but we were inside. Soon it would be two months since I'd last paid my rent, I wondered if I'd find my suitcases in front of the door or in the trash when I got back. If I got back.

Judit's silence ended up making me crazy. February was freezing; an icy wind swooped through the Strait, the sea was invariably gray-green and covered with whitecaps. All my comrades were depressed. Even Saadi looked glum, his beard was turning grey, he had stopped shaving. He spent most of his time sleeping.

"We can't stay like this till Judgment Day," I said.

He jumped from his cot, straightened up.

"No, that's true, little one, we can't. At least you can't. Me, you know, I could stay like this until I retire. They'll end up finding a solution eventually. We're in the way, a hundred sailors and four ferries stuck in the port."

"Don't you miss your wife? Don't you want to go home?"

"You know I've spent nine-tenths of my life far from home. This isn't much of a change. I'm used to it."

"I feel like I'm in prison. I can't take it anymore. I'm going to go crazy here, pacing back and forth between the boats and cleaning."

He looked at me a little more softly.

"I can see you're going crazy, yes. That's a possibility that shouldn't be ignored. I remember the time I was sailing on the *Kairouan*, one of the sailors went mad. He couldn't leave the gangway or the bridge. It was impossible to make him go down to the lower decks or the engine rooms, impossible. He was suddenly horribly claus-trophobic. We decided to ignore it, we didn't worry about him, we did his job for him. Waiting for him to get better, you know? And then it got worse: he curled up into a ball in a corner of the bridge. He was outside, sitting down, soaked the whole time by the sea spray, the rain. We forced a raincoat onto his shoulders. The captain began to get worried, saying, but he's completely crazy, that one, he'll catch pneumonia, we have to do something, take him down to the infirmary. We replied that might not be a good idea to shut him up, because of the sudden claustrophobia, but the officers didn't want to hear it. It took five hefty guys to carry him, he didn't give in, he braced himself against the pipes, clung desperately to the doors. Finally they managed to get him inside, he shouted with terror when they locked the door, he pounded with his fists for hours, begging them to open it, it made you sick to your stomach; I saw quite a few guys with tears in their eyes when they heard him and finally the captain ordered him to be freed immediately. When we went in he was just a moaning bundle of nerves, had pissed himself, was shaking like an epileptic. We took him gently to bring him back outside, but it was too late, he was totally broken: as soon as we let go of him he leaped over the railing and threw himself into the sea—we couldn't save him."

"That's awful. I hope I won't go mad like that. At the same time, if I throw myself into the harbor, I won't have to smell fuel oil till the end of my days, but I won't be missing much else."

He looked at me, laughing from his cot.

"Son, I actually think it's time you made yourself scarce."

IT took more time than expected to organize "my escape," as Saadi called it, but once again, chance, Fate, or the Devil smiled on me and, two weeks later, in mid-February, I was walking for the first time on European soil, and not just between containers; I remember going by foot, without any luggage, to the center of Algeciras, and I spent my first euros there, in a bar, on a beer and a tuna sandwich. No one paid any attention to me, no one looked at me, I was a poor Moor like any other; I tried to read the paper, but I was too feverish to concentrate. The beer tasted like happiness, may God forgive me. On my passport I had a one-month visa granted "for humanitarian reasons," that is, to go make my life miserable somewhere else—I neither had the right to work nor to go to another European country; I could only crawl to Tarifa to board a ferry for Tangier. But before that I wanted to go to Barcelona to see Judit.

As I left the bar I asked the owner where there was an Internet café, he pointed me toward a kind of telecommunications office with free computers. The place was managed by Moroccans—I don't know why, I was a little ashamed, I'd have preferred the owners to be Spanish. I sent an email to Judit: Ya habibati, *I'm on my way, if you want me. I have a visa, I've left the port. I can take a bus from Algeciras and be in Barcelona tomorrow. If you want.* I didn't ask her all the questions that had been eating away at me about her silence, but the slightly despairing phrasing of the message, I thought, did it for me. Then I made the rounds of Algeciras; I looked at the shops, people-watched. I bought myself another beer in a bar I found rather chic. There were women in the café; all kinds of women. Young women, talking in groups with their friends; older ones looked like they were having a drink on their way back from work. And even a waitress, who must have been my age; she's the one who brought me my draft beer. I was trying to pass unseen, to pretend as if all this weren't new—the language, the faces. I felt as if I had passed into a television and all of a sudden, with my khaki parka slightly blackened at the elbows, I imagined that everyone was staring at me, guessing it came from the Salvation Army.

Two hours later I went back to see if Judit had given a sign of life, but no reply. I decided to give her a little more time, I crossed the city looking for the least expensive hotel. I found it—it was pathetic, not to say disgusting; there were hairs on the pillow, pubic hairs in the shower, it stank of frying oil from the restaurant downstairs, and you had to pay in advance, but the rates were almost Moroccan.

Freedom had a taste of sadness. I thought about Saadi and my friends on the boat, about Jean-François Bourrelier, about Sheikh Nureddin, Bassam, all the people who had helped me before disappearing. About Judit too, of course.

I had made one more huge mistake, I was alone, with two hundred euros loaned by Saadi, I had nothing on me except a Koran, a thriller, and a rotten parka, I had to reconstruct everything, with a charity visa, gotten as a special favor from the port authorities. My life seemed extraordinarily fragile to me; I saw myself begging in the markets as I'd done two years earlier, back to square one.

I spent the night in a bar called El Estrecho, which was well-named, narrow as the Strait itself; it had a TV, Real Madrid had played to a 1-1 draw in Moscow, it took up my entire evening.

On my way back I returned to glance at my emails and Facebook, still no news from Judit. I decided to call her on her cell, it was 11:30; there was a line of phone booths in the *locutorio*. I dialed her number and she answered almost immediately.

"*Hola*, it's Lakhdar," I said. "I'm in Algeciras."

I tried to control my voice, to seem cheerful, so she wouldn't guess my anxiety.

"Lakhdar, ¿*qué tal? Kayfa-l hal?*"

"Everything's fine," I said. "I have a visa, did you get my email?"

I could sense she was embarrassed, that something wasn't right.

"No . . . Or yes, I saw your email . . ." She hesitated for an instant. "But I haven't had time to answer."

I knew right away she was lying.

The conversation was full of silences, she made an effort to ask me what was new, suddenly I didn't really know what to say.

"Do you . . . do you want me to come to Barcelona?"

I already knew the answer, but I waited, like a deserter facing the execution squad.

"Um, yes, of course . . ."

We were in the process of humiliating each other; she was humiliating me by lying and I was humiliating her by forcing her to lie.

I tried to smile as I spoke: that's okay, don't worry, I'll call back in a few days, in the meantime, we can write; and then whereas usually it took us many minutes to bring ourselves to end the conversation, I sensed her relief when she said see you soon then, and hung up.

I didn't leave the tiny phone booth right away; I looked at the dial for a while, my head empty. Then I thought that the Moroccans outside were making fun of me, calling me little cuckolded prick, tittering; I was ashamed that my eyes were burning. I left the cabin to pay.

I returned to my luxury hotel after stopping on the way in a grocery store that was still open to buy a couple of beers, which I drank, lying on the bed, thinking I really was all alone now. I tore out the pages from an old tourist magazine to try to write a long poem or a letter to Judit, but I was incapable of doing either.

She was with someone else, you feel these things; little by little my rage grew with the alcohol, a desperate rage, in the emptiness and bustle of a continent that had just lost all its meaning, all I had left was this pathetic room, my whole life was summarized in this shitty craphole, I was locked up again, there was nothing for it, nothing, you're never free, you always collide with things, with walls. I thought about this world on fire, about a Europe that would burn again someday like Libya, like Syria, a world of dogs, of abandoned beggars—it's hard to resist mediocrity, in the constant humiliation life holds us in, and I was angry at Judit, I was angry at Judit for the pain of abandonment, the blackness of solitude and the betrayal I imagined behind her embarrassed words, the future was a stormy sky, a sky of steel, leaden in the north; Fate plays in little spurts, little movements, the sum of minute mistakes in a direction that hurls you onto the rocks instead of reaching the paradisiacal island so desired, the Leeward Islands or the catlike Celebes. I thought of Saadi, of Ibn Battuta, of Casanova, of happy travelers—I alone was stuck with a lukewarm beer and a heart of sadness, in the Western darkness, and there was no beacon in the night of Algeciras, none, the lights of Barcelona, of Paris, were all out, I had nothing left but to go back to Tangier, Tangier and kilometrically typing the names of dead soldiers, conquered by too many shipwrecks.

THIS whole series of coincidences, chances, I don't know how to interpret them; call them God, Allah, Fate, predestination, karma, life, good luck, bad luck, whatever you like—I didn't go to Barcelona right away, I didn't run to find Judit, because I was convinced she was with another guy, true, but also because I was afraid, afraid of falling back into wandering, poverty, because I was a little cowardly too; who knows. I was tired. No revolution, no books, no future. I couldn't go back to Tangier because I knew it would be impossible for me to leave it again, not northward, at least, or illegally; on board the *Ibn Battuta* I had heard a lot of stories, terrible stories of exile, of men drowned in the Strait or the Atlantic coast, between Morocco and the Canaries—Africans preferred the Canaries because the archipelago was harder to monitor. Since all those blacks and North Africans wandering around the streets with nothing to do were bad for tourism, the Canary government sent them packing somewhere else by plane, to the continent, at its own expense, and the sub-Saharans, Moors, Nigerians, and Ugandans wound up in Madrid or Barcelona, trying their chances in a country with the highest unemployment rate in Europe—the girls became whores, the men ended up in illegal, squalid camps out in the country, in Aragon or La Mancha, stuck between a couple of trees, living out in the open in the middle of garbage dumps, discarded trash, and the cold, and they developed magnificent diseases of the skin, abscesses, parasites, chilblains, waiting for a farmer to give them a little menial work in exchange for stale bread and potato peelings for their soup, they cleared stones out of fields in the winter, picked cherries and peaches in the summer—not for me, thanks. You always find people worse off than you, compared to these galley slaves I was well-off, I had a little education, a little money, and a country where, in the worst case, you could scrape together a living—I was a city boy, I had read books, I spoke foreign languages, I knew how to use a computer, I'd end up finding something, and in fact I did very quickly find a job near Algeciras, thanks to Saadi of course, it would never have occurred to me to explore that branch, supposing such a branch actually exists: when I was moping around in my stinking hovel a few hundred meters away from the *Ibn Battuta*, picturing Judit with her new guy, he sent me a text asking me to call, which I did right away. At the port he had spoken to an "entrepreneur" from the region who needed a Moroccan for a small job, and that's how I entered the service of Marcelo Cruz, funeral services: my Fortune was playing tricks on me, it hadn't had its fill, it always wanted more. Señor Cruz scheduled a meeting with me in a café in the center of Algeciras, he had a black SUV which he unhesitatingly double-parked, he recognized me because of the green parka, said is that you Lakhdar? Yes, I answered and smiled, that's me, I'm a friend of Saadi's. Of who?, he asked. I said of the sailor on the *Ibn Battuta*, oh yes, good, he said, would you like to work for me, I answered, of course, of course, what exactly is involved? Well it's a very simple job, he said, you have to look after dead people.

Mr. Cruz had a mournful, sweaty face, a shirt open to the middle of his chest, and a black leather jacket.

I didn't quite see what that meant, looking after dead people, aside from my experience with the poilus, but I accepted, obviously.

Marcelo Cruz's business had been flourishing; for years, he was the one who gathered, stored, and repatriated all the bodies of illegal immigrants in the Strait—drowned men, men who died from fear or hypothermia, bodies the Guardia Civil gathered on the beaches, from Cadiz to Almeria. After the judge and the pathologist, when they were assured the poor guy or guys had indeed croaked, their faces turned gray by the sea, their bodies swollen, they would call Marcelo Cruz; he would then put the remains in his cold-storage room and would try to guess the stiff's origins, which wasn't a piece of cake, as he said. *There aren't any easy jobs*, Señor Cruz repeated to me during the trip in his SUV, which brought me to the funeral enterprise, a few kilometers away from Algeciras toward Tarifa. If there weren't any material leads and no surviving witnesses, if it was impossible to put a name to the corpse, they'd end up burying the body at the expense of the State in an anonymous grave in one of the cemeteries along the coast; when they guessed its origins, either because it had a passport on it, or a handwritten note, or a telephone number, they'd keep it cold until its possible repatriation in a fine lead-lined, zinc coffin: Mr. Cruz would then climb into his hearse, take the ferry in Algeciras and bring the deceased to his final resting place. He knew Morocco like the back of his hand, most of his "clients" were Moroccan; entire villages would start mourning when they saw his wagon of death arriving. According to him, Marcelo Cruz was sadly famous there.

Lately, the crisis and better radar at sea had obviously put a slight dent in his business, so he was mostly repatriating workers who had died entirely legally in Spain—accidents, illnesses, or old age, whatever the Grim Reaper was willing to hand him, who mowed down my compatriots along with everyone else, thank God; but he always hoped, at the end of winter, for a good cargo of illegal corpses—the waters of the Strait were dangerous in that season, the *pateras* were going farther east to avoid patrols and were taking more risks: they sailed when the heavy swells made radar observation difficult. My work would be simple, it would mainly involve warehousing, loading, unloading, placing the bodies in coffins, etc.; he needed a Muslim, he explained, so the remains would be treated with respect for religion—the Imam from the neighborhood mosque would come and give me a hand.

So I would be a Muslim dogsbody. Paid on the black market. Housed on site. I was replacing another young Moroccan who had left him not long before, to try his luck in Madrid.

I thought of that bastard Saadi, who hadn't warned me about the nature of this job. Three hundred euros plus room and board, with laundry included. It wasn't that bad.

The idea of sending real stiffs back to Morocco after having imported dead soldiers to it virtually was rather amusing, I thought. I had never seen a corpse. I wondered how I would react. I thought about Judit, I wasn't at all sure of wanting to tell her what my new job entailed. In any case it would be all the same to her.

THE weeks with Mr. Cruz were an abyss of unhappiness. I lived in death. I stayed in a garden shed in back of the business, a cubbyhole full of tools and jugs of weed-killer, it stank of lawnmower gas; the generator for the cold-storage chamber was behind my wall and its vibrations woke me up every night. Mr. Cruz would lock me up in the enclosure when he went out at night, and would free me when he arrived in the morning—with rare exceptions he limited my movements, from fear of identity checks by the cops or social services. When I needed something—clothes, toiletries—he'd buy it for me himself. I didn't have any visitors. After 7 PM, when Mr. Cruz got into his SUV to go home, I was alone with the coffins.

I never got used to contact with the corpses, which fortunately didn't come in very often—you had to unload them, take them out of their plastic bags, while wearing a mask over your nose; the first time I almost fainted, it was a poor drowned guy, a young one, in a horrible state; fortunately Cruz was there—it was he who gently turned the body over on the stainless steel table, who placed the remains in the waterproof zinc box, who got out the electric screwdriver to seal the casket, all in silence. I couldn't breathe. The special mask was suffocating, its camphor or bleach smell mingled in my throat with the mustiness of the Strait, and the cadaverous fetidness of sadness, and the decay of the forgotten carcass, and even today, sometimes, years later, the smell of cleaning products makes the stench of those poor creatures come again to the back of my throat, creatures that Cruz manipulated without blinking an eye, without trembling, respectfully, calmly.

Then the Imam would come, and we would pray in front of the remains or the coffin, depending on the state of the body, one behind the other, as is the custom; Cruz would leave us. The Imam was a Moroccan from Casablanca, a middle-aged man to whom the solemnity of the task gave the aged and well-worn appearance of serious business, without a smile, without a mark of sympathy or antipathy, sure as he was of the equality of all before God, perhaps.

Praying for unknown dead people, for the vague remains of the existences of total strangers, was sadly abstract. Some of them we weren't even sure were Muslim; it was presumed, and maybe we were sending them to the wrong God, to a Paradise in which they'd be illegal immigrants yet again.

After praying, we would line the waterproof zinc coffins up in the cold-storage room, where they joined the other "pending" deceased. The oldest one had been there for three years, another drowned man from the Strait.

The government paid sixty euros per body and per day of storage: that was Señor Cruz's cut.

When Mr. Cruz had received the money for repatriation or had discovered the origin of an unknown body, he would organize "a loading"; he'd put two or three macabre boxes in his van and would take the ferry in Algeciras; the customs formalities were fussy, he had to seal the mortuary crates with lead, declare the freight, etc.

The business was surrounded by tall walls surmounted by broken bottles, which encircled a little garden; Mr. Cruz's house was a few hundred meters away—at night, I was locked up with the dead, in this suburb next to the highway, and it was sad, sad and frightening.

I also took care of the cleaning and gardening; I washed Mr. Cruz's car and fed his dogs, two handsome, blue-eyed, polar mutts that looked like wolves of the steppes—these animals were wild and gentle, they seemed to come from another world. I wondered how they bore the crushing summers of Andalusia with so much fur. Cruz was a mystery, somber and shifty; his face was yellow, his eyes wrinkled; when no bodies arrived, he would spend all day behind his desk, whiskey in hand, listening absent-mindedly to the police radio scanner so as to be the first one on the scene in case a body was discovered; he drank nothing but Cutty Sark, hypnotized by the Internet and hundreds of videos, war reports, atrocious clips of accidents and violent deaths: this spectacle didn't seem to excite him, on the contrary; he spent his time in a kind of lethargy, of digital apathy—only his hand on the mouse seemed alive; he was stupefied by bestiality and whiskey all day long and, when night fell, he staggered a little when he got up, he'd put on his leather jacket and leave without saying a word, bolting the door with two turns of the key. He called me his little Lakhdar, when he addressed me; he had a tiny voice that contrasted with his large size, his corpulence, his thick face: he spoke like a child and this false note made him even more frightening.

He was a poor guy, and I didn't know if he inspired fear or pity in me; he was exploiting me, locking me up like a slave; he spread a terrible sadness, the rotten smell of a soul in solitude.

I had to get out of there; the first time he let me stroll around town one afternoon, I thought for a while of disappearing without leaving a trace, of getting into a bus headed north, or a ferry to go back to Morocco—but I had nothing, no money, no papers, he had kept my passport, which I had been idiotic enough to give him, and I would probably have been arrested and thrown in jail before being expelled if I was asked to produce my documents.

I confided in the Imam from the mosque who came to pray for our dead; I explained to him that this Mr. Cruz was pretty strange, which he did not deny, only shrugging his shoulders with an air of powerlessness. He told me he thought my predecessor had run away for this excellent reason, because Cruz was a strange man, but one who had respect for the dead and for religion. That's all.

Seen from here, the long days on board the *Ibn Battuta* seemed like paradise.

I imagined climbing the wall, after all it wasn't so hard, Cruz wouldn't go so far as to run after me; but first I had to get back my papers and some money.

One day, Mr. Cruz left at dawn with the hearse; he returned with a load of dead bodies—seventeen, a *patera* had capsized off of Tarifa and the current had dotted the beaches with corpses. He was very happy with this harvest; a strange happiness, he didn't want to seem happy to be getting fat off the backs of these poor stiffs, but I could sense, behind his mask for the occasion, from the way he stroked his dogs, and called me *my little Lakhdar*, that he was delighted with the resumption of business, but was ashamed at the same time.

Seventeen. That's a huge little number. You don't realize, when you listen to the radio or the TV, the number of corpses left by some catastrophe or other, what seventeen bodies represent. You say, oh, seventeen, that's not so much, tell me about a thousand, two thousand, three thousand stiffs, but seventeen, seventeen isn't anything extraordinary, and yet, and yet, it's an enormous quantity of vanished life, dead meat, it's cumbersome, in memory as well as in the cold-storage room, it's seventeen faces and over a ton of flesh and bone, tens of thousands of hours of existence, billions of memories gone, hundreds of people touched by mourning, between Tangier and Mombasa.

One by one, I wrapped these guys up in their shrouds, and wept; most of them were young, my age, or even younger; some had broken limbs or bruises on their face. The great majority looked Arab. Among these bodies was a girl's. She had tattooed a telephone number in henna on her arm, a Moroccan number. She had long hair, very black, a gray face. I was disturbed; I didn't want to see her breasts, her sex; normally I shouldn't have placed her in the casket myself, a woman was supposed to do that. I was afraid of my own gaze on this female body; I imagined Meryem dead—it was her I was placing in the coffin, her I was burying finally, alone in the night of my nightmares, I imagined the police calling this tattooed phone number, a mother or brother picking up, an almost mechanical voice informing them, repeating very loudly to be understood, of the end of their sister, their daughter, just as the phone must have rung at my uncle's house, one day, to announce this terrible news, just as it will ring one day for us, too, one after the other, and shyly, tenderly, fraternally, I placed this unknown girl in her metal sarcophagus.

Perhaps we can't really picture death unless we see our own corpse in others' bodies, young as me, Moroccan as me, candidates for exile like me.

At night I would write poems for all these dead people, secret poems that I would then slip into their coffins, a little note that would disappear with them, a homage, a *ritha'*; I gave them names, tried to imagine them alive, to guess their lives, their hopes, their last moments. Sometimes I saw them in my dreams.

I never forgot their faces.

My hatred for Cruz grew; it was irrational; aside from my semi-captivity, he wasn't mean; he was crumbling beneath the weight of the corpses; he just had this strange perversion that consisted in looking at, scrutinizing all day, extraordinarily violent videos; beheadings in Afghanistan, hangings from the Second World War, all kinds of car accidents, bodies incinerated by a bomb.

I had to get away as soon as possible.

I missed Casanova and my soldiers every day. I thought of Judit, sometimes I sent her texts and called her; most of the time she didn't reply to the messages or pick up the phone, and I felt as if I were in limbo, in the *barzakh*, unreachable between life and the beyond.

For books, all I had was the Koran and two Spanish thrillers bought used in town, not great, but OK, they helped pass the time.

Then I had three days of vacation because Cruz left to deliver a load of corpses on the other side of the Strait. He couldn't leave me locked up the whole time, so he gave me a little pocket money (until then I hadn't yet seen the color of my wages) to amuse myself in town, as he said. I spent my days at sidewalk cafés, quietly reading and drinking my small beer.

I went to check my email and there, surprise: a message from Sheikh Nureddin. He was writing to me from Arabia, where he was working for a pious foundation; he asked me for news. I replied saying I was in Spain, without telling him about my pitiful activity. I hesitated about telling him about the fire at the Propagation for Koranic Thought, I wondered if he knew about it. His letter was kind, even brotherly; my suspicions about his possible participation in the Marrakesh attack seemed ridiculous to me now, even if the mystery of his sudden disappearance remained intact—I asked him if he knew where Bassam was.

I thought nostalgically about the long reading sessions at the Group, lying on the rugs. Tangier was far away, in another world.

I wrote a long note to Judit explaining in brief my slave's life in Algeciras; I didn't mention the corpses, just the gardening, cleaning, and the strange Cruz. I told her I hoped to see her soon.

I called Saadi, inviting him for coffee in downtown Algeciras; he had a visa, he could come and go as he liked, that was the injustice of the administration: the older you were and the less you wanted to, the easier it was to move around.

He was happy to see me again, as was I. I asked him if there was news of the company—he told me the Moroccan government was going to find a solution any day now. I still had time to profit from it, he said.

I hesitated. That was one way to leave Cruz; it would also mean saying goodbye to Judit. I was sure that if I returned to Tangier it would be almost impossible for me to return to Spain.

If Saadi guessed the reason for my hesitation, he didn't insist.

I told him about my days with Cruz, the great sadness of this terrible job, he listened, opening his eyes wide and shaking his gray head; well son, he said, if I had known, I wouldn't have sent you into that cesspit—I tried to reassure him, without much conviction, telling him it would allow me to make a little money to go to Barcelona in a month or two.

We stayed there till evening, sitting in the same café, taking advantage of the breeze, of the slow swaying of the palm trees that shed a little shadow on the square. And then he left. He hugged me and said, sure you don't want to come back with me on the boat? It's not easy for me sending you back there.

I hesitated for a second, it was tempting to stay with him, to rediscover the floating cage of the *Ibn Battuta*, where nothing could happen to you, aside from inadvertently crushing a cockroach with your bare feet.

Finally I refused; I promised to call him very soon, and after a final embrace I left to catch my bus.

I also took advantage of my boss's absence to sketch out a plan. I knew he kept—at least when he was there—a certain sum of money in a little safe, so he could pay people without a middleman, that this safe had a key, and that he kept it on his key ring.

The idea of stealing it came to me from the thriller I was reading, from all the thrillers I had read; after all, wasn't I locked up in a novel, a very noir one? It was only logical that it was these books that suggested a way out.

IBN Battuta recounts in his travels how, during his visit to Mecca, he meets a strange character, a mute whom the Meccans all know and call Hassan the Mad, who was touched with madness under strange circumstances: when he was still of sound mind, Hassan was completing his ritual circumambulations around the Kaaba at night and, every evening, he'd pass a beggar in the sanctuary—they never saw each other during the day, only at night. One night, then, the beggar addressed Hassan: Hey, Hassan, your mother misses you and is crying, wouldn't you like to see her again? My mother? Of course, Hassan replied, whose heart had sunk at the memory of her, of course, but it's not possible, she's far away. One day the beggar offered to meet him at the cemetery, and Hassan the Mad agreed; the beggar asked him to hold onto the beggar's robes and close his eyes, and when he opened them again, Hassan was in front of his house, in Iraq. He spent two weeks with his mother. Two weeks later, he met the beggar at the village cemetery; the beggar offered to bring him back to Mecca, to Hassam's master Najm Ed-Din Isfahani, by the same means, his eyes closed, his hands clutching the beggar's linsey-woolsey robe. He made Hassan promise never to reveal anything about this journey. In Mecca, Isfahani was worried about the long absence of his servant, two weeks isn't nothing—so Hassan ended up telling the beggar's story and Isfahani, at night, wanted to see the man in question: Hassan took him to the Kaaba and pointed to the vagabond with a cry to his master, it's him! It's him! Immediately the beggar placed his hand on Hassan's throat and said, By God, you will never speak again, and his will was done; the beggar disappeared and Hassan, mad and mute, paced around the sanctuary for years on end, without saying any prayers, without making any ablutions: the people of Mecca took care of him, fed him like a strange saint, for Hassan's blessing increased sales and profits; Hassan the Mad circled around and around the black stone, in orbit, in eternal silence, for having wanted to see his mother again, for having betrayed a secret. And in my shadows, near Cruz's little corpses, among the dogs, I prayed that a magic beggar would take me out of the darkness for a while, would bring me back, to the light of Tangier, to my mother's, into the arms of Meryem, of Judit, before leaving me spinning like a fragile meteorite around the planet, for years on end. I think today of that dark parenthesis, that first imprisonment in Algeciras, that antechamber, when around me spin the lost ones, walking, blind, without the help of books; Cruz was actually taking advantage of the world's possibilities, of the pomp of death; he was living like those dung beetles, those worms, those insects that swarm over corpses, and he had his own sort of conscience, no doubt, he thought he was doing Good; he was being of service; he was living as a parasite on misery: might as well reproach a dog for biting. He was the guard of the castle, the ferryman of the Strait, a lost man, himself, in the depths of his deadly forest, who spun, endlessly, in the dark.

PERHAPS it was this long familiarity with corpses that facilitated things; those two months of death made the prospect of robbing Señor Cruz easier to imagine—he had returned as planned after three days, exhausted, he said, by the truck journey into the depths of Morocco. He seemed happy to see me again.

He told me about his trip, which had gone well, he had brought his five corpses to Beni Mellal, all by chance to the same place, it was both practical and horrible. As usual, the women had cried terribly, their wailing had bored into his ears, the men had dug the graves, and that was it. He had only enough time to stop in Casa for a night to pig out, he said these words with such sadness in his reedy voice, *pig out*, that it could just have easily have been referring to his last meal.

Cruz poured himself some whiskey.

He had me sit down across from him in an armchair, offered me a drink, which I refused.

He said nothing, the whole scene seemed to call for conversation, confidences, but he was silent; he drank his Cutty Sark, glancing at me from time to time, and I felt more and more nervous.

I tried to speak, to ask questions about his trip to Morocco, but when he replied his answers were monosyllabic.

He finished his drink and politely offered me another before helping himself again.

After an endless quarter of an hour of silence, which I spent looking in turn at my knees and at his impassive face, I left, asking him to excuse me, I had to feed the dogs; he motioned with his head, accompanied with a brief smile.

Once in the yard I breathed a sigh of relief, I was trembling like a frail thing. Through the window, I saw Cruz's fat face, haloed by the electric blue of the computer screen, resume his stupefied contemplation of the forms of death.

I felt in danger; fear overcame me, powerful, irrational; I went to kneel down with the mutts, their muzzles nosed into my armpits, the softness of their fur and their clear gaze comforted me a little.

CRUZ always seemed to be hovering on the verge of speech.

I had never encountered madness before, if Cruz was mad—he didn't launch into unreasonable diatribes, didn't bang his head against the walls, didn't eat his excrement, wasn't overcome with delirium or visions; he lived in the screen, and in the screen, there were terrible images—old photos of Chinese tortures where men bled, attached to posts, their chests cut open, their limbs amputated by executioners with long knives; Afghan and Bosnian decapitations; stonings, stomachs ripped open, defenestrations, and countless war reports—strange, I thought, fiction is much better filmed, much more realistic than documentaries or the photos from the beginning of the century, and I wondered why, above all, Cruz always looked for the mention of "reality" in his pictures; he wanted the truth, but what difference could it make: he had his storage room full of corpses, he knew them intimately, he had frequented them for years, and I still wonder today what could have motivated this pathological virtual observation, he should have been cured of death yet he was gorging on miles of scenes of tortures and massacres. What was he looking for, an answer to his questions, to the questions the stiffs didn't answer, a questioning about the moment of death, the instant of passage, perhaps?—or perhaps he had simply been engulfed by the image, the bodies had made him leave reality and so he was burrowing into cyber-reality to find there, in vain, something of life.

As the days went by, he frightened me more and more, for no reason—he was the most inoffensive of creatures; he was gentle with me, gentle with his dogs, respectful of the dead. Every day I thought about asking him for my passport and up and leaving, too bad about the cash, farewell Mr. Cruz, the drowned and the bluish light of tortures on YouTube, come what may—but every night, in my cubbyhole, reassured by the company of the dogs, by the softness of their fur, by their panting calm, I would resume my dreams of theft, of the two or three thousand euros that Cruz's safe might deliver to me. I had sketched out a plan, one of those schemes that only work in books, until you try them: go into town to buy a similar key, it might be a common model, and substitute it on the key ring, which he often left in the entryway—of course the new key wouldn't open the safe, but when he realized it, with a little luck I'd be far away.

All the corpses I washed and put into their boxes justified my petty theft, I thought—but Mr. Cruz had an honest profession, he wasn't killing these poor people himself, he was charitable, he didn't bleed the families of the deceased, his prey was the State, the autonomous Community of Andalusia that paid his per diem for the carcasses of my compatriots, but all the riches I saw him accumulating, his gold rings, the chains around his neck, his black shirts, his car, his two huskies with their blue eyes in the sheltering shade of his creeping vines, all that seemed to me to be stolen from the Dead, seemed to belong to those nameless stiffs who had dreamed for a while of a better life, who had thought, like me, that they could make themselves a place in the world, and out of respect for this dream I thought I could appropriate some of his cash, as a little revenge for these poor martyrs who had known the pangs of drowning, experienced agony in the black solitude of the waves.

The more my determination increased, the more the possibility of putting my thoughts into action kept me awake at night; how could I get hold of the key to the safe, when should I run away, how—I had to go by foot to the bus stop, three hundred meters away, and I had to await the pleasure of the very erratic Andalusian intercity transportation system. That's when I would be most vulnerable, just like in novels. Books and prisons were full of guys who made huge blunders and who were nabbed without any difficulty whatsoever, just like that, at a bus stop or a sidewalk café. That wouldn't be my way. The bus, the bus station, the 11 PM coach, and the next day I'd be in Barcelona, lost in the crowd.

I couldn't make up my mind to act. Cruz was hypnotized by the Internet more and more; he stayed late, sometimes till ten at night, exploring videos—he had discovered a site called *faces of death* where hundreds of violent deaths could be found: a young Iranian demonstrator killed by the forces of order, Egyptian revolutionaries beaten to death by the police, Libyan soldiers burned alive in their Jeep, Syrian children massacred—current events filled the Internet with documents for Cruz.

One particularly dark day, the Strait vomited up an old, very damaged corpse that people walking on the beach had discovered— the judge visited, gave notice that this detritus on the sand could be chucked, the pathologist concluded death by drowning, and Cruz rushed there with his hearse to take charge of the remains before any of the competition: it was very sad and very gruesome, the guy had tattooed "Selma" in Arabic over his heart, that's all that could be used to identify him: he no longer had a face, at least nothing recognizable, and we quickly, very quickly closed him up in his zinc box so as not to see him anymore. Señor Cruz threw on his rubber gloves, then his mask; he had a little tear in the corner of his right eye, which he erased by rubbing his face against his bicep, arm outstretched. He sighed, turned toward me, without saying anything, he crossed the yard to walk to my hut, the dogs followed him wagging their tails, thinking he wanted to play or give them some food; he re-emerged from the garden shed holding a bottle, I wondered if he had hidden a liter of Scotch there without my ever noticing it, but the container looked smaller than his eternal Cutty Sark. He made a sign to me to follow him into the office; he said in his tiny voice:

"We've earned a drink, haven't we, Lakhdar?"

He sat down as usual behind his screen, shook the mouse, entered his password; I remained standing.

"Sit down, sit down, we'll have a drink and talk a little."

I searched for an excuse to escape, but couldn't find any; I was too exhausted from taking care of the corpse to think—I ended up worn out every time.

I sat on the sofa. I looked at the bottle he had placed on his desk; it was a half-liter glass flask, the label was facing him. Mr. Cruz needed a stiff one; his long face was pale, his eyes red-rimmed. He put on a video, out of force of habit—he stared at the screen for a second before stopping the procession of images of death that I couldn't see.

"So, Lakhdar, a little whiskey?"

Suddenly he was extraordinarily nervous, he went to the kitchen, returned with two glasses and some ice in a metal bucket.

I didn't want to annoy him, so I agreed. It might do me good, too.

He immediately seized a bottle of Cutty on the shelf, opened it, poured whiskey into two glasses, threw two ice cubes into each, and downed his in one gulp, even before I could pick mine up. He breathed out an ahhh of relief, poured himself another, handed me my glass before collapsing into his armchair, looking relaxed.

I emptied half the liquid in one gulp as well. I had never drunk whiskey. For me it was a legendary drink you had to taste in a bar in London, or Paris, with a girl at your side. Taste of crushed bedbugs, burning sensation in the esophagus. Hard to understand the interest of my authors in this beverage. Especially in a situation like this.

Cruz was watching me, as usual, on the verge of speech; he always seemed on the point of saying something that never came out, an eternal stammer. He began a phrase with my first name, said,

Lakhdar? I answered yes Mr. Cruz, and then nothing, he stared at me in silence.

I prayed to get out of this place as soon as possible. Too bad about the money, too bad about everything; I was going to get my passport back and leave. Go back to Morocco, find Tangier again, forget Algeciras, forget the dead, forget Judit and Barcelona.

I was just about to say to Cruz that I wanted to go home. It was the right moment, he looked a little placated by the alcohol; he hesitated again, articulated Lakhdar? without saying anything else. He seized the little flask, poured himself a large swig, and added a hefty dose of whiskey until the glass was three-quarters full. Then he stared at the mixture; he swirled around the ice that hadn't melted yet.

I got up, I couldn't sit still anymore. I said Mr. Cruz . . . He looked at me with such a look of pain, such suffering marked his fat face, all of a sudden, that I muttered that I had to go feed the dogs.

He passed his hands over his face, as if to wipe away some absent sweat.

"Lakhdar?"

"Yes, Mr. Cruz?"

"Come back soon, I'll wait for you."

And he downed his cocktail all at once, with an air of relief.

He had one of his silences, as if he were hesitating about adding something, and then he whispered:

"You're in luck, you'll see."

The phrase was cryptic; I imagined, as I played a little with the huskies before getting out their food bowl, that Cruz had realized I wanted to leave, that he wanted to wish me luck for the future.

When I went back to the office after feeding the dogs, he wasn't there; I heard a noise in the bathroom, of vomiting; he came out staggering.

"Are you okay, Mr. Cruz?"

He swallowed with difficulty, his mouth twisted, his face so tense that his eyes were rolling around like marbles.

"It's starting, Lakhdar."

He's dead drunk, I said to myself.

He sat down on the sofa facing the desk; he seemed to be having trouble breathing; he crossed his arms over his stomach, looked as if he were in great pain.

"It won't last very long . . . Watch closely . . ."

His lips were drawn out, he was grating his teeth; his face reddened, his shoulders were overcome with tremors, he lifted his knees to his stomach to relieve the pain.

"Mr. Cruz? Are you sick?"

He looked as if he wanted to answer, but no sound managed to form in his throat; he lifted his chin toward me, his hands were nervously patting each other. A dew of sweat covered his forehead, a drop of blood trickled from his nose, his lips turned purple, his head began to shake from right to left, leaning forward, as if to chase away the suffering, as if he couldn't believe what was happening to him—but the movement transformed into a terrifying contraction of the tendons in his neck, to the side first, then backward; his Adam's apple rose and fell, vibrated along his taut throat, like a big insect.

He was suddenly seized by a huge spasm that threw him onto the floor, his arm flung out, his legs arced as if he wanted to jump, he began shouting, I went over to him:

"Mr. Cruz, can you hear me?"

He still couldn't manage to answer and I was overcome with terror—he couldn't swallow, his neck was stiff, his chest lifted up, his back arched, his eyes looked as if they were about to explode. His body was a steel cable tensed with suffering, he was trying to speak, trying to grab my arm, but his wide-open hands twisted outward, the fingers stiffly spread apart—it lasted about twenty seconds, maybe a little more, and he went limp; he went limp, sighing, groaning, breathing very loudly, I shouted Mr. Cruz, what is the number for emergencies? The number for an ambulance? He didn't answer, I rushed to the telephone, feverishly tried dialing 1-5, as in Morocco, nothing happened; I looked quickly at his desk to see if there was a phone book, but no.

Cruz was suddenly overcome by a second convulsion, even more violent than the first, if that was possible; his eyelids drew almost completely back into the sockets, disappeared behind the eyeballs, it was horrible to see, his face was blue, his feet managed to fold the thick plastic of his soles like cardboard, he rose up, moved by the absolute tension of all the muscles, in a sharp cry that seemed to come from the depths of his thoracic cage—tears started to well up in my eyes, Señor Cruz, Señor Cruz, I didn't know what to do, I thought I should go find a neighbor, ran outside, ready to run the two hundred meters that separated us from the nearest house, or to stop a car passing by on the highway; once in the yard I remembered that bitch of a fence was always locked, instead of going all out and climbing it I chose to turn back and take the key from Cruz's pocket, to be able to open it for the ambulance.

Cruz was resting on his left side, his body formed a horrible half-circle, his back curved like a bow without a string, pelvis forward, feet extraordinarily convex; he was a monstrous ballet dancer, whose round neck and wide-open mouth completed the atrocious pose. Even the tips of his fingers took part in this fixed contraction, whose energy could no longer be discerned. He was dead. I approached him, nothing came to my mind, not even a prayer.

Cruz had joined the drowned of the Strait.

The only movement on this mass of flesh was the second hand of his watch, which showed 6:43.

I remained stunned for a few minutes, kneeling before the inert body, before I gathered my wits, of course I didn't understand, it took me years to try to understand the leprosy that was eating away at Cruz in his solitude; he had sprinkled me with his death, he had offered me his agony, an atrocious gift—I realized that he had poisoned himself right in front of my eyes; I went to splash water on my face, thousands, millions of contradictory thoughts were spinning in my head, now what, I saw the little bottle on the desk, the label bore a white skull on a red background. I paced in circles for a while, come on, now you have to act; I recovered Cruz's key ring. I conscientiously searched through the desk drawers, but didn't find anything important aside from my passport; I opened the little safe with the help of a key shaped like a cross, it contained a number of papers that had nothing to do with me, and almost five thousand euros in cash. I was becoming a thief. I had enough to live on for a while in Barcelona or elsewhere. The money of the dead, that's the kind of idiotic thing I said to myself.

Of course there were the police. I had left my fingerprints everywhere, even on the bottle of poison, I was the king of dunces.

I gathered my things together and put them in a pretty ridiculous looking yellow and blue Cádiz soccer club sport bag that I found in the shed.

Anguish was becoming more remote. I avoided glancing one last time at Cruz, stroked the dogs for a long time to say goodbye to them, and left to wait for the bus.

A little later on in his travels, when he's in the city of Bolghar, Ibn Battuta wants to visit the Land of Darkness, mentioned in the legend of Alexander the Great; he finally decides not to go there when he learns that in order to reach it you need a sled drawn by huge dogs, to cross the ice that surrounds it—he will be content to hear talk of it, to learn that the fur merchants trade for skins from its mysterious inhabitants, who live in total night: "After forty days of crossing this desert of ice, the travelers reach the Land of Darkness. The merchants leave large bags of merchandise some distance from their camp. The next day, they return to inspect their bags and discover in place of their things the skins of martens, squirrels, and ermines. If they like the skins, they take them, and if not, they leave them there for one more night. In that case the inhabitants of the Land of Darkness increase the quantity of furs or, if they don't agree with the terms of exchange, replace the travelers' merchandise. That is how one does business in the Land of Darkness, and the people who go there don't know if they're dealing with men or djinns, for they never see a soul."

I left Algeciras with the sensation that the world was empty, peopled exclusively by phantoms that appeared at night to die or kill, to leave or take, without ever seeing each other or communicating with each other, and in the long night of the bus that brought me to Barcelona, city of Fate and Death, I had the terrible impression of crossing into the Land of Darkness, the real darkness, our own, and the further the bus advanced into obscurity on the highway in the middle of the desert, between Almeria and Murcia, the deeper the horror I had just witnessed seeped into me; Cruz's face, moist and purple in its contractions, appeared to me among the flashes of truck headlights, in the midst of the reflections on my window.

Cruz was among the shadows, and so was I.

Unable to close my eyes, pursued by funereal images, bodies shriveled by the sea and the face of Cruz projecting his agony onto me, I waited for the liberation of dawn, when the bus was already drawing closer to Alicante.

III

THE STREET OF THIEVES

I arrived in Barcelona on March 3rd—I had left Tangier more than four months before. I didn't know where to go. I must have looked like the poorest of the poor in my green parka and with my '80s sport bag, haggard eyes, thick beard—if the cops ever arrested and searched me, I'd have trouble justifying the thousands of euros in cash I was carrying. Sheikh Nureddin's money, Cruz's cash, as if God always arranged to give me the means for my travels; I ate from the hand of Fate.

The bus went down Avinguda Diagonal, Diagonal Avenue, palm trees caressed the banks, the noble buildings of past centuries were reflected in the glass and steel of modern skyscrapers, the yellow and black taxis were countless wasps scattering at the sound of the bus's horn; elegant and disciplined pedestrians waited patiently at the crossroads, without using their superiority in numbers to invade the road; the cars themselves respected the zebra crossings and, stopping carefully at a blinking yellow light, let those traveling on foot cross when their turn came. The shop windows all looked luxurious to me; the city was intimidating but, despite my fatigue, finally arriving filled me with a new energy, as if the huge sparkling phallus of that multicolored skyscraper of the Torre Agbar over there in the distance, that pagan divinity, were transmitting its strength to me.

I blinked my eyes in the noon light and picked up my bag; the station serving points north, *Estació del Nord*, was apparently adjacent to a large park; a little lower down near the sea was the station for France, and then, to the right, the harbor. I found a phone booth and called Judit; she answered, and when I heard her voice I began crying like a kid, I must have been so exhausted. I said it's me, it's Lakhdar, I'm in Barcelona. She seemed happy to hear me, despite my sniveling; she asked me where I was, I replied at the Estació del Nord; she said she'd meet me not far from there, in a neighborhood called the Born, and then she added no, that's complicated, you'll never find it, don't move, I'll come get you, give me a quarter of an hour. I said thank you, thank you, and I hung up, I was overcome with a kind of dizzy spell and had to sit down on the ground, next to the phone booth. I thanked God, I said a brief prayer, and felt a little ashamed at addressing Him.

I stayed like that, my eyes closed, my head in my hands, for minutes on end, before gathering my wits. I wanted to look strong when Judit arrived—I felt dirty, as if I stank of corpses, the morgue, hatred; I hadn't seen her since last summer, was she going to recognize me?

And then the energy of the Torre Abgar returned to me.

The energy of desire.

The first minutes were very strange.

We didn't kiss, but smiled; we were both equally embarrassed. We exchanged a few banalities, she stared at me from head to toe, without coming to any conclusion—or at least, without revealing any of her conclusions; she just said, you want to have lunch? Which seemed a bizarre question to me, I answered yes, why not, and we began walking toward the center of town.

I told her about my last weeks with Cruz, obviously without mentioning the horrible end. She sympathized, and my cowardliness was such that I wanted her to feel sorry for me, to soften her. Seeing her again made my heart pound; I had only one desire, that she take me in her arms; I wanted to lie down next to her, right up against her, and sleep like that, in her warmth, for at least two days. On the way we had passed a triumphal arch in red brick that opened onto a wide promenade bordered with palm trees and elegant buildings. I secretly hoped the place where we were going wouldn't be too chic, I didn't want to be ashamed of my clothing. Fortunately she brought me to a bar on a pretty, quiet, shaded little square. I had to force myself to eat.

I couldn't bring myself to ask Judit any questions, at least not the ones I wanted to ask; I questioned her about Barcelona, about the geography of the city, the neighborhoods, no personal questions; it all was terribly artificial. She avoided looking me in the eyes. Sadness began to invade me. I felt as if the ground were disappearing beneath my feet, time became thick, something heavy and tangible, Judit's face seemed to have gotten darker, she had cut her hair, which made her look tougher. She spoke to me mostly of current politics; of the crisis in Europe, its harshness, of unemployment, of poverty that was coming back, as if from the depths of Spanish history, she said, of conflicts, racism, tensions, the insurrection that was being prepared. She had gotten very involved in the Movement of the Indignants, for some months. Also very involved in the Spanish Occupy movement, *los Okupas*, she said. Repression had never been so violent. The other day a twenty-year-old student lost an eye from being hit with a rubber bullet when the cops broke up a peaceful sit-in, she said. Spain is heading for its end, Europe too. Ultra-liberal propaganda would have us believe we can't resist the diktat of the markets. Here they won't take care anymore of the poor, the old, the foreigners. Right now the revolution is delayed because of soccer, Real, Barça; but when that's not enough to make up for frustration and poverty, then there'll be riots, she said.

I watched her, I wanted to take her hand, not talk about the crisis. At times, Cruz's face came back to me, appearing between Judit and me; I had to shake my head to make it disappear.

She was fed up with school. She was in her last year, wasn't taking many courses, didn't have many class hours, and she felt her Arabic was still just as bad. She didn't really know what to do, she wanted to spend some time abroad, maybe in Egypt or Lebanon, since Syria was in flames—I was hurt that she didn't mention Morocco, I must've made a funny face; she immediately changed the subject.

"And you, what're your plans? What are you going to do, are you going to try to stay here?"

"I don't know, it depends a little on you."

She lowered her eyes, and I knew then that everything I had imagined was true—she was with someone else.

She was suddenly shifting about nervously.

She didn't say anything.

I was so tired, worried, broken by my stay with Cruz, the long hours awake in the bus, and the emotion of seeing Judit again that I got annoyed, it was the first time I raised my voice with her, I shouted something like you could tell me that you don't want to see me anymore, shit, and I half-rose from my chair—the people at the table next to ours (bourgeois couple, sunglasses perched atop their heads, checked shirt, V-neck over shoulders) turned to us, I screamed at them to mind their own business, they looked offended.

Judit looked me in the eyes as if to say sit down, stop your histrionics. I became aware of my ridiculousness and sat back down.

"Listen, there's no point getting worked up like that."

She was whispering. She was ashamed. I took my courage in my hands, the courage that she didn't have.

"You have someone else, don't you?"

She denied it. She shook her head, repeating no, no.

"You're a fucking slut."

I had made use of my lowbrow detective-novel vocabulary, to make her react. She must not have understood what I said, since she didn't get angry. She just added I don't want to be with anyone at the moment, that's all, which seemed to me an incredible piece of crap, a lie, a stupid remark.

I looked at the small oval plaza. Opposite, under the trees, there was a beautiful wooden porte cochere from another era, a chic restaurant; in front of me a pretty fountain shaped like a vase, with gold spigots; an old lady went by pulling a wheeled shopping bag.

We stayed for a while in silence, I didn't know what to do or say. She felt bad about leaving me like that, I could sense it.

"Where are you sleeping?"

"What the fuck do you care."

No need even to add "bitch" or "cow," since the phrase sounded so much like a bruise.

"Don't get mad, it's stupid. I'm just trying to help you."

I didn't know what I wanted anymore, I felt sorry for provoking her anger. The lady with the cart had crossed the entire square; a baguette stuck out of her cart; the couple next to us with the sunglasses asked for the bill.

She had only one desire, to leave, I knew that; she must have been tortured by guilt; I saw myself, with my poorly-shaved African mug, in my shitty khaki parka, without a goal, without anything, the world wasn't even the world, it was a television set, a fake. I had a sudden burst of memories, Tangier, our neighborhood, Meryem and Bassam, I wondered what the hell I was doing there, on this square that was so pretty, so cute, facing Judit who didn't want me anymore, God alone knows why.

I began talking in Moroccan.

I begged her, without articulating, very fast; I spoke to her of love, of my fatigue, of the *Ibn Battuta*, of Cruz, of the darkness of Algeciras, of our week in Tunis, of the memories on our balcony in Tangier, I told her she couldn't throw all that away in one fell swoop, she'd kill me.

She looked at me with a pained air. I wasn't at all sure she had understood what I had just said.

She took my hand; she said something sort of definitive, like "I don't have the strength," which sounded dramatic and theatrical in Arabic; I felt as if we were acting in an Egyptian soap opera.

I was too exhausted, I muttered, whatever you want, I won't bother you anymore; just point the way to a mosque, that's all.

Judit looked at me with big eyes: a mosque?

A mosque, a bookseller, and a hotel that's not too expensive, I added.

A supermarket, I'll find that on my own.

I called the waiter, got out a nice, brand-new fifty-euro note, and didn't let Judit pay, even though she wanted to.

CITIES can be tamed, or rather they tame us; they teach us how to behave, they make us lose, little by little, our foreign surface; they tear our outer yokel shell away from us, melt us into themselves, shape us in their image—very quickly, we abandon our way of walking, we stop looking in the air, we no longer hesitate when we enter a subway station, we have the right rhythm, we advance at the right pace, and whether you're Moroccan, Pakistani, English, German, French, Andalusian, Catalan, or Philippine, in the end Barcelona, London, or Paris train us like dogs. We surprise ourselves one day, waiting at the pedestrian crossing for the signal to walk; we learn the language, the words of the city, its smells, its clamor—Barcelona woke up to the racket of the gas canisters being changed, to the Pakistani handling the propane gas and shouting *Butaaanooooooooo* in his orange uniform, accursed color, color of the worst profession in the world, since you had to cart 30-kilo canisters up the narrow staircases of apartment buildings, with no elevator, to the fifth or sixth floor for a tiny commission per bottle sold: in my neighborhood, the "Pakis," whether they were actually Pakistani or Bengali, Indian or even Sri Lankan, were bottled gas peddlers, rose sellers, beer sellers late at night, grocers or telephone operators in the *locutorios*, the talking-places, that mix of phone-booth-equipped telecommunications office and internet café. In the beginning I went often, on the Rambla del Raval, right near my place, to that sort of establishment to consult the Internet—the rates were ludicrously low, and all countries and nationalities could be found there: Moroccans, Algerians, Western Saharans, Ecuadorans, Peruvians, Gambians, Senegalese, Guineans, and Chinese who called their families or sent money to their country by an international transfer system of liquid cash, from hand to hand, a system that came close to a racket since the commissions were so high, but which had the poetry of the modern world: you gave a hundred, two hundred or a thousand euros to a ticket office in Barcelona with the identity of the recipient, and the sum was immediately available in Quito or Lahore; dough doesn't recognize the same boundaries as its owners, money that the migrants weren't yet able to borrow by themselves in Spain could dematerialize in the innards of the Internet to transform into electrons, pulses, electronic mail, leave Dhaka and appear, instantaneously, in a computer in Barcelona.

My street was one of the worst in the neighborhood, or one of the most picturesque if you like, it answered to the flowery name of Carrer Robadors, Street of Thieves, a headache for the district's town hall—street of whores, of drug addicts, drunkards, of dropouts of all kinds who spent their days in this narrow citadel that smelled of urine, stale beer, tagine, and samosas. It was our palace, our fortress; you entered through the little bottleneck on Carrer de Hospital, and you emerged on the esplanade of modern buildings at the corner of Carrer de Sant Rafael, which opened onto the Rambla del Raval; opposite, on the other side of Carrer Sant Pau, began Carrer de Sant Ramon, another fortress—between the two, the new movie theater, supposed to transform the neighborhood by the lights of culture and draw the bourgeois from the North, the well-to-do from Eixample who, without the geographical-cultural initiatives of the City, would never come down here. Of course the lovers of auteur films and the clients of the four-star hotel on the Rambla del Raval had to be protected not only from the excesses of the rabble, but also from the temptation of going to the whores or buying drugs, and so the zone was patrolled 24/7 by the cops, who often parked their van at the end of our Palace of Thieves: their presence, far from being reassuring, on the contrary gave the impression that this region was under surveillance, that there was real danger, especially when the patrol was large, armed to the teeth, and in bulletproof vests.

By day, whoring was present, but somewhat limited; by night in the high season, dead-drunk foreign tourists got lost in our alleys and sometimes let themselves be tempted by a pretty black chick they'd take from behind, in a doorway, out in the open: I often saw, late at night, the moving shimmer of white buttocks breaking through the penumbra of corner spaces.

Our building was at the start of the Street of Thieves, at its narrowest part, close to Hospital Street; it was a typical neighborhood building, old, ruined; one of those that, despite the efforts of the owners and the city hall, seemed to resist any renovation: the steps in the stairway had lost half their tiles, the woodwork was warped, the walls were ridding themselves of their coating in large sections whose debris littered the landings; electric wires hung from the ceiling, the old ceramic sockets hadn't seen the nose of a light bulb for ages, and the rusty, dented mailboxes gaped apart, disjointed or wide open, when they still had a door. The stairway was peopled with cockroaches and rats and it wasn't rare, climbing upstairs at night, to surprise a fat black rodent sucking at the needle of an abandoned syringe, to extract the little drop of blood—the creature would skitter away through a hole in the wall of an apartment, and you'd always shiver, thinking the same thing could happen on our floor.

The drug addicts came from the social aid center that was reserved for them a little farther down the street, and they'd look for a place to shoot up; in adjacent streets, a lot of them resold the methadone the municipality gave them. They entered buildings whose doors didn't close properly, climbed up as far as their physical condition allowed them, sometimes to the roof, where they didn't risk being chased out by the occupant with kicks or a broom handle. You felt sorry for them. Most of them were wrecks of stupefying thinness; they had abscesses on their arms, pustules on their faces; a lot of them spoke to themselves, cursed, swore, crushed their cans of beer, which they emptied one after the other, waiting for better; sometimes you saw them staggering, silent, blissful, emerging from a building, and you knew they had just injected themselves, in a hurry, sitting in the midst of roaches, with their dose of happiness. When they had money, they'd buy themselves a bowl of soup at the Moroccan restaurant a little farther down the street, and would stay there a long time, watching TV, looking absent; the restaurant owners were generous, they tolerated these phantoms who paid and stole nothing but teaspoons—they just didn't let them use the bathrooms. The drug addicts even had a little park to themselves, a corner of greenery that no one denied them, not even City Hall: a little more to the south, near the harbor, against the ramparts of the Gothic Arsenal, behind an embankment that must once have protected an old moat, there was, two meters down, a square of grass invisible from the street—agents of municipal cleanliness didn't often go down there, and even the cops, on the principle that anything invisible isn't annoying and thus does not exist, only rarely bothered the junkies. There were women and men, even though it was sometimes hard to tell what sex they were; they lived among themselves, argued among themselves, died among themselves, and if they weren't the most elegant or the cleanest inhabitants of the neighborhood, they were, along with the rodents and insects, among the most harmless.

Except sometimes, just as a dog at bay can show its teeth and try to bite an aggressor, you saw some of them turn violent; I remember an incredible fit of madness, one day, when I was on my balcony calmly observing the goings-on in the street, one of those guys emerged from his methadone stupor in a rage; he began shouting, then screaming incomprehensible curses, hitting his fist against the wall, then against a passing Pakistani who didn't understand what earned him this deluge of bruises; two people came to his aid: despite his skinniness, the addict had immense, almost divine strength, three young men couldn't manage to control him but just tear him away, trying to grab him around the waist, his clothes were much less resistant than he—first his T-shirt tore, then his belt gave out, he fought like a demon and sent his aggressors rolling with huge vengeful kicks in the shins, the balls, until he was just in his underwear, he fought in his underwear like a ridiculous warrior, thin and meager, his legs covered with sores, his arms crusted with scabs and tattoos, and it took five people, two cops, and an ambulance to bring it to an end: the fuzz managed to handcuff him, the men in white gave him an injection and then strapped him to a stretcher to take him God knows where—there was a real sad beauty in this last battle of the poor naked man, dispossessed of his brain and his body by heroin; he was fighting against himself, against God, and the social services, which to him were identical.

The whores also provoked pity, but of another kind. Some were nasty pieces of work, sharp, dangerous she-wolves who didn't think twice about robbing customers or scratching the eyes out of a bad payer; they showered insults on males who refused their advances, calling them homos, fairies, impotents. Most of the women came from Africa, but there were also a few Romanians and even one or two Spaniards, including the one sitting under a porch at the entrance to the street, Maria, something of a concierge for our palace. Maria was in her forties, somewhat plump, usually smiling, not very pretty, but nice; she sat there in front of her door every afternoon and evening; she would spread her legs and show us her thong, calling us her little darlings when we walked by her: I would always politely reply, hello Maria, quickly checking out her cunt, it did no harm to anyone, it was good neighborliness. I never dared go up with her—because of the age difference, first of all, which intimidated me, and because of the memory of Zahra, the little whore in Tangier, which saddened me. Most of the regular customers were immigrants, broke foreigners who haggled over the price, which made Maria shout: she'd spit on the ground, screaming like a pig, Then go see the black girls, at that price! The sex business was in mid-crisis, too, apparently. Maria lived with a guy who was a truck driver, or a sailor, I forget—in any case he wasn't there much. The African girls had pimps, mafiosi to whom they had sold their bodies in their native countries, for the price of the crossing to Europe: I don't know how long they had to get laid by the poor and the tourists before they could get their freedom back—if they ever did.

There was also a bicycle repair shop, a poultry dealer, some illegal fridges for the beer-selling Pakistanis, some storehouses for roses for the rose-selling Pakistanis, some poor Moroccan families, some poor Bengali families, some old Spanish ladies (who had known the neighborhood since before the war and who said that, aside from the nationality of the whores and thieves, few things had changed), and some young illegal immigrants like us, mostly Moroccan, some of them underage, kids hanging around waiting for a low trick to dispel their boredom as much as to make themselves a little dough: rob tourists, sell them fake hash, nick a bicycle.

And just at the corner, a mosque, the Mosque of Tariq ibn Ziyad, glorious Conqueror of Andalusia, which was why I had ended up in the neighborhood: it was the only one Judit knew, one of the oldest in Barcelona, situated on the ground floor of a renovated building. It was clean and quite large.

There were also two booksellers not far away, a big underground supermarket nearby, and a used-book market every Sunday within walking distance, so I was content. Sad, my heart broken by Judit, but content.

I looked for news of Cruz's death; the only thing I could find was a tiny item in the *Diario Sur*:

Tragedy in Algeciras
Poisoned by One of His Employees

The owner of a funeral enterprise, Marcelo Cruz, was found dead at his place of work from strychnine poisoning. It was one of his neighbors and collaborators, the Imam of the Algeciras mosque, who called emergency services. The precise circumstances of the tragedy are still unknown but, according to the National Police, Mr. Cruz was poisoned by one of his employees, who fled after robbing him.

So I was being sought for murder and theft.

It wasn't a surprise, but seeing it in the paper brought a lump to my throat. Fortunately, Cruz hadn't told the authorities about my presence; he didn't have a work permit for me, hadn't photocopied my identity papers, so there was no clue, aside, no doubt, from my fingerprints and my DNA—the Imam didn't know my last name: but he could still describe me, indicate my name was Lakhdar and that I came from Tangier. That was much more than the cops needed to recognize me in case of arrest, especially with a first name as uncommon as mine.

I thought again of Cruz's dogs, I wondered who would take care of them. Maybe because they were the only glimmer of light in the darkness of the last weeks, I missed their mechanical tenderness, their fur and their breathing.

To keep from being arrested, I had to lay low on the Street of Thieves.

Everything seemed very far away to me.

Judit, closer than ever, seemed far away.

Tangier was far away.

Meryem was far away, Bassam was far away; Jean-François Bourrelier's soldiers were far away; Casanova was far away; I had found a new prison for myself, Carrer Robadors, where I could hide; you never leave prison.

Life was far away.

The first days were hard—I stayed in a hotel for students, totally unthinking: I had to leave my passport at the desk, the cops could have easily found me and collected me first thing in the morning. But nothing ever happens the way it does in books. Whatever the case, well hidden in the Raval, in the lower depths, between the whores and the thieves, I felt as if I had nothing to fear.

The Tariq ibn Ziyad Mosque was in the hands of the Pakis; I also ran into a few Arabs there, but few in comparison. The Imam was from the Punjab. I spent some time there, in the beginning, in order to meet people, to rest in prayer and reading. When you have no home and know no one, you have to start somewhere: bars or mosques—and I chose well: it was thanks to the mosque that I found my room in the dilapidated but livable apartment, in the heart of the Raval fortress: thirty square meters all lengthwise, with a little balcony. I shared the apartment with a Tunisian named Mounir. I paid three hundred euros per month, everything included—in fact we didn't know who was in charge of electricity, if there was an electric bill; as to water, it came from large reservoirs on the roof, and there were no meters. I never managed to find out who the owner was—we settled the rent in cash in a bar on Sant Ramon Street, and that was it. When Mounir couldn't pay, at the end of April, two guys gave him a good thrashing; that encouraged him to find dough quickly, he got by, took some risks to steal four nice bicycles which he sold off cheaply, nothing else.

My relationship with Judit was strange. We saw each other almost every day. She helped me with everything; she even went so far as to open an account in a savings bank in her name so I could deposit my money—she gave me the debit card and the PIN, it was all cash of course, given where I lived. It was she herself who made the deposit for me, she didn't ask me where the cash came from and I didn't tell her.

Judit seemed to me the most beautiful and noblest of women, even if, for a reason that was entirely obscure, she no longer wanted me. She immediately arranged to find me work—teacher of Arabic. Twice a week, I gave a special class to Judit, Elena, and Francesc, one of their schoolmates, for ten euros an hour. I was very proud. I explained the subtleties of grammar to them; I commented on classical verses with them. Often, I learned that same morning from a book what I explained in the afternoon; all of a sudden I was reading a lot in Arabic to prepare for the classes, it was enjoyable. We learned by heart some poems by Abu Nuwas, in my opinion the greatest, most subversive, and funniest of the Arab poets; I explained to them, almost line by line, the great novels of Naguib Mahfouz or Tayeb Salih which I had never read, but which were on their class list.

Judit lived with her parents, at the top of the city, in Gràcia; it was a mostly middle-class, well-kept neighborhood, an old village attached to Barcelona in the nineteenth century, with narrow streets and pleasant squares; local tradition had it that the children of these bourgeois people were mostly rebellious and alternative: there were a lot of activist organizations, there was even a squat, right in the middle of the neighborhood—youth will have its fling. Up there, the Arabs too were more fashionable, more bourgeois; the restaurants mostly Syrian, Lebanese, or Palestinian; right next door to Judit's home was also a Mesopotamian establishment and a Phoenician one—all that was a little intimidating and, stuck between Catalanity and Antiquity, I preferred to take refuge in the darkness of my alleyways. Judit of course felt very much at ease up there. She had her friends there, her school, the streets where she'd grown up; sometimes she insisted on taking me out to lunch, after the Arab class, in one of those noble, ancient restaurants: the owner at the

Phoenician one hadn't come straight out of a sarcophagus in Sidon, he was a Lebanese from the mountains; he talked politics with Judit for a while, about Syria, mainly, the civil war underway, the difficult role Turkey, Saudi Arabia, and Qatar would play in it—it was all a little depressing, I felt that whatever we did, the Arabs were condemned to violence and oppression. I have to admit he was pretty intelligent and very nice, that Phoenician, which only increased my jealousy—I didn't open my mouth, he must have taken me for a grouch or a half-wit.

Judit grew more mysterious every day. She seemed sad, profoundly sad at times, absent, but I couldn't figure out why; at other times, though, she was bubbling with energy, laughed, spoke to me of her plans, suggested we go out for a walk or a drink. The first days I bugged her to make her confess she was with someone else, but she kept denying it, I stopped persecuting her, and after a while I knew so well how she used her time that I had to face facts: there was no one else in her life, aside from a few university friends and me.

That was all the more incomprehensible.

I told myself I had to give her time, she'd end up coming back to me. Sometimes, when we went out, I'd take her hand; she wouldn't withdraw it—I just felt as if it was all the same to her. And even, on one occasion, and only one, we slept together: I had invited her to see my glorious new room in the afternoon; she let herself be kissed and undressed without putting up any resistance—and I mean *without putting up any resistance*, mechanically, and all my caresses, all my love came to nothing, so much that once my business was done, she got dressed in silence, and I was overcome with shame, shame and guilt as if I had raped her. She reassured me, saying I was being ridiculous, she just didn't want to at the time, that's all.

"I told you, I don't have the strength to be with someone."

For me, it was absolutely unfathomable, it must have been some kind of illness. So I spoiled her; I wrote her poems, gave her books, reminded her of the perfect times in Tangier and Tunis. Those memories plunged her into melancholy. She seemed fragile, as if the slightest thing could make her crumble.

I never took my eyes off her.

BARCELONA was beautiful and wild, I loved the elegance, the rhythm, the sounds of the city, the diversity of the neighborhoods, from Gràcia to Poble Sec, from the harbor to the mountain, the strange unity there existed in the differences and the out-of-the-way places, the surprises the city offered—a stone's throw from my place, for instance, hidden by walls, behind an arched stone gate, was the Holy Cross Hospice and its magnificent garden, planted with orange trees, its beautiful fountain and the wonderful stone staircases of the National Library of Catalonia—as soon as a ray of sunshine appeared, I would be sitting on a bench there reading, in the perfume of the orange flowers; the pretty students from the applied arts school would come out and smoke cigarettes, sitting on the steps, and it was nice to watch them for a while; a few steps away, under the porticos of the old cloister, a group of bums guzzled beers and bottles of red; they too looked as if they found the place to their liking, just like the junkies on the Street of Thieves, the hash-sellers, the tourist-robbers, everyone liked this place—though of course for different reasons. The medieval hospice continued to fulfill its fundamental purpose: it sheltered poor things, books, artists, drunks, and thieves.

At night, when Judit couldn't be bothered to go out, I would stroll for a while on the Rambla del Raval, a long oblong square planted with palm trees, dotted with benches, with a huge bronze cat, an improbable statue, at one end—Pakis walked about in their *salwar kameez*, families took their children out in strollers, women and little Indian girls wore their beautiful multicolored dresses, gypsies got out chairs and argued on the sidewalk in front of a restaurant where there dined, before normal hours, some Brits who, from the color of their shoulders, looked as if they'd spent the day at the beach—this whole little clutch of people took the air, taking advantage of the truce of evening, and you could've believed, going up and down the Rambla del Raval, that there were no antagonisms, no hatred, no racism, no poverty—the illusion didn't last long; usually an Arab started annoying a Paki, or vice-versa, and you'd end up hearing shouts, which sometimes degenerated into something worse.

When the sun was low, I would go home; I had a new ritual: I would buy a bottle of Catalan red wine at the supermarket, some olives, and a can of tuna; I would settle myself on my tiny balcony on the fifth floor, open the bottle, the can, and the package of olives, take a book, and wait for night to fall, gently; I was the king of the world. Better than Abu Nuwas at the Baghdad court, better than Ibn Zaydún in the gardens of Andalusia, I was getting a little foretaste of Paradise, may God forgive me, I lacked only the houris. I would read a Spanish thriller (you have to make do with what's at hand) or classical Arabic poetry, with the help of the dictionary Judit had lent me—deciphering an obscure verse full of forgotten words was an immense pleasure.

I had discovered wine. A sin, indeed, I admit, but one of the most pleasant and least expensive: depending on the bottle I chose, it cost me between 1.50 and 3 euros. The powerful Kingdom of Morocco taxed alcohol pitilessly, so before I had to content myself with coffee with milk; here, beautiful Spain placed the fruit of its vines within reach of all budgets.

The sun ended up sinking almost directly opposite me, near the Sant Pau Church, I still had a mere half-hour of daylight left, then it was too dark to read on the balcony, so I would watch the street for a little while; on the weekends, dozens of people would line up in front of the premises of the Evangelical, or Adventist, sect, or some similar minor heresy, our neighbors—they were very successful with the indigent, because they gave out free meals after service. One obviously can't prejudge the sincerity of the faith that animated these ragged flocks, who for all anyone knew might be real Protestants. In any case, this church (a former butcher shop) always had a full house—you could hear them singing hymns; then they spoke of love, the Lord and his lambs, and of Christ, who would return bringing justice at the Day of Resurrection.

It was strange to think that all our religions were essentially tales: fables in which some believed and others not, an immense storybook, where everyone could choose what he liked—there was a collection called *Islam* which didn't entirely tally with the versions contained in *Christianity*, which itself differed from the *Judaism* collection; these Protestants singing for the poor must have had their version too—I had picked up one of their instruments for evangelizing, it was a comic book in color, about a dozen pages long, in simple lines; all the characters were black, except for Christ, golden and haloed, with a beard and long hair: you saw a man building a wooden house with a hammer, getting married, having a family; his children grew up around his hut; everyone worked the earth. Then the man grew old, his hair turned white; finally he died and a gleaming Jesus accompanied him to heaven, among the angels.

The whores came out when the streetlights came on. They would arrange themselves at the entrance to the street, on the esplanade side; the Tariq ibn Ziyad Mosque must have been the only one in the world before which Amazons black as night, armed with sequined miniskirts, spangled bras, and high heels accosted the faithful—who to be sure paid them no heed. They were part of the decor, like the cops who were also starting their patrol at nightfall, in threes or fours, in rows, proud, very proud of exhibiting all the force of order and the harshness of the law. The truth was that this was how they accelerated most illegal activities: as soon as they had turned the corner, you knew, as sure as you could tell from a watch hand or from a star, that they'd take a good five minutes to return. There were surveillance cameras, of course, but I never heard anyone in the street say they should be paid any attention to: just as God sees us all, Mr. Mayor could just as well observe us from his office on Plaça Sant Jaume—no one would find anything to object to, not the drunks who knocked back beers and raved almost directly beneath the camera in question, not the hash dealer, in the same spot all the blessed day, not the blacks, owners of a whole stable of prostitutes who were slaving away a little farther down the street for their profit, not the junkies who yelled at each other in front of the closed social aid center, not the Pakistanis who came, late at night, looking for beers in the underground coolers. No one looked the least bit bothered by these white, visible cameras attached to each side of the lane. They were the price you had to pay for fame.

And then, around eleven o'clock or midnight, I'd go for a little walk with Mounir, my co-renter. Mounir was one of the escapees from Lampedusa, one of the Tunisians who had landed in France during the Revolution thanks to the generosity of Berlusconi, to the great displeasure of the French government, ready to share anything except debts and indigents. Mounir had spent some months in Paris, well, Paris is easy to say, it was more like the suburbs, he was stuck in a wasteland next to the canal, left there to freeze and die of hunger. Those French bastards didn't even give me a single sandwich, you understand? Not even a sandwich! Ah it's a fine thing, democracy! Impossible to find work, we wandered around all day, from Stalingrad to Belleville to the République, we were willing to accept any job to survive. Nothing, nothing to do, no one helps you, over there, especially not the Arabs, they think there are too many of them already, one more poor darkie is bad for everyone. They think the Tunisian Revolution is very nice from far away, they say, But now that you've done the Revolution, stay there, in your jasmine paradise full of Islamists and don't come bothering us with your useless mouths. You know what I think, my brother Lakhdar, all these Arab Revolutions are American machinations to bust our balls a little more.

He exaggerated about the French: he told me he had survived thanks to the *Restos du Coeur* and the *Soupe Populaire*, soup kitchens for the homeless, where if you stood in line long enough you ended up eating some beans or leaving with a package of pasta without anyone asking you any questions. The picture he painted of Paris was not an enticing one—battalions of poor to whom they handed out individual tents so they could sleep on the sidewalks, right in the middle of the streets; endless suburbs, abandoned by God and man, where everyone was unemployed, where there was nothing to do except burn cars to avoid boredom on the weekend—and above all, hatred, he said, the hatred and violence that you feel in that city, you have no idea. Every day on the news you hear about the rising hatred. I'm telling you, they don't realize it, they're headed straight for an explosion.

He added a little more than that, true, but it wasn't reassuring. The French Right wanted to close the borders, blindfold their eyes with a tricolor flag, and be hermetically sealed against everything, except cash.

Mounir had ended up leaving Paris, disgusted, to try his luck farther south—what about Marseille, did you see Marseille? I had my memories of thrillers by Izzo and I felt as if I knew Marseille. But no, Mounir hadn't stopped in Marseille, he had his face smashed in by two guys in front of the Montpellier train station, who had attacked him just like that, for the pleasure of it, he said. Ever since then, I never go out without a knife, he added, and it was true: he always carried a blade on him, short but sharp.

The real good fortune of Barcelona, the only thing that still made the city a city and not an ensemble of bloodthirsty ghettos, was the tourists. A blessing from God. Everyone lived off them, in one way or another. The restaurant owners lived off them, the hotel owners lived off them, the café owners and the vendors of soccer jerseys lived off them, the butchers lived off them, and even the bookstores, which had branches in museums to pump their share of this pink-skinned gold that irrigated the center of town. The beer hawkers lived off them, the peddlers of birdcalls, whistles, magic spinning tops, and blinking pins lived off them—Mounir lived off them too. After all, as he said, everyone steals from these tourists. Everyone robs them. They pay eight euros for their beers on La Rambla. I don't see why taking a camera, a wallet, or a handbag from them is necessarily more evil. Because it's *haram*, actually, it's theft. No, he replied, if Al-Qaida allows infidels to be beheaded, I don't see why it's forbidden to pickpocket them, and he let out a big laugh.

The truth is that it was hard to contradict him: you sometimes felt as if it was God himself (may He forgive me) who sent these creatures into our alleyways, with their innocent airs, looking up in the sky as Mounir calmly slipped his hand into their backpacks.

Manna. The poorest survived thanks to tourism, the city survived thanks to tourism, it always wanted more, always attracted more, increased the number of hotels, of inns, of planes to bring these sheep to be fleeced, it all reminded me of Morocco, because at that period there was a promotional campaign for tourism in Marrakesh in the Barcelona subway, an assortment of orientalist photographs with a pretty slogan like "Marrakesh, the city that travels inside you," or "Where your heart takes you," and I said to myself that tourism was a curse, like gasoline, a trap, which brought false wealth, corruption and violence; in the Barcelona subway I thought again of the explosion in Marrakesh, of Sheikh Nureddin somewhere in Arabia, and of Bassam, somewhere in the Land of Darkness, of the attack in Tangier where that student had met death by sword—of course, Barcelona was different, it was a democracy, but you felt it was all at a tipping point, that it wouldn't take much for the whole country to fall into violence and hatred as well, that France would follow, then Germany, and all of Europe would catch fire like the Arab world; the obscenity of this poster in the subway was proof of it, there was nothing else for Marrakesh to do than invest money in ad campaigns so that their lost manna would return, even if they knew perfectly well that it was the money from tourism that provoked underdevelopment, corruption and neo-colonialism, just as in Barcelona, little by little, you felt resentment against foreign cash mounting, cash from within as well as from without; money pitted the poor against each other, humiliation was slowly changing into hatred; everyone hated the Chinese, who were buying up the bars, restaurants, markets, one by one with the money of entire families who came from regions whose poverty couldn't even be imagined; everyone despised the British louts who came to quench their thirst with cheap beer, fuck in doorways, and, still drunk, take a plane back that had cost them the price of a pint of ale in their obscure suburb; everyone silently desired those very young Nordic girls the color of chalk who, because of the difference in temperature, broke out their miniskirts and flip-flops in February—one quarter of Catalonia was out of work, the papers overflowed with terrifying stories about the crisis, about families kicked out of apartments they couldn't pay for anymore, which the banks sold off cheaply while still continuing to claim their debt, about suicides, sacrifices, discouragement: you could feel the pressure mounting, violence mounting, even on the Street of Thieves among the poorest of the poor, even in Gràcia among the sons of the middle class, you could feel the city ready for anything, for resignation as well as for insurrection.

Mounir told me about Sidi Bouzid, about the gesture of despair that had set off the Revolution: you had to lift your hand against yourself to make the masses react, as if only that ultimate motion could finally set things off—someone had to burn himself to death for people to find the courage to act; it took the irreversible death of another to realize you had nothing to lose yourself. This question tormented me; it brought me back to Morocco, to my expedition at night with Bassam and Sheikh Nureddin, to my cowardliness, a movement exactly opposite that of Sidi Bouzid, as if on one hand there was suicide and on the other the dictatorship of cudgels, as if the whole world were on the point of toppling into the dictatorship of cudgels and as if all that was left was the prospect of setting yourself on fire—or staying on a balcony reading books, the ones that weren't burned in the meantime, or going with Mounir to sell a camera to his fence, then drink a beer or two in a neighborhood bar, bowing low to the cops when you passed them.

At that time, in France, in Toulouse, a maniac killed three children and an adult in a Jewish school, with a pistol, point-blank; a few days earlier, he'd cut down some unarmed soldiers in the same way; it was impossible to find any sense in these shots, which resounded throughout the world. The story was spread across two or three pages in the Barcelona papers. A mad dog had stood up, had killed before dropping dead himself, what else could be said, aside from that this madman's first name was the Prophet's, that he had tried to take part in the Jihad, God knows where; Mounir thought the cops who had shot him had been too gentle with this degenerate, that he should have been impaled very slowly in a public square—or quartered like Damien, the regicide in Casanova's Memoirs, perhaps, but what would that have changed. I thought of Bassam, lost somewhere in his own personal Jihad, who might have killed a student with a sword in Tangier, sometimes explaining serves no purpose; there's nothing to understand in violence, the violence of animals, mad from fear, from hatred, from blind stupidity that motivates a guy my age to coolly place the barrel of a gun to the temple of a little eight-year-old girl in a school, to change his weapons when the first one jams, with the calm that implies determination, and to fire in order to win the respect of some rats in Afghan caves. I remembered the words of Sheikh Nureddin, provoking clashes, setting off revenges that would fan the fires of the world, would launch dogs against each other, journalists and writers at the lead, who hurried to *understand* and *explain* as if there were something truly *interesting* in the paranoid ravings from the brain of a bastard so frazzled that even Al-Qaida didn't want him.

Mounir thought that these attacks were secretly supported by the fascist extreme right to increase the hatred and mistrust of Islam and to justify the attacks on North Africans to come; I remembered the expression of Manchette in I forget which book, *the two jaws of the same idiocy.*

A sky of infinite blackness, that was what was waiting for us— today in my library, where the fury of the world has been muffled by the walls, I watch the series of cataclysms like one who, in a supposedly safe shelter, feels the floor vibrating, the walls trembling, and wonders how much longer he'll be able to preserve his life: outside, everything seems to be nothing but darkness.

NO *se puede vivir sin amar*, that's what I kept repeating to Judit, you can't live without loving, I had found this phrase in a beautiful novel, dark and complex; she had to pull herself together, rediscover her energy, her strength, and I had only one desire, to offer her these glimmers, this fire of tenderness with which I was overflowing—offer it to her through books, through poems, through everyday gestures; I had let Meryem die, I didn't want Judit to sink into her own darkness. I spoke to Elena about it, one day when we were walking together after class, through the strangely-named streets of Gràcia—Stream-of-Footlight Street, Flood Street, Danger Street—and she agreed with me, she could see that Judit wasn't doing well, that she seemed more and more absent, reclusive, shut up inside herself; Elena had suggested they both go traveling together again, for the Holy Week, to go somewhere in the Arab world, to Cairo, why not, or Jordan, but no success—Judit replied that she didn't want to ask her parents for money, her father owned a little construction company that had been flourishing before but was now on the verge of bankruptcy, and her mother, a university professor, had seen her salary reduced twice the year before. But I don't think it's matter of money, Elena said; it's something else—nothing interests her anymore. Even Arabic, she keeps at it, as you see, but without passion. She stopped looking for graduate programs and translating schools for next year. She almost never goes out anymore, aside from with you from time to time. Last year we still went to clubs, to concerts, but now not at all. She got involved with the *Oku-pas*, she took part in meetings of the Indignants, she had a whole bunch of activities and today almost none. She still goes to classes, but that's it. I feel like most of the time she stays locked up in her bedroom, she walks a little around the neighborhood, to get some air, and that's it. Elena seemed sad and worried about her friend, all the more so since she didn't see what could have provoked this change in attitude. When she got back from Tunis, she said, she spoke of almost nothing except you, the both of you, Morocco, the huge progress she had made in Arabic, and so on—and in the fall, it began going not so well; she was worried you didn't write to her a lot, even though she knew of course that you were on your boat without Internet most of the time; little by little she got tired of the Indignants, she found their movement a little empty; the festive side of the *Okupas* movement bored her as well, she went less and less to the sit-in on the Plaça del Sol. In short, little by little, she stopped doing much, she sank into sadness.

That seemed exaggerated, to me, as a description, it was just a passing thing, I was sure.

As for me, even though I was happy with my setup in Barcelona, even though I liked my readings on the balcony, the life of the neighborhood, the Arabic classes, and everything I was discovering about life in Europe, languages, newspapers, books, my situation was not an easy one. They must still be looking for me for the Cruz affair, I couldn't reasonably go see the cops to ask them about news of their investigation or explain to them that I had not (as they probably suspected) killed the gentleman: that meant I was stuck in Barcelona, locked up once again, but in a larger territory. This absence of future was a little heavy: I'd have liked to enroll in the university, but without a residence permit it wasn't possible; and neither was working legally. I had to wait—I had in front of me a long wait of several years, so the police could forget me and for the economic situation in Europe could improve, which didn't seem likely to happen anytime soon. Just as someone who has a slowly-progressing illness, almost painless in the early stages, readily forgets it in daily life, these questions didn't torment me—at least not often. Cruz had joined the world of my nightmares, of my dead. From time to time I smoked some joints, in the middle of the night, when some too-horrible dream prevented me from falling back asleep: still the same themes, blood, drowning, death.

I missed Bassam's smile when we watched the Strait, his cheery, laughing peasant-face.

With university ruled out, I tried to cultivate myself, to keep from wasting my time. I was aware that it was books that had procured the best jobs I had ever had, at the Propagation for Koranic Thought and with Mr. Bourrelier; I sensed confusedly that they gave me a painful superiority over my companions in misfortune, illegal like me—not to speak of an almost free pastime. Soccer and TV weren't much more expensive, true, but I found it hard to get passionate about the saga of Barça, which had become, who knows why, the team of the Just and the Oppressed faced with the evil Whites of Madrid. I sometimes went with Mounir to watch a match in a bar—but without much enthusiasm.

I went to the library, read essays on the history of Spain, of Europe, I took notes in a big notebook; I tried to learn a little Catalan, I had a little notebook for vocabulary where I wrote words, fragments of sentences, verbs. God knows why, but Catalan seemed a very ancient language to me, a very old little language, spoken by medieval knights and merciless crusaders—maybe because of all those Xs and strange phonemes.

I also improved my Spanish and kept up my French, even if my kind of books were somewhat hard to find—I sometimes came across a few in used bookstores. I thought about buying an e-reader, but I hadn't yet made up my mind. There were thousands of titles available for free online, all of French literature practically. It was tempting, even if according to my research there weren't that many thrillers available. Under the pseudonym Eugène Tarpon, I took part from time to time in an online forum devoted to "Detective Literature"; I made virtual friends there who knew all the web's thriller-resources.

So I was reasonably well occupied, the intellectual of the Street of Thieves.

At this rate, I'd soon be sprouting glasses.

AND then on March 29th, the insurrection started, just as a pressure cooker left on the stove explodes when no one attends to it.

The day before, Mounir had brought me to a bar to watch Barça play Milan in the Champions League, 0-0, a pretty boring spectacle but pleasant company: there were four of us Arabs sitting at a table drinking beers, cracking jokes and snacking on *patatas bravas*, a nice time, even if the soccer fans would've liked to see some goals and a win for their team. What always impressed me in these soccer bars is that there were girls, pretty young women who wore the Barça jersey, drank beers straight from the bottle and yelled at least as much as the men, it was wonderful—we talked about them among ourselves in a lingo that was a mixture of Moroccan, Tunisian, French, and Spanish, which is the language of the future, a new language, born in the bars of the lower depths of Barcelona; we all agreed, laughing, that there was a lack of girls in our joints at home—that's because we don't know how to play soccer, said Muhammed, the Rif native with his Berber accent, when we have a club like Barça, we'll have chicks drinking beers and watching the matches too. That's how it is. The two go together.

His explanation was actually convincing, but Mounir raised an objection: that has nothing to do with it, look at France. They don't know how to play soccer, they don't have a decent team, but they still have girls with beers in the bars.

"Yes, that is troublesome," I said. "But France already won the World Cup. So you can establish a positive correlation between the general socceristic level and the number of females in bars."

"Doesn't the African Cup count?"

"For Tunisians, maybe; you Moroccans lost in the finals because there weren't enough chicks in your bars, no doubt about it. Plus now we have freedom, and you don't."

"True, and Egypt's won the African Cup so often that Cairo is famous for its bikini-wearing supporters, who shout and throw beers at the screen during the rebroadcasts."

"Just look at the seventy supporters who died in the last match in Egypt, it was exclusively women, and cute ones at that, apparently."

"Who won the African Cup this year?"

"Zambia."

"Are you messing with me? Where is that, Zambia?"

"Those must be some girls they have in their cafés."

We laughed a lot. It did good to forget the daily petty thefts, the dishwashing in restaurants, the bags of cement, or simply exile.

The unity of the Arab world existed only in Europe.

The next morning, the whirr of a helicopter woke me up. A helicopter that was circling, quite low, above the center of Barcelona—we would hear it for twenty-four hours. We had gone to bed late, with our jokes about beers, girls, and soccer, we had even smoked a pair of joints together before going to sleep and all of a sudden I had completely forgotten there was a general strike. Strange idea, in any case, a general strike, planned, organized, with a fixed date, and for only twenty-four hours. If refusal to work has a weight, I thought from the height of my twenty years, it's in the length of time, in the threat of its continuation. Not in Spain. Here the unions fought against the government for a single day, just one, and by dint of numbers: their leaders viewed the strike as a *success* or a *failure* not because they had achieved anything, which would have been a real success, but when they reached such-or-such a percentage of strikers. So the strike was an immense success for the unions (eighty percent of strikers, hundreds of thousands of demonstrators) but also for the government: it didn't have to stray one iota from its policy, and didn't even offer to negotiate, on any point. I don't even know if that idea was on the agenda. The principle of the strike was that no one goes to work, that everyone demonstrates, and that's that. One could see that Spain was beyond politics, in a world beyond such things, where the leaders no longer gave a shit about anyone, they just announced the weather, like the King of France in Casanova's day: my friends, the coffers are empty, today it's the functionaries who are going to pay the price. They've lived too well for years, their time has come. Tomorrow, filthy weather for health. Storms over schools. Put your kids in private schools. The last remaining employees of heavy industry who haven't died of cancer have been fired. We've made the job market flexible, reformed contracts. The trial period is extended to a year: if you're shown the door after three hundred sixty-four days you don't qualify for unemployment compensation. This backhand notion of a minimum wage is profoundly leftist and binds the hands of entrepreneurs who want to create jobs, it must be fought. The minimum wage per hour of work is now at the level of Morocco, which has just increased it: it's too high already to compete effectively against the competition. To fight the competition we need slaves, Catholic slaves who are content with their lot. Malcontents shouldn't vote. Malcontents are dangerous alternatives and as such are excluded from democracy, they deserve nothing but clubbings and mass arrests. The Spanish Episcopal Conference recommends Catholics to be parsimonious in matters of fertility, since a high birth rate in times of crisis unreasonably increases the expenses of the State: His Holiness Pope Benedict advocates a whole series of ecumenical measures like Mass and self-flagellation to overcome the excess of desire.

All these things were in the papers, on TV; I even saw a report one day asserting that "the fingers of black people, which *are not*

exemplary in the quality of their manicures, shouldn't handle condoms, since it's dangerous, they risk puncturing them, and for that
reason the Pope has forbidden blacks to use condoms; what's more,"
added the commentator, "they don't know how to read, so aren't up
to the task of understanding the instructions, which explains," he
said, "why there is more AIDS where condoms *are* distributed than
where they are not available."

A real load of crap. When you heard things like that, it wasn't the
strike that loomed, but the Revolution. The media here seemed to
fabricate the Kingdom from hatred, lies, and bad faith. The Spanish
should have had their Arab Spring, started burning themselves alive,
maybe then everything would have been different.

There was something I didn't understand: Europe was admitting
that it didn't have the wherewithal for its development, that it was
all just an illusion, that Spain in fact was an African country like
the others and everything we saw, the highways, the bridges, the
skyscrapers, the hospitals, the schools, the daycare centers, was just
a mirage bought on credit that was threatening to be retaken by
the creditors. Would everything disappear, burn up, get swallowed
by the markets, corruption and the demonstrators? If that was the
case, a lot of people would end up on the Street of Thieves; a lot of
people would fail, change their lives, die young, for lack of money
to take care of themselves, lose their savings; their children would
inherit a kick in the ass, would no longer go to nice schools, but to
sheds where everyone would huddle around a wood stove—no one
saw that coming. You had to come from far away to imagine what
this transformation would be, you had to come from Morocco,
from Sheikh Nureddin, from Cruz and his corpses.

The helicopter wasn't there for nothing, everything must have
seemed more beautiful seen from the sky, which was clear that day.
In the street it was quite otherwise. I hadn't cancelled my class for
the day: I was a strike-breaker. I had to go there on foot, since there
was no subway. It was ten in the morning, and there were already

gatherings, groups of guys with caps, flags, megaphones, and cops everywhere. Half the streets in the city were blocked off. The big brand names were closed, just a few small businesses braved the picket lines—to their detriment: I saw a baker forced to close by a dozen unhappy union members shouting "Strike, strike!" and threatening to smash in his window with axe handles, he took less than ten minutes to abdicate and give his employees the day off. On the other hand, explaining to the Chinese in the Ronda shops the concept of *picketing* was more complicated:

"No work today."

"No work?"

"No, it's a general strike."

"We not on strike."

"Yes, it's a general strike."

"We not on strike."

"Exactly, you have to close."

"We have to go strike?"

But in the end, used to the proletarian struggles of the Single Party, the Chinese could also recognize a big stick when they saw one, and ended up lowering their shutters, for a few hours at least.

Their job became even more clandestine than usual.

In Gràcia, everything seemed calm. The streets were bathed in the blue-tinged coolness of a spring morning; Judit was waiting for the class, I arrived a little out of breath. Elena and Francesc couldn't make it, they lived too far away to come by foot. Judit's mother was there, it was the first time I met her; I was introduced as "Lakhdar, my Arabic professor." She seemed much younger than I'd have thought; she wore skinny jeans, a blue T-shirt on which was written *I would prefer not to*; her name was Núria. I thought of my own mother, they must have been about the same age—but they didn't have the same life, you just had to look at them to see that.

The one-on-one class went well, even though Judit was a little absent. We had read a passage by Ibn Battuta that seemed to suit current events. Ibn Battuta is in India, with the Sultan Muhammed Shah, and he relates how a Sheikh named Shihab-ud-dun, very powerful and well-respected, refused to appear before the Sultan when he had been summoned; the Sheikh explains to the court messenger that "he would never serve a tyrant." So the Sultan sent for him to be taken by force:

"You say I'm a tyrant?"

"Yes," replied the Sheikh, "you are a tyrant, and among your tyrannies, there is this and that," and he began to enumerate on a number of them, like the destruction of the city of Delhi and the expulsion of its inhabitants.

The Sultan held his sword out to his vizier, saying:

"If I am a tyrant, cut off my head!"

"The man who calls you a tyrant is a dead man, but you yourself know perfectly well that you are one," interrupted the Sheikh.

The Sultan had him arrested and locked up for fourteen days with nothing to eat or drink; every day he was brought to the courtroom, where the judges asked him to withdraw what he had said.

"I will not retract my words. I am made of the same cloth as the martyrs."

On the fourteenth day, the Sultan had a meal sent to him, but the Sheikh refused:

"My belongings are already no longer of this world, take away this food."

When the Sultan heard this, he ordered that they make the Sheikh ingest four pounds of fecal matter; some idolatrous Hindus were in charge of executing the order: they spread open the Sheikh's jaw with pincers, mixed the excrement with water, and made him swallow it.

The next day, they brought him before a gathering of higher-ups and foreign ambassadors, so he would repent and withdraw what he had said—he refused once again, and was decapitated.

May God have mercy on his soul.

Once the text was translated, as an exercise, we discussed, in literary Arabic, the Sheikh's determination and this question: Should one give in to the powerful? I said I didn't think the Sheikh's sacrifice served much purpose. He would certainly have been more useful had he stayed alive and continued the struggle, even if it meant going back on his statement. Judit was wiser than me, and more courageous too, perhaps:

"I think his sacrifice was useful—tyrants have to know what they are. The Sheikh's determination even to the point of death showed the Sultan that there are ideas and people who cannot be conquered. What's more, if the Sheikh had retracted, Ibn Battuta would not have told this story, and his struggle would have remained unknown to all, whereas his example is of great benefit."

She expressed herself well, her Arabic was fluid, with fine expressions and no grammatical errors.

We began talking politics; I thought of the Syrians, tortured and bombed every day, and of the courage they needed to continue fighting, in the long war against their Sultan who must also have known perfectly well that he was a tyrant.

I left Judit around one o'clock; I suggested we go out for a walk, or a coffee; she declined with a pretty smile. She had plans in the afternoon to go to the demonstration with her friends.

So I was free as the air, I went to sit on the Plaça del Sol, on a bench, I read a thriller by Vázquez Montalbán for a few hours; his detective, Pepe Carvalho, was the most disillusioned, pretentious, antipathetic guy on earth; his plots were incredibly boring, but his passion for food, sex, and the city ended up making his books amusing. In the end, I learned quite a few things about Spain and Barcelona, and some new words and expressions that were always useful. Once I'd finished the book, I made my way to the center of town. The helicopter was still wheeling around, lower down; the wind carried a burnt smell, layers of smoke weighed down the air; distant police sirens ripped through the seeming calm of the streets

and when I emerged at the corner of Avinguda Diagonal, in front
of one of the largest hotels in Barcelona, I encountered hundreds
of people with signs; black and red anarchist flags floated on the
obelisk, brandished by dozens of demonstrators who had climbed
the pedestal; the crowd seemed to be occupying the entire Passeig de
Gràcia. The window of the Deutsche Bank had been shattered by a
hammer; I saw a group of young people attacking the savings bank
next door, chanting and spraying graffiti with red spray-paint—the
helicopter was very close now, above us, it must have been observing
the activists; down below, toward the Plaça de Catalunya, immense
columns of smoke rose to the sky and you could see the glimmer of
flames—the city was burning, to the sound of loudspeakers shouting slogans, chants, music of all sorts, sirens, it was a deafening,
brutal, blinding spectacle, which made your heart beat in unison
with hundreds of thousands of motionless spectators, prevented
from moving by their own numbers; the closer I got to the heart
of Barcelona, along side streets, the more fires there were—in the
middle of an avenue, a barricade of trashcans was burning itself out
with a hellish smell. On Plaça Urquinaona, there was a pitched battle—in the flames and smoke, a multitude of young people, compact and moving, were advancing against two police vans, throwing
their flagstaffs, bottles, trash at them, then spreading out in disorder
when the vehicles began moving, two fat marine-blue creatures,
their eyes covered by metal grills, which quickly belched out their
occupants, helmeted, wearing gas masks: some were carrying rifles,
they began shooting into the crowd, flashing detonations from the
barrels of their weapons—the young people moved back under the
hail of rubber bullets and the tear gas; some of them, scarves over
faces to protect themselves from the gas, continued their offensive—
they had nothing left to throw except insults.

I was at the side of the street, sheltering with some other passersby in a doorway. Opposite us, a fire-truck was trying to control the
flames emerging from a Starbucks, a glaring symbol of American

capitalism, whose windows hung in tatters, a strange cloth of broken glass. From time to time, a cop would advance, shoulder his weapon, and aim calmly, before falling back in with his colleagues, like a hunter or a soldier, and one wondered what effect these projectiles could have, so extraordinarily violent and frightening were the shots.

To get to the Street of Thieves, I had to cross the police line—or else retrace my steps, walk toward the university and from there burrow into the Raval, but I thought the university square would also be on fire, if not under fire and sword.

Subversion was everywhere, you could feel the violence and hatred of the boys in blue rising: they were rushing around, restlessly brandishing their long clubs, their rifles, their shields—opposite them, the young people lowered their pants to show their asses, called the cops assholes and sons of whores; a little group dismantled some metal trashcans to throw at them, others, oddly, attacked a tree, maybe to turn it into a giant spear. The confrontation was unequal and reminded me of a battle of conquistadors, with armor and harquebuses, against a troop of Mayan or Aztec civilians I had seen an engraving of in a history book. Conquest was on the march.

The moment I decided to go behind the forces of order to try to cross, the charge began. About fifteen of the fuzz ran forward, clubs in hand; four others covered their flanks and headed toward us, shoved us bluntly aside, a respectable gentleman in his fifties began shouting, saying he lived on the other side of the street; the masked cop yelled Clear the way clear the way, he landed his club in the gentleman's back, who ended up taking to his heels, indignant, tears of rage in his eyes—we had to surge back to the upper part of the city, which is precisely the opposite of where I had to go. Violence and hatred; I felt rage rising within me, rage and fear; I tried to call Judit on her cellphone to find out where she was—no signal. The police must have cut off the networks to prevent demonstrators from coordinating with each other via texts.

The city was wavering between insurrection and festivity—the Gran Via was still full of people, I passed an old lady carrying a sign saying "He who sows poverty reaps rage," a little girl holding the string of a balloon that read "Enough budget cuts," students chanting *Rajoy, chulo, te damos por culo,* Rajoy, you pimp, we'll give it to you from behind, and other pleasantries along those lines, in the stench of burning trash and tear gas—strangely, a little bar tucked behind some scaffolding was open, I decided to take a rest and wait for things to calm down a little. I ordered a coffee which I eked out—the TV was showing the day's events live, I saw the battle scene I had just been part of on Plaça Urquinaona, taken from a different angle: it was a very strange sensation to think that behind those policemen, on the left, at the corner of Carrer Pau Claris, they could have seen me. The TV was the periscope of a lost submarine.

Night fell. I was afraid of being arrested along with a group of activists by accident, so I decided to make a big detour to get to my neighborhood, my fortress, the Palace of Thieves: to go by Carrer Diputació to Villaroel, go down to the Sant Antoni Market and enter the Raval by Carrer Riera Alta. A detour that took a good forty-five minutes, but that should prevent me from finding myself by chance in the midst of a club-wielding horde of police. On Diputació, at every street corner, you could see, five hundred meters lower down on the left, around Plaça de Catalunya, the white emanations of gas mingling with the black smoke of trashcans on fire. I managed to meet up with Judit—she had left the demonstration to go back up to her place when the cops charged at the corner of Diagonal and Passeig de Gràcia; her voice was hoarse; I asked her if she was all right, yes yes, she answered, of course; I didn't press further.

The detour was a good idea—aside from local policemen on motorbikes who prevented the cars from reaching the center, I passed only groups of store owners talking in front of their half-closed shops, or young people with grave, frightened faces climbing up from University Square.

The two temporary buildings of the Sant Antoni Market were a gateway in imaginary ramparts; behind them opened the Raval and, in its heart, the Street of Thieves—I was safe. God knows why, the neighborhood was blacked out. No street lights. Maybe an effect of the strike, or a coincidence; a few shops were open and threw a strange wavering glow onto the asphalt, adding an even more medieval look to our castle of the poor. On Carrer Robadors, nothing had changed: our blacks were keeping a lookout at the corner, waiting for God knows what that never arrived; Maria was in front of her door, skirt hiked up to mid-thigh; fat cockroaches scurried out of my way as I climbed the stairs; Mounir was in front of the TV, feet up on the coffee table, in socks. I collapsed next to him on the sofa, worn out—I had walked for almost four hours.

The TV showed the images of the day on loop.

I began to play mechanically with the knife that Mounir had placed on the table as usual; it was a short but wide weapon, very sharp; a spur of metal kept the blade from folding back in once opened, a very powerful spring you had to release to close it back up. The handle was short, steel, covered with two pieces of red wood. Solid, sharp, dangerous. I asked Mounir if he'd used it yet, he said no, in your dreams, I haven't even taken it out of my pocket in front of anyone. It's just a security measure, you never know.

You do, in fact, never know.

On TV, the commentaries remained the same.

The unions were delighted with the strike's great success.

The government was delighted to be able, starting tomorrow, to resume its indispensable economic reforms.

In the distance, the helicopter still circled.

THE next day the city awoke feverish and in disbelief; the wave of violence was still trembling in the morning—curious onlookers stared at the broken windows in little groups, making comments in low voices; cleaning teams tried to erase all traces of fire as quickly as possible. In the papers, the only thing they talked about was the cost of the damage, the number of arrests.

The difference from Tunis, Mounir said to me, possibly the only difference, is that in Tunis the chaos continued the next day, the day after that, and the day after that. Here, it's as if nothing had happened. They repair the bank façades, the government continues its work, the revolutionaries return to their skateboards, and the tourists resume control of Plaça de Catalunya.

Here, everyone still has too much to lose to launch an insurrection, believe me.

Of course, at the time, we couldn't know.

Mounir was desperately trying to earn some money, more money—he took insane risks to steal cameras that were increasingly expensive, wallets that were never fat enough, I suggested a kind of association with him, so he wouldn't have to steal so much, I had an idea, which came from Casanova's memoirs—the Venetian was like Mounir, he too was always in need of money and, in Paris, he invented something extraordinary for the King of France: the lottery, that is, a money game where everyone emerged a winner, or almost. I explained to Mounir how you could earn dough by organizing the Lottery of Thieves, a nice, neat, underground operation—we were on that sidewalk café on Carrer del Cid that we liked for its quietness, five hundred meters from the Carrer Robadors, and I was making him laugh with my lottery stories, he found it hard to believe that it could work. If we don't try, we'll never know, I said. Of course money games are a sin, but for the player, not for the organizer, I suppose.

You think there's a lottery in Saudi Arabia?

I found it extraordinarily funny that it was old Casanova who provided us with this magnificent idea. Of course a little investment was necessary, at least for the winnings from the first drawing, if we didn't sell enough tickets the first time around. We'd be much less greedy than the State and we'd reinvest most of our earnings, keeping just a profit of twenty percent of the stakes—the rest would go to the owner of the winning ticket.

Mounir strongly doubted that clients would trust us, but the projections made him salivate: look, if we sell, let's say, 50 tickets at 10 euros each, that makes 500 euros. We give 400 euros in winnings, and we keep 100 euros. If 10 euros seems too much to you, we can do the same with 5 euros.

Mounir began to understand all the magic of this beautiful invention. He made calculations. Hey, he was a clever one, your Casanova. Did he really invent that? Yes, I think so, I replied. At least that's what he says.

Putting this plan into action was obviously more complicated than we'd thought, but one week later we had printed our tickets for our underground lottery—I was the investor, so I had taken charge of this material part of the business. In the end, we found it simpler to use the results of an existing lottery instead of organizing our own, and this way had the additional advantage of giving us a certain legitimacy: everyone could check, via the paper or the special kiosks, if he had won or lost.

This activity was very Spanish, people told me: at Christmas, everyone (associations, businesses, supermarkets, administrations) organizes lots of lotteries. So ours would have the particularity of being out of season and Casanovan.

Of course, this initiative was an almost complete fiasco: we sold three tickets, two in the Moroccan restaurant on the Street of Thieves and a third to Judit's mother, which was a little shameful—on his side Mounir couldn't manage to palm off a single one on his own, making the rounds of all the Chinese outfits on the Raval, and this when the (supposed) Chinese passion for gambling was going to make our fortune.

Our tickets were handsome, though, in color and in Catalan, because I thought that looked more serious: *Loteria Robadors* was not, on the other hand, perhaps the best name in the world.

Still, the fact is that this Casanovan action brought us thirty euros (after checking that none of the tickets was the winning one, which would have been a catastrophe, or bankruptcy) from which we had to subtract some euros for a color copier to print a hundred tickets: enough to drink some coffee and lunch lavishly with Mounir, but that's it. .

I was a far cry from Casanova.

LOCKED up waiting for violence: the month of April passed, between reading sessions, a few rare excursions to the beach (paradise peopled with pink-breasted Brits, Nordic girls blonde as the sand, Brazilians with provocative thongs) and soccer disappointments that were quite serious for my comrades but that didn't affect me much—I was settled in my routine; I was still trying to remain vigilant, not to leave the neighborhood too much. I couldn't lower my guard: Mounir had been arrested by a bad stroke of luck on Plaça de Catalunya when he was trying to snatch a tourist's wallet. Of course he didn't have his passport on him, he said he was homeless and a Palestinian from Gaza, which, according to him, was supposed to earn the sympathy of the boys in blue and make his expulsion more difficult. He spent a day in lockup before being released with a summons to appear at court the next day, with which he of course did not comply—he showed it to me, it was addressed to Mounir Arafat. When I asked him why he had chosen such a pseudonym, he answered it was the only purely Palestinian surname that had come to mind, which cracked us up. The interpreter sent to the police station had obviously glimpsed the hoax right away, but, Mounir said, he was a nice guy, a Syrian, who hadn't given it away.

He'd been quite surprised: he was expecting a beating, but aside from a few friendly slaps and one or two humiliations, the fuzz had been pretty civil.

So Mounir was like me now, twice a fugitive, clandestine, and an established thief.

He knew that the next time, he wouldn't get off so easily.

Aside from these legal delights, I had another cause for worry, more serious in another way: Judit's state was becoming more and more alarming. She had almost stopped eating, spent her days in the dark because, she said, the light gave her migraines; the doctor wavered between diagnosing sinusitis and a pollen allergy, which would explain the congestion, aggravated by a depressive state. She was given masses of all kinds of medications and slept for most of the day. She no longer had the strength to concentrate on her Arabic classes: so I was content to visit her and stay with her for an hour or two. I would read her some texts, tell her a story from Ibn Battuta's travels, and often she would fall asleep on the sofa, lulled by my voice, and woke only when I left. She told me she often had strange dreams, where she thought she was awake and struggling to find sleep: this obsession would pursue her until she actually awoke and realized that this insomnia was a dream.

Leaving Judit was heart-wrenching—I would always go down to Carrer Robadors on foot, to avoid any possible identity checks in the subway, that hostile underground world peopled with guards and muzzled dogs, and it took the entire trip to rid me somewhat of the sorrow and pain her condition caused me. Even if, according to her doctor, there was nothing alarming, just a passing weakness, a result of various factors, this illness was an unfair piece of shittiness that deprived me of the only presence that mattered to me.

So I began writing again—poems that were so bad compared to those of my role models that I destroyed them right away, which made this activity at least as distressing as the absence of Judit, locked away in her eternal drowsiness.

The world seemed suspended, arrested; I was waiting for it to topple over, for something to happen—its destruction in the flames of the Revolution, or a new blow of Fate.

Often, I would lunch alone in a little Moroccan restaurant on the Street of Thieves, where you could imagine you were in Tangier: same food, same waiters, same colors, it reminded me of the cafeteria where Sheikh Nureddin took us out to lunch after the Friday mosque, except now I went there alone; in the dining room a couple of junkies ordered a chorba for two, they sat side by side, shoulder to shoulder to support each other, and couldn't even manage to finish the single dish.

The place filled me with nostalgia, and every time I was angry with myself: I had wanted to come to Barcelona, I didn't come here to cry into my plate at the memory of Tangier. I thought of my mother, my family, Bassam of course.

I realized I wasn't going to the mosque very often, just Fridays at noon, if that, from time to time. I read the Koran and its commentary, sometimes, it's true, but less and less often. It was hard for me to find the concentration necessary for prayer; I felt as if I was no longer available for God, as if I were carrying out a mechanical imitation. Faith was a dead skin that Cruz and reading books had sloughed off me; all that was left to me was religious practice that seemed very empty, simple prostrations done by rote.

Sometimes I got caught up in imagining myself in Paris, or Venice; if I'd had a passport in order I'd have liked to go there: Paris to buy some thrillers, see the Seine; Venice to visit Casanova's city, discover the sites of his escapades, navigate the lagoon.

At no time, in his travels, does Ibn Battuta speak of a passport, or papers, or safe-conducts; he seems to travel as he pleases and to fear nothing but bandits, just as Saadi the sailor feared pirates. It was distressing to think that today, if you were a murderer, a thief, or even just an Arab, you couldn't so easily visit La Serenissima or the City of Light. I thought for a while of using the networks on the Street of Thieves to establish a new identity for myself, but what I knew purely from the experience of books is that it was very difficult and often not very effective, things being as they were, unless you chose a Libyan, Sudanese or Ethiopian passport and that too, without the shimmering bronze sticker of the Schengen visa, was good for nothing. If it weren't for Judit, I think I'd have tried my chances, I'd have gone back to Algeciras, tried to cross illegally through customs in the other direction, which must not have been very complicated, and once in Morocco I would just have had to pray that the customs officers of the Motherland had never heard of me and would let me return to the cradle. Then, I'd have settled in Tangier with my loot, before returning to my dead soldiers and to Jean-François Bourrelier, the champion of typing by the kilometer. And a few years later, once my crimes had reached their statute of limitations, having gotten rich off of one million three hundred thousand dead poilus, I'd ask for a tourist visa to go to Venice and Paris, and that was it.

But I still had hope that one of my kisses would cure Judit of her illness, that one day she would wake up and decide to be with me again, full-time. And after all, despite the conditions, despite the great poverty of the Street of Thieves, I wasn't that badly off—I just felt I was on a stopover; real life still hadn't begun, it was endlessly postponed: deferred at the Propagation for Koranic Thought, which disappeared in flames; delayed on board the *Ibn Battuta*, lost craft; put off at chez Cruz, dog among dogs; suspended in Barcelona at the mercy of the crisis and Judit. On the run, always. There were accounts that still weren't settled and today, in my noisy monastery, my convent of thieving dervishes, when everything outside has burned, Europe, the Arab world, when flames have devoured the books, when hatred has invaded us, destroying the world of yesterday with the furious doggedness of stupidity, when the dogs are growling, attacking blindly to kill each other, the last weeks on the Street of Thieves seem to me like a somber happiness, the edge of a razor, and you don't know whose throat it's going to cut: just as the tightrope walker must defy the possibility of falling in order to concentrate on his footsteps—he looks in front of him, gently maneuvers the pole that saves him from the abyss, advances toward the unknown—I was walking without thinking about the fate that had pushed me toward Barcelona; like an animal, I could sense the storm to come, around me, inside me, while at the same time putting it all out of mind so I'd be able to cross the void.

IT was Sheikh Nureddin who warned me, via a brief email; life is a funny thing, a mysterious arrangement, a merciless logic of a futile destiny. He was coming to visit me. He had to pass through Barcelona for a meeting, on business. I confess I was happy to see him again, a little worried, too—the echo of the Marrakesh attack still hovered, a year later. The fire at the Group for Propagation of Koranic Thought, too. Questions that I had turned over in my mind for so long—little by little they had emptied themselves of meaning.

Sheikh Nureddin was powerful—he disappeared whenever he pleased and reappeared whenever he thought fit, from Arabia or Qatar, the non-combatant branch of a pious foundation, without any passport, visa, or money problems. Always elegant, in a suit, with a white shirt, no tie of course, a short well-trimmed beard, a little black briefcase; he spoke calmly, smiled, even laughed sometimes; his voice could glide from the gentleness of brotherhood to the shouts of battle, I can still hear them sometimes in my sleep, those speeches on the battle of Badr, *I will come to your aid, with a thousand angels following each other,* إِذْ تَسْتَغِيثُونَ رَبَّكُمْ فَاسْتَجَابَ لَكُمْ أَنِّي مُمِدُّكُم بِأَلْفٍ مِّنَ الْمَلَائِكَةِ مُرْدِفِينَ, it seemed as if he knew the entire Koran by heart, وَلَقَدْ نَصَرَكُمُ اللَّهُ بِبَدْرٍ وَأَنتُمْ أَذِلَّةٌ, *God gave you victory in Badr when you were at your weakest,* and the Text shone forth from his mouth, gleamed with a thousand lights of those angels promised by the Lord; he would spend hours telling us the story of Bilal, the slave tortured for his Faith, who became the first muezzin in Islam and whose voice, his voice alone, could draw tears from the inhabitants of Medina when he made the call to prayer—all those stories filled us with strength, joy, or anger, depending on their themes.

Seeing Sheikh Nureddin again was a Sign: a part of me, of my life, of my childhood reappeared in Barcelona, and despite the doubts, the mysteries, the shame linked to the nocturnal expedition of the bruisers of Tangier, a little light entered the Street of Thieves.

I had told Mounir everything, without mentioning the most worrisome details, and even though he was anything but religious, I managed to transmit a little of Sheikh Nureddin's energy to him; Mounir was anxious to meet him. I secretly hoped the reason for his trip was to open an office-bookstore in Barcelona I could take charge of, like in Tangier; that would explain why he had gotten back in touch. I pictured a little shop in the Raval, with books in Spanish, in Arabic, why not, in French—a miracle. A bookstore whose stock would have been mainly made up of books from Arabia, but with one or two shelves of thrillers and a shelf in homage to Casanova—a place, in short, that would somewhat resemble me. Yes of course, I was an illegal and a fugitive, but in my dreams I saw myself registering this little business in Judit's name and staying there, for years, in that special scent—ink, dust, old thoughts—of books, confident in the knowledge that the boys in blue are not much interested in the written word and, in general, leave bookstores pretty much alone, just as here, today, I'm hardly bothered at all in my library: it's the only zone of freedom around here, where sometimes even the screws come to chew the fat. Few readers, a lot of books. Of course our joint is far from being one of the largest jails in Spain, but it's undoubtedly one of the most modern; around me the dogs are strolling down the hallways.

Life is a tomb, it's the Street of Thieves, the end of the line, a promise without content, empty words.

Sheikh Nureddin's arrival coincided with the diagnosis of Judit's tumor. The doctor suspected that allergies, sinusitis, or God knows what depression could be the symptoms of a more serious disorder; her parents had paid for the MRI out of their own pockets to avoid the state health care system delays and the results were back; something was growing on the side of her brain. They still had to wait to find out if this "thing" was treatable, operable, malignant, benign, if there was any hope or if her *prognosis* as the docs say *was very poor*—I took the news like a physical blow. Judit told me gently, though, as if she were more worried about me than about herself, an effect of the illness perhaps. Her mother could barely hold back her tears, her eyes seemed to be constantly shimmering. Judit, lying on the sofa, gently took my hand, and I wanted to bawl too, to shout, to pray, I thought *ya Rabb*, don't take Judit away to death, please, you can't take all the women I've loved, I thought of Meryem again, maybe I was the one who was transmitting the malady of death to them, have pity, Lord, let Judit live, I'd have easily traded my shitty existence for her life, but I knew my offer was good for nothing.

On my way back I stopped to use the Internet, I looked at dozens of pages on brain tumors, there were all kinds, terrifying descriptions of the evolution of symptoms in certain cases, great stories of cures in others, I said to myself it's impossible, Judit is twenty-three, according to this statistic serious cancers are very rare at that age, that's definite, it's all just a false alarm, and I was so caught up by this macabre wandering through descriptions of the nooks and crannies of death that I arrived late to my meeting with Nureddin, near Plaça de Catalunya, out of breath, tense, sad, and worried.

The Sheikh hadn't changed, he was sitting at a table on the terrace in front of a café, looking noble and well-dressed; a young guy was with him, with a shaved head and a black beard; he got up as I approached and threw himself into my arms: Bassam, Bassam good Lord, I was overcome with joy, Bassam, wow, Bassam, he said Lakhdar my brother, clutched me to his chest and for a little while I forgot to greet Nureddin who laughed at the warmth of our reunion, I said Bassam my friend, even your mother wouldn't recognize you, he replied and you with your white hair, you look like you've become a miller. It does me good to see you, thanks be to God.

Full of emotion, I also embraced the Sheikh—and right away we no longer knew what to say, where to begin. Bassam was sitting down again, he had stopped smiling; he had the disturbing gaze of a blind man or certain animals with frightened, fragile eyes which always seem to be staring off into the distance. Sheikh Nureddin began questioning me about my life in Barcelona; he wanted to know how I had arrived here. I told them a little of my adventures; of course I hid the end of the Cruz episode from them. When I mentioned the fire at the Propagation for Koranic Thought, the Sheikh nodded with a look of disgust: the cowardly revenge of an impious one, a bastard who took advantage of our absence to attack the Book itself, what dishonor. He said this point-blank, with accents of rage in his voice—I suddenly remembered the bookseller, his mute surprise when he had seen me entering his store; maybe he had taken revenge. It was possible. Life is nothing but a series of wrong answers and misunderstandings.

Bassam continued to be silent; he swayed his head from time to time, stared at passersby, looked at girls' legs, his eyes always just as empty.

I had a slew of questions for Bassam and Nureddin—I dared to ask the first, what had happened, why had they disappeared all of a sudden? The Sheikh looked surprised, but you were the one who was no longer there, son. When we came back from that meeting in Casablanca, I discovered our headquarters had burned down—you hadn't left an address. We even suspected you for a while. Then I learned through Bassam (who shook himself a little when he heard his name, as if he were waking up) that you had a relationship with a young Spanish woman and you had left without leaving a trace.

This in a reproachful tone, before adding but that's ancient history, we forgave you.

I was so stunned that I searched my memory for this meeting in Casablanca, though without success. But still I apologized for this misunderstanding; I said I had become afraid after the attack in Marrakesh and the fire.

The Sheikh swept it all aside with a motion of his hand.

I realized I wouldn't learn any more.

I asked Bassam where he had been this whole time; he looked at me with empty eyes, his blind man's eyes, his dog's eyes. It was Nureddin who answered for him: he was with me, completing his training.

Bassam nodded.

Then the Sheikh invited us out to lunch at a Lebanese restaurant near University Square. Bassam followed. He was a phantom— maybe he's exhausted from jet lag, I thought.

He perked up again at the sight of food: at least he hadn't lost his appetite, that reassured me. He wolfed down a plate of hummus, a salad, and three skewers of meat as if his life depended on it; a vague smile played over his face between mouthfuls.

During the meal, we mostly discussed politics, as was usual, during the days of the Group; a victory for Islam at the elections in Tunisia and Egypt was excellent news; in Syria, he foresaw a defeat of the regime in a little while, *inshallah*, after a bloody war. Curiously, he didn't talk about Morocco, as if that terrain had ceased to interest him. I asked him what brought him to Spain—nothing special, he replied. A meeting of charity associations, donors. A gala dinner. In a luxury hotel. With some soccer players from Barça. At the invitation of the Queen of Spain.

I couldn't believe my ears. Nureddin in a fancy hotel with princes for a charity event.

The foundation I'm working for now runs all kinds of activities, he added, smiling.

I asked Bassam how long he thought he would stay; he shook himself, as if my question surprised him, before replying I don't know, a few days at least.

That was good news.

I convinced Bassam to leave his hotel and move back with me to the Street of Thieves—he'd gain in friendship what he'd lose in comfort. Sheikh Nureddin encouraged him, it's better to discover a city with its inhabitants, he said, laughing. I found it hard to imagine that he would be in the midst of a crowd of nobility and gentry in elegant salons that very night, glass of orange juice in hand, shaking hands with all those Bourbon-Parmas—him, the beater-up of miscreants, the man who fired us up and urged us to revolt, was perhaps going to dine at the same table as Juan Carlos, the one all the papers were talking about: the King had recently distinguished himself on an elephant safari, in Africa, and photos of the monarch in the company of a dead pachyderm had made the rounds online—it reminded me of Casanova's Memoirs, from another era. As if monarchies could never rid themselves of violence and cruelty; Fate pushed them to it: in his youth, Juan Carlos had accidentally killed his brother with a gun; his grandson had just accidentally shot himself in the foot; an entire regiment of dead elephants bore witness to the royal passion for firearms. At least the King of Morocco next door had the merit of discretion.

I wondered what the reason was for Nureddin's trip from the Persian Gulf to this gala dinner straight out of the eighteenth century, but I didn't dare ask him.

He had brought me Bassam, and that was enough for me.

We decided to walk around a little before going back to Carrer Robadors, Bassam seemed to have emerged from his torpor and opened his eyes wide upon discovering the city he'd been dreaming about for so long, poor guy, muttering Fuck, fuck, in front of the luxury shops, the avenues, the buildings; he turned around to look at the girls on bikes whose skirts lifted up as they pedaled, at the mannequins in the shop windows, at the heavily made-up passersby, lifted his face to the modernist office buildings, shook himself incredulously faced with all this luxury and liberty, it was good to see, I almost forgot about Judit's illness, as Bassam communicated his childlike enthusiasm to me as he'd done before, he kept exclaiming wow, insane, will you look at her, what a knockout, my God what a fucking knockout, it's just insane, and I'd reply that's nothing, you haven't seen anything yet, pal, you haven't seen anything, wait, wait. We happily went up Rambla Catalunya, beneath the trees; I bought him a coffee on a terrace so he could enjoy the girls and the nice spring weather, I felt as if we'd gone backward, to the blessed time of our adolescence, transported in Bassam's dreams as we contemplated the Strait—he used to talk to me about the lights of Barcelona, the girls of Barcelona, the bars of Barcelona: thanks to his presence I finally felt as if I was there, as if I had arrived somewhere, as if I had finally reached my destination. He kept cracking up in delight on his own like a kid, and it was a real joy to see his big fat bearded yokel's head smiling at the world.

"So my friend, where were you, all this time? What's the story with those lousy emails you sent me?"

"What? Whoa, take a look at that rack. Nothing, I was out East, with Nureddin."

"But why did you disappear like that? What the hell were you doing in Marrakesh?"

"In Marrakesh? In Casa, you mean? Check out those legs, they're incredible."

"No, in Marrakesh, you remember, the day of the attack? Judit saw you over there."

"The Marrakesh attack, yes of course I remember. I don't know anymore, I think we were on our way south."

Impossible to tear him away from his urban contemplation. Too bad, we'd talk about it later.

We headed off for the lower part of the city, and a bit further on Bassam pulled up short opposite the display window for an art gallery, in front of an immense photograph that measured two meters by three: a strange scene, eight people behind a table loaded with empty cans of beer, drained glasses, bottles of wine, leftovers, dirty bowls and spoons, crumpled wrappers, bottles of spirits, containers of fruit juice, ashtrays overflowing with butts and burnt matches: two girls in bras standing, holding joints; three guys with bare chests, one of them very hairy, in the background, who had climbed up on chairs, the picture cut off at his shoulders; a pensive bearded guy, on the right, with a cigarette, his head turned to the others, absorbed in contemplation of the disaster, and opposite him, at the left edge, a naked guy smiling at the camera, hat on his head, while at his side an elegant couple—jacket, light-colored shirt, black cardigan for the woman—seemed so drunk that they had to support each other, shoulder to shoulder, like the junkies on the Street of Thieves. In the back on the left, a window showed a glimpse of an orangey glow, an apocalyptic lighting, you couldn't tell if it came from a sunset, a sunrise, or a light bulb in the stairwell. The whole group, in these giant proportions, gave off an extraordinary force; a movement rose diagonally from the smile of the guy in the hat to the hairy chest in the opposite corner; the hairs shone on the yellowish skins, the red cans of beer exploded on the table; the girls in lacy bras had rolls of flesh, tired faces, heavy breasts; the well-dressed woman was closing her wrinkled eyes, her long, dirty-blonde hair spilled onto the filth on the table, into the tobacco ash, old fries, wine stains.

Bassam was very close to the image, he looked at each of these characters and then shook his head incredulously, muttering; he stepped back to look at the entire photo and turned to me, questioningly—he asked with an air of disgust, what is this? An ad? I replied, laughing, I don't think so, it's art, my friend. Bassam wasn't laughing, he seemed frightened, he said to me Lakhdar if you stay here you'll end up like that, like them, that made me laugh even harder, I said Bassam you're completely crazy, but he said don't you see, it's a parody of the Sura of the Laden Table, *O God Our Lord, said Issa, son of Maryam, make a laden table come down from heaven that will be a celebration, for the first of us as well as for the last,* it's a disgrace. He looked completely serious, frightened and angry at the same time.

I didn't know much about art, but aside from the table, obviously, it was hard to see anything religious in this photo, on the contrary, it was totally decadent, obscene and decadent.

"Come on buddy, you're raving, let's go."

But he couldn't manage to tear his eyes away from the image; he was staring with hatred at the girls in underwear, the bottles of wine, and the man with the hat—if he could have he would no doubt have broken the window.

"You want us to buy it, is that it? You want me to ask them to make a little copy for your place? Should I take a picture of it with my cell?"

He shot me a furious look, this thing is an offence to God, this country is an offence to God, he raised his eyes to the sky.

"Come on, let's go."

I began walking and he ended up following me; he was muttering curses.

I knew where to take him to make it pass away. So much for the risks of shared transport, we took a bus headed for La Barceloneta— when Bassam asked me where we were going, I replied, to Paradise. That didn't make him laugh at all and he barked, stop with your blasphemies, before returning to that silence of his from the beginning of our afternoon.

When we arrived, he couldn't hold back a whistle of admiration at the immense sail-shaped hotel, at the edge of the embankment, at the façades glimmering in the sun, and at the cable car that crossed the harbor, off to the right, disappearing in the greenness of the hill of Montjuïc.

"Wait, you haven't seen anything yet."

A Saturday, I knew the beach would be swarming with people. I took off my shoes and dragged Bassam toward the sea.

"What the hell are you up to, you're not going swimming are you?"

I walked straight ahead, in the burning sand; the light was blinding despite the late hour; the sun hadn't set yet, over there in the west, behind the Street of Thieves. I knew, as I started walking, that I was missing Bassam's expression and exclamations; the bodies were so close together that we had to set one foot in front of the other to pass between the bare breasts and oiled thighs. I found an open spot, a dozen meters from the water; I threw myself onto the ground. Bassam sat cross-legged, facing the sea; over there's where the show is, I said. Turn around and look.

I was generously offering him the most beautiful collection of asses on earth. Lying in the same direction, taking advantage of the slight slope of the beach, head facing the top of the slope, in rows, on their stomachs mostly but sometimes on their backs, breasts bare or not, some in thongs, others in modest one-pieces, a whole rainbow of girls unfurled before us—milk-white ones applying sunscreen; pink ones wearing hats to protect their faces; slightly tanned ones, bronze ones, black ones, many shades of ass, the triangular mounds hidden under swimsuits, breasts of all shapes and sizes and colors; I lay down on the sand, hands under my chin: a meter away from me I had, thighs slightly spread on a multicolored towel, a Nordic girl whose round ass was beginning to turn pink past the edges of her suit—you could make out her sex where the material puckered slightly, dented it into waves of softness where there peeked out, at the edge of the cloth, against the flesh, a few tiny blond hairs; her feet were charming, toes buried in the sand; I felt as if my head were between her legs and I wondered if my gaze had any effect on this cunt, so close; if, by staring at it for a long time, I could manage to make it warm, the way the sun sets fire to straw with its rays—with eyeglasses by way of magnifying glass, who knows. The girl from the North scratched her lower back, as if I had disturbed her, and I quickly looked away, by an idiotic reflex—unless Odin had provided his creatures with unheard-of abilities, the single eye that observed me from behind the garnet polyester was blind.

I tore myself away from my contemplation: Bassam was smiling blissfully, still cross-legged, hands on his knees; he swept his eyes across the beach like a spotlight, from one side to the other; skateboarders and bicyclists passed by on the jetty; strolling vendors paced the sand, by the water's edge, offering beer, soda, henna tattoos, cheap baubles, sunglasses, Barça decals, caps, scarves, beach towels, African gris-gris, doughnuts, foot massages, or all of the above, it was impossible to stay by the sea for over five minutes without someone taking advantage of your immobility to try to sell you something—those hundreds of prone people comprised an infinite reservoir of potential clients stupefied by the sun. Bassam looked at all that, all those asses, all those breasts, all those Senegalese carrying their merchandise, all those neo-hippies passing by on the jetty; on the left, the brilliant colossus of the Hotel Vela protected these people with its glass and steel sail; on the right, at the other edge of the promenade, near the Olympic harbor, a welded metal whale seemed to be melting on the beach, between the Torre Mapfre and the Arts Hotel; in the distance, the chimneys of the Centrale de Badalona were lost in a halo of pollution, behind the sheet of hazy cement of the Forum of Cultures.

Suddenly I thought of Judit, of that tumor, that injustice of the body. This powerlessness was as bitter as Cruz's poison.

We stayed a long time, absorbed by the beauty of the city, the infinite sea punctuated with white sailboats, until the sun sank behind Montjuïc and the sunbathers got dressed one by one: some just slipped a dress over their swimsuits; others, more elegant, older, or more bourgeois, undertook slow metamorphoses, hidden by a towel; one could take stock of their underwear, held out in a charitable hand by a husband or girlfriend, note their loss of balance as they slipped it on, standing on one leg, strange, clumsy birds clutching a pareo to their chest. A slight breeze had picked up, I told Bassam it was time to get back to the Street of Thieves, on foot this time. He brushed himself to get rid of the sand and began walking, seemed disoriented again—ever since we had arrived he hadn't said a word, so that I thought he'd fallen asleep, cross-legged, like a Buddha in meditation.

He remained just as silent on the way back; he stared at the asphalt, head lowered, lifting it only to check if I was indeed still next to him.

We entered the Raval by the Arsenal, the gateway to the neighborhood from the sea, before going back up to Sant Pau and La Rambla. Suddenly Bassam seemed more interested; the Pakis were strolling around, in little groups; Arabs were chatting in front of the sandwich joints; children were playing near the giant metal cat, swung disrespectfully from its steel whiskers, tried to ride it like an elephant, perched between its ears. I thought of inviting Bassam for dinner in the Moroccan restaurant on Carrer Robadors, in memory of Tangier and the good old times—but first we had to go upstairs to drop off his bag. He had been lugging it around all afternoon without batting an eye. It was a simple travel bag, canvas with two leather handles; I don't know why, it made me think again of the attack in Marrakesh, that bag. I realized I didn't know what Bassam was doing in Barcelona. Or when he would leave. Or even precisely where he was coming from.

At the corner of Robadors, by the Tariq ibn Ziyad mosque, two black whores were perched on parking stanchions; blue faux-leather miniskirts, high heels, bras, breasts almost popping out.

Bassam seemed to walk into an invisible wall when he saw them; he changed sidewalks.

The entrance to our building cracked him up. Say, my friend, some class your hotel has. A real luxury hotel, *khouya*. Even at our place we don't have anything this rotten, *la samah Allah*.

I didn't take the bait. I just hoped we wouldn't pass a rat roaming around.

I showed Bassam around our apartment; I introduced him to Mounir, who was calmly scratching his toes with the tip of his knife in front of the TV—Bassam barely said a word to him. Just a greeting, an empty phrase, a hand on his chest, his gaze distant. Mounir looked at me questioningly. A childhood friend, I said. He's going to sleep on the couch for a few days.

Bassam made the rounds of the flat three times, sat down on the balcony, watched the street.

I suggested we go out for a bite to eat, he agreed.

On our way out, we passed two drunkards who were pissing copiously against the façade, provoking the shouts of the beggars waiting for the evangelists to open for their hymns and sandwiches.

It was Saturday, streetwalking activity was at its height at the crossroads; two or three dealers were pacing in the night; a junkie in need of his fix vomited a stream of bile onto the base of a lamppost, splattering two cockroaches fat as frogs emerging lazily from the restaurant next door.

The joint was almost empty—I greeted the managers warmly, introduced them to Bassam, a childhood friend from Tangier. They welcomed him to Barcelona. We sat at a table on the side; in the back of the room, Al-Jazeera was broadcasting images of various massacres in a loop, in Syria or Palestine, intercut with violent demonstrations, in Greece or Spain.

"It's great you're here."

He was in a hurry to order dinner.

The prospect of food from home brought a smile back to Bassam's face. Having him opposite me, like that, like the old days, took me back to Tangier, to Meryem. I didn't know how to begin. Beneath the table, my leg jiggled nervously.

"Your mother accidentally gave me an old letter from you. With Meryem's inside it. You should have told me."

He looked very surprised, all of a sudden, wide-eyed, he wasn't expecting that at all; he ended up saying:

"I was afraid of hurting you. When you came back I didn't dare. Afterward it was too late. I should've destroyed all that, so you'd never know."

He was looking at the tablecloth.

"Everything ends up known eventually," I said stupidly. And I was ashamed of evoking the memory of Meryem this way, of betraying her, as if her death were a banal piece of news, a kind of weather report or the result of the Thieves' Lottery.

"Is the tagine good here?"

"Better than at your house, asshole."

That cracked him up.

"That's not hard to do, you know."

The portions were huge, Moroccan. Bassam threw himself onto the food like a wild thing.

"Judit is sick," I said.

He looked at me for an instant, between mouthfuls, without understanding; in the end I didn't want to explain. I'd have liked to tell him in detail about the *Ibn Battuta*, the Algeciras port, Cruz, the corpses; Cruz's death throes, which I had kept secret for so long.

"What the hell have you been up to all this time?"

I repeated the question three or four times, to the rhythm of his spoon; he gulped down half his Coke, ended up mumbling nothing special, didn't ask me any more questions, before returning to the regular ingestion of vegetables, to the greedy gnawing of chicken bones; he was still hungry, he ordered a serving of rice with dried fruit; I raised my head to the TV, reflexively, where had he gone, to Yemen, to Afghanistan, to Mali, to Syria even, possibly, who knows, there were so many places where you could fight, for what cause, the cause of God no doubt, the prime cause, I found it difficult to picture Bassam traipsing about the burning desert, rifle in hand— physically, he hadn't changed much, he might be a tiny bit thinner, but nothing striking and once you'd gotten used to his shaved head he was the same, the same but more silent, tenser, and older. All that was unreal. His beaten mongrel's gaze returned to his plate, was he thinking of war, no, he must've been content to chew, his head empty.

The name of that Frenchman, the mass killer of Jewish children in Toulouse, came to mind; unthinkable to associate Bassam with such a cowardly act—for a second I imagined a journalist questioning me about him, I'd have replied he was a nice guy, kind of funny, who liked looking at girls and eating well. If he was still the same.

"Was that you in Tangier, at the Café Hafa?"

He raised his head from his plate, fixed his empty eyes on mine, I looked away.

I didn't want to know anymore.

I didn't want to know what the war was, his war; I didn't want to know his lies, or his truth.

I thought of Cruz again, hypnotized in front of his screen by the knives of jihadists.

I asked one final question:

"What did you come here to do?"

There was a look of great pain on his face, all of a sudden, a great sadness or a great indifference.

"Nothing special, *khouya*; to see you. To see Barcelona."

It was impossible to guess if he had been hurt by my suspicions or if his own fate saddened him, like an incurable disease.

DISTANCING, in friendship as in love. Bassam was distancing himself; I was too, probably—I was no longer the backward child of Tangier, full of mediocre dreams; I was on my way to my prison, already locked up in the ivory tower of books, which is the only place on earth where life is good. Judit was disappearing into illness; I needed superhuman effort to go to the Clinic, where she was being cared for; the smell of the hallways, the cynical distance of the personnel, the false silence of those rooms murmuring secretly with death caused me a terrible, atrocious anguish; Cruz's little morgue kept coming to mind, those bodies no longer left me; I saw the hospital like a huge factory of dead flesh: women and men went in through the main door and exited out the back, dead dogs you drag behind you to burn them out of sight. I didn't want Judit to disappear, it couldn't happen. She shared her room with a woman in her fifties who had a whole regiment of mourners by her bedside and was pretty quickly transferred to another part of the building: in a hospital you have to be dying to get a private room, to keep from depressing your neighbor, still struggling for life amid your death-rattles and your family's moaning—and even though Judit's tumor was benign, she had to undergo a whole series of treatments before the operation itself; for a little while I would've begun praying again, if I hadn't been convinced, more and more, of the injustice of God, which seems a great deal like an absence. Despite everything, Judit seemed to be keeping her spirits up—she had hope, the doctors were optimistic, and only her mother, Núria, whom I saw at each of my visits, seemed to be aging visibly. She almost never left her daughter's room, received the visitors, gave explanations on the progression of the illness, as if she herself were suffering from it; Judit was sometimes confined to bed, sometimes sitting in an armchair; I would stay for a quarter of an hour and then leave. We'd talk about any old thing, the weather, the state of the Arabic world, the war in Syria, our memories, too—of Tangier, of Tunis, and thinking back to those vanished happinesses made my voice wobble in a slightly ridiculous way, and my eyes water, so I'd leave, I'd say goodbye to Núria and gently kiss Judit, who would hug me close, I'd reenter the hallways reeking of death, between the nurses, the sick people on drips, a whole troop of guys in nightshirts, each one leaning on his IV stand with its glass bottle and tube burrowed into their veins, at the wrist or under the elbow, there they stood around smoking and talking, accompanied by a few nurses or good-natured doctors, it was the festival of bandaging and scars, of hanging catheters and cotton gowns, so I fled, I fled dreaming of being able to carry Judit away with me into a well-guarded room on the Carrer Robadors, with Bassam, who was going round in circles without any IV drip between the mosque, the Moroccan restaurant, the bicycle thieves, and the whores, whom he observed from afar, like a sort of attractive, strange fauna, like the King of Spain's elephants. I had my own little zoo at home: Bassam and Mounir hated each other. Ideologically, personally, everything put up walls between them; Mounir saw in Bassam nothing but a narrow-minded, taciturn, uncivilized Islamist; Bassam scorned Mounir because he was a failure, a thief, a miscreant. They were both right, in a sense; I thought they could have gotten closer on other levels, girls, soccer, life, but no, there was nothing to be done—they only talked to each other when forced to, and Mounir asked me almost every day when Bassam was leaving. Life was wavering, and I could feel it; Bassam was immersed in prayer and waiting; Judit was supposed to have surgery any day now; the crisis precipitated the rhythm of strikes, demonstrations, helicopter noises; the first heat of the end of spring was making the junkies, the poor, and the mad go crazy; every day new corpses would flower somewhere, a bank would fail, a cataclysm would carry away one more scrap from this ruined world, or maybe I'm the one who, today, am tempted to read these events in the light of what followed; to think that the worst was yet to come, that the worst has come—everything was dancing before my eyes, Judit in the hospital, Bassam at the Tariq ibn Ziyad Mosque, Meryem in the grave, the world was demanding something, a movement, a change, one more step toward Fate; I sensed that soon we would have to choose our camp, that one day or another I would have to choose, that it was up to me to revolt, to make a move for once in my life, a real decisive move, and of course it's easy to think of that today, from my prison library, surrounded by all the certainty of books, hundreds of texts, by dint of all my reading, since the man of yesterday has disappeared; the Lakhdar of the Street of Thieves has disappeared, he has been transformed, he is trying to restore their lost meaning to his actions; he is reflecting, I am reflecting, but I am going round in circles in my prison for I can never rediscover who I was before, the lover of Meryem, the son of my mother, the child of Tangier, the friend of Bassam; life has gone on since, God has deserted, conscience has gone its way, and identity along with it—I am what I have read, I am what I have seen, I have as much Arabic in me as Spanish and French, I have been multiplied in those mirrors until I have been lost or rebuilt, fragile image, image in motion. *No se puede vivir sin amar*, I said to Judit, and I was wrong, you can live without loving, love is one more book, one more mirror, a trace on our wax tablet, marks on our hands, lifelines, fingerprints that appear once it's over, once the game has been played—I enjoy seeing Judit again, she comes here once a week, we talk for a long time, we exchange long cybernetic letters in which I talk to her some more about Arabic literature, about the unsurpassable beauty of Ibn Zay-dún, of Jahiz the immense, of Sayyab the sad, who died of a strange illness from which only poets know how to die, and I know that Judit only visits me or writes to me out of fidelity to what we were, in that hotel in Tangier, in that apartment in Tunis, which exist only for us. I still think often of that story of Hassan the Mad, which Ibn Battuta tells when he is in Mecca—even if it means I'd have to go round in circles for eternity, I'd have liked to return for fifteen days to my mother's house, or to the past, to relive the weeks in Tangier or Tunis with Judit; maybe it will return, the time of madmen and prodigious beggars, someday, the day that oil runs dry, the day that Mecca is once again a month away by horse and sail; a day of glory, when I'll emerge into the new sun, when I'll stop my mute convolutions to rediscover Judit's arms.

Bassam was also going around in circles. He had almost stopped talking; he just opened his eyes and mouth wide when Maria's thighs unclenched, on her threshold at the entrance to the Street of Thieves; he would stay there for three, five, ten, or even fifteen eternal seconds, stunned, his lower jaw hanging down like a halfwit's, his gaze lost between her legs, and Maria had to make fun of him or insult him to set him on his way, grumbling; it didn't matter that I told him it wasn't right, to stay there like that all agog, that he could simply pay a few euros and go upstairs with her, he could have seen, touched, penetrated, and come, and that's that, but no, he shook his head like a child caught with his hand in the cookie jar, as if he had seen the devil, no no, Lakhdar *khouya*, he said, we don't pay for that kind of thing, and I sort of agreed, we don't pay, not with money so much, but with the sad memory of the dead smell of Zahra the little whore in Tangier whom he didn't know. Then he'd go back to the restaurant to wolf down a tagine or some skewers of meat, then he'd go to the mosque, hands in his pockets, he'd spit on the addicts and thieves, ogle the black whores with a mixture of scorn and desire, try to forget them by making his ablutions, prayed, then he'd talk with some Pakistanis, always the same ones, his friends he said, then he'd come home, sit with his eyes glued to the TV, make Mounir flee in the midst of his ritual pedicure—Mounir would close his knife, sighing, get up, then slam the door to his room with a bang.

Sheikh Nureddin had only stayed for three days, as planned; he had met all the high society of Barcelona, princes and soccer players included, had stuffed himself with petit-fours in a luxury hotel, and then had left, not without inviting us, Bassam and me, one last time out to lunch—I felt as if I were sharing the meal with an uncle from America; he was very elegant, in a dark blue jacket with a white shirt with a stand-up collar; he had money, rhetoric, and a business class ticket to the Gulf. I felt a little like his personal yokel; I couldn't stop myself from speaking Moroccan with him, while he told us about his charity evenings in a classical Arabic mixed with eastern touches. Bassam remained silent; his gaze gave off admiration, boundless servitude. I don't know why, I hated Sheikh Nureddin, that day; maybe because that same morning I had gone to see Judit in the hospital, and that had put me off a little, who knows. In any case, I was happy at the time to say goodbye to him. I remember his last words well, before he flagged down a taxi to get his luggage at the hotel: don't hesitate, he said, if you want to join us, don't hesitate, we'll always have work for you. I thanked him without daring to mention my dream to him, that little religious-cum-pagan bookstore on the Raval in Barcelona. Then I thought how that dog had created and torn apart my life, that he had a valid passport full of visas, that he had never known either Cruz or the Street of Thieves, and that he deserved a good kick in the ass, to teach him to live—Bassam threw himself around his neck as if he were his father; I thought I could hear the Sheikh's words murmured into his ear, *be strong, the Hour may be near,* لَعَلَّ السَّاعَة تَكونُ قريباً, it reminded me of a verse from the Koran, it was very strange and solemn as a goodbye. Nureddin saw I had heard, he smiled saying be good, don't forget God and your Brothers, and drove off in a yellow-and-black taxi.

Bassam watched him go as if the Prophet himself were disappearing.

It was time to take him in hand again, as before; I said to him okay, now we'll go down a few beers and hit on some girls, my treat.

He looked infinitely sad, shifted from foot to foot as if he suddenly had to pee, and took my hand, like a lost girl.

"Come on," I said, "we'll live it up."

He let himself be dragged along like the puppy or child he had never stopped being.

IF *people question you about the Final Hour, reply: "Only God knows about it." What do you know about it? It could be that the Hour is near. God has cursed the Infidels and has prepared a burning furnace for them, where they will remain for eternity, without finding either ally or aid.* يَسْأَلُكَ النَّاسُ عَن السَّاعَةِ قُلْ إِنَّمَا عِلْمُهَا عِندَ اللَّهِ وَمَا يُدْرِيكَ لَعَلَّ السَّاعَةَ تَكُونُ قَرِيبًا/ إِنَّ اللَّهَ لَعَنَ الْكَافِرِينَ وَأَعَدَّ لَهُمْ سَعِيرًا/ خَالِدِينَ فِيهَا أَبَدًا لَّا يَجِدُونَ وَلِيًّا وَلَا نَصِيرًا, I looked it up in the Koran the next day, after a night watching Bassam sink into silence behind a Coke, as we enjoyed the crowded terraces around the MACBA, in the overwhelming noise of skateboarders, a cascade of boards hitting the pavement, endless, dis-ordered clatter—Bassam watched the skateboarders with an incredu-lous air, and it's true that for a novice their activity was extremely perplexing; they would travel just a few feet on the square, try a move—a leap or a hop—which looked ridiculous and always ended up in the same result: the board would flip over, fall to the ground, and its owner would find himself on foot, only to recover his device and start over again, like Hassan the Mad eternally circling; the rumbling and clashing of those dozens of skateboards rose from the square with a fierce regularity; the spectators sitting on the low mar-ble perimeter enjoyed the constant spectacle of these sonorous evo-lutions, tourists resting with legs dangling, loaded with cameras and backpacks, teenagers emptying beers, smoking joints, flea-ridden bums tippling their bottles on blankets stiff with filth, cheerful cops surveying the lot with an eye as skeptical as Bassam's—after a while the noise ended up getting on your nerves; constant but irregular, it was impossible to get used to it. Bassam eyed this circus with a look of scorn; he didn't say much, content to gesture to me when a pair of tight shorts, a miniskirt, or a particularly well-developed chest passed by. I tried to talk to him, but the conversational subjects were exhausted one after the other; he refused to discuss the past, aside from our childhood years in Tangier, a few anecdotes from elementary or high school, as if we were old men.

I was relieved when he wanted to go to bed.

So the next day I looked through a digital database for Nureddin's words, لَعَلَّ السّاعَةَ تَكونُ قَريباً, the verse was in the Al Ahzab Sura, "The Allies"; it was about the final hour, the hour of Judgment, when an eternal fire was promised for non-believers. I wondered if I was being paranoid, yet again; it seemed to me that this harmless verse, in Nureddin's mouth, was a coded message; Bassam must be waiting for the time to spark the flames of the apocalypse, which would explain why he was going round in circles in Barcelona without managing to explain to me what he was doing there; I knew he had a tourist visa for a month—he was just as incapable of telling me by what miracle he had obtained it.

I imagined an attack, an explosion, with his Pakistani friends from the mosque, as he called them; a revenge for the death of Bin Laden, a coup to destabilize Europe further at a time when it seemed to be wavering, cracking like a beautiful, fragile vase, vengeance for the dead Syrian children, for the dead Palestinian children, for dead children in general, that whole absurd rhetoric, the spiral of stupidity, or simply for the pleasure of destruction and fire, what do I know, I watched Bassam in his solitude and his seclusion, ricocheting like a billiard ball in the Street of Thieves against the sad whores, the addicts, the verminous, and the bearded men of the mosque, I saw him again absorbed in resentment in front of that decadent photograph on Rambla Catalunya, لَعَلَّ السّاعَةَ تَكونُ قَريباً,

I saw him ogling Maria's sex on her doorstep, I pictured him carrying suitcases to Marrakesh, and as the killer with the sword in Tangier, and as a fighter in Mali or Afghanistan, or maybe none of the above, maybe just a man just like me lost in the whirl of the Carrer Robadors, a hollow man, a walking tomb, a man who sought in flames the end of an already dead world, a warrior from a theater of shadows, who felt confusedly that there was no more reality around him, nothing tangible, nothing true, and who was struggling, moved by the last breath of hatred, in a cottony emptiness, a cloud, a silent man, a mute man who would blow up in a train, in a plane, in a subway line, for no one, لَعَلَّ السّاعَةَ تَكونُ قَريباً, perhaps the Hour is approaching, I saw Bassam's perfectly round head in prayer, I no longer expected answers to my questions, no more answers, an unknown surgeon would soon open Judit's skull to remove the disease from it, around us the world was on fire and Bassam was standing there, motionless like a snake charmer's cobra, an empty man whose hour would soon toll, a soldier of despair who carried his corpses in his eyes, just like Cruz.

لَعَلَّ السَّاعَة تَكونُ قريباً, the days were long and silent—Bassam followed his ritual, without saying anything, he was waiting, waiting for a sign or for the end of the world, just as I was waiting for Judit's operation, which looked as though it was going to be longer and more difficult than foreseen; in the evening I'd go out for a walk with Mounir in Barcelona's warm humidity, which was like Tangier or Tunis—relieved, we'd leave Bassam on the Street of Thieves to go to our little sidewalk café a little farther south, on Calle del Cid; we'd drink some beers there, nicely tucked away in that forgotten lane, and Mounir was a great comfort, he'd always end up cracking me up: despite his fragile situation, he kept his sense of humor, his energy, and he managed to communicate some of it to me, make me forget everything I'd lost, everything that had broken, despite the world around us; Spain, sinking into crisis, Europe, destroying itself before our eyes, and the Arab world, not escaping from its contradictions. Mounir had been relieved by the victory of the Left in the French presidential elections, he saw hope in it, he was optimistic, nothing for it, him the small-time thief, the dealer, he thought the Revolution was still underway, that it hadn't been crushed once and for all by stupidity and blindness, and he laughed, he laughed at the millions of euros swallowed up in the banks or in bankrupt nations, he laughed, he was confident, all these misfortunes were nothing, his poverty in Paris, his misery in Barcelona, he still had the strength of the poor and the revolutionary, he said One day, Lakhdar, one day I'll be able to live decently in Tunisia, I won't need Milan, Paris or Barcelona anymore, one day you'll see, and I who had never really wanted to leave Tangier, who had never really shared these dreams of emigration, I'd reply that we'd always be better off tucked away in the Raval, in our palace of lepers, watching the world collapse, لَعَلَّ السّاعَة تَكونُ قريباً, and that made him laugh.

I was increasingly convinced that the Hour was near; that Bassam was waiting for a signal to play his part in the end of the world—he would disappear for much of the day, during prayer times; he pretended to be happy when I suggested we go out for a bit, change neighborhoods, enjoy the city that held its arms out to us; he managed to pretend for half an hour, to go into raptures over one or two girls and three shop windows, then he'd become silent again, snapped up by his memories, his plans, or his hatred. When I grilled him he'd look at me with his simpleton's face, his eyes incredulous, as if he didn't have the slightest clue as to what I was talking about, and I began to doubt, I told myself I was exaggerating, that the ambiance, the Street of Thieves, and Judit's illness were beginning to get to me, so I'd promise myself not to mention it to him again— until night came, when he'd disappear for two or three hours, God knows where, in the company of his random Pakistani pals and he'd return, silent, with the lost, tremulous gaze of someone wanting to ask a question, taking Mounir's place on the sofa, and my doubts and questions would reappear. One day I noticed that he had come back with a plastic bag, bizarre for someone who never bought himself anything, who owned almost nothing, aside from a few pieces of clothing which he ritually washed by hand every night before bed—I glanced into it when he went to piss; the package contained four new cellphones of a very simple model, I remembered the modus operandi of the Marrakesh attack, of course I couldn't resist, I asked him the question, he didn't seem angry that I'd searched through his things, just a little tired of my suspicions, he answered very simply it's a little business with my pals from down there, if you like I can get you one free of charge—the naturalness of his answer disarmed me, and I fell silent.

I was probably going mad, completely paranoid.

ONE day I couldn't stand it anymore, I talked about it with Judit. She was still in the hospital, the operation kept being delayed: major budget cuts had forced the hospital to close a wing of its operating theaters—and there were always more urgent cases to be operated on.

Núria wasn't there, we were alone in her room; she was sitting in the visitor's chair, and I was on the floor next to her. I hesitated for a long time, and I said to her, you know, I wonder if Bassam is preparing for something.

She leaned toward me.

"Something dangerous, you mean?"

"Yes, something like Marrakesh or Tangier. But I'm not sure. It's just a possibility."

I thought of Bassam's new gaze, so empty, so lost, so suffering.

Judit sighed, and we stayed silent like that for a while.

"And what're you going to do?"

"I don't know."

She leaned over to stroke my forehead, and then she sat down next to me, on the floor, her back leaning against the bed, she held me tight and we embraced for a long time.

"Don't worry, I know you'll make the right decision."

In the end she had to gently dismiss me so I'd go back to the Street of Thieves, leaving behind me the horde of intubated smokers on the hospital's plaza.

WHETHER it was dereliction or violence, it doesn't matter. Bassam circled, eaten away by a leprocy of the soul, a disease of despair, abandoned—what could he have seen over there in the East, what had happened, what horror had destroyed him, I haven't a clue; was it the sword attack in Tangier, the dead in Marrakesh, the fighting, the summary executions in the Afghan underground, or none of the above, nothing but solitude and the silence of God, that absence of a master that drives dogs crazy—I felt as if he were appealing to me, asking me something, as if his eyes were seeking me out, as if he wanted me to cure him, as if the end of the world had to be stopped, as if the flames had to be stopped from rising and invading everything, and Bassam was one of those birds of the apocalypse who keep circling, just as Cruz watched violent death videos online all day, and I was sure of nothing, nothing aside from that summons, that force of violence—that question that Cruz asked as he swallowed his poison in front of me, deciding to end it all in the most horrible way, I thought I saw it again in Bassam's eyes. That will to end it all. Sometimes you have to act, when the flames flare up too high, too pressing; I watched Bassam return from the mosque after prayer, say a few words, hello Lakhdar my brother, throw himself on the sofa—Mounir had locked himself in his room; I'd exchange a few banalities with Bassam before taking refuge in my cubbyhole and watch the circus of the Street of Thieves for hours on end, all those people going round in circles in the night.

HIS eyes were closed.

I stroked his rough skull, I thought of Tangier, of the Strait, of the Propagation for Koranic Thought, of the Café Hafa, of girls, the sea, I saw Tangier again streaming in the rain, in the fall, in the spring; I pictured us walking, pacing up and down the city, from the cliffs to the beach; I went over our childhood, our adolescence, we hadn't lived very long.

Mounir came out of his room two hours later, saw the body, then looked at his bloodied knife on the floor, horrified; he shouted but I didn't hear him; I saw him gesticulating, panicked; he quickly gathered up his things, I saw his lips moving, he said something that I didn't understand and took to his heels.

I fell asleep, on the sofa, next to the corpse.

In the afternoon I called the cops from my cellphone. I gave the address almost smiling, 13 Street of Thieves, fourth on the left.

That night, at the station, I learned from her mother that Judit's surgery had taken place, that she'd come through. It couldn't have been a coincidence.

Two or three days later Núria came to see me in custody.

She assured me that Judit would visit me as soon as she got out of the hospital.

They questioned me; one by one, they wove all the threads of my existence together on endless pieces of paper.

The psychiatrist declared me of sound mind.

And a few months later, once the prosecutor had uttered his long and lugubrious summation in which the darkness of premeditation glared, after my lawyer had pleaded, arguing that I was a lost child, young, too young to spend twenty years in prison, that I had sought to defend society, that I had, she said, *struggled poorly for the good*, which deserved the leniency of the jury, when the presiding magistrate asked me if I wanted to add anything, contrary to the advice of my lawyer who rolled angry eyes behind her glasses, I rose; I looked at Judit in the audience, Judit, more beautiful than ever despite her pallor, a worried but encouraging smile on her lips; I turned to the judges and said calmly, hoping my voice wouldn't tremble too much:

"I am not a murderer, I am more than that.

"I am not a Moroccan, I am not a Frenchman, I'm not a Spaniard, I'm more than that.

"I am not a Muslim, I am more than that.

"Do what you will with me."

ON his way home, Ibn Battuta goes back through Syria; he wants to meet his son there, born soon after he left Damascus, twenty years before—the country is at the time decimated by the Black Death, two thousand four hundred people are dying there every day and, from Gaza to Aleppo, the region is devastated by the epidemic; Ibn Battuta's son died too. The traveler asks an old man from Tangier for news of the country and learns that his father left this world fifteen years ago and that his mother has just died, over there in the West. Then he goes to Alexandria, where the plague causes one thousand one hundred deaths in a single day, then Cairo, where twenty thousand people, he says, have perished; none of the Sheikhs he had met on his way out are still alive. He goes to Morocco and passes through Tangier to pray at his mother's grave, before settling once and for all in Fez.

Today when the plague is here again, when its breath roars over much of the world, when I watch the successors of Hassan the Mad circling in the yard, all those who want to see their mothers again before they pass, their city, their world before it's erased, in the sweet company of books, of the monastically regulated life of prison, I look at myself in the mirror; I examine the white hair at my temples, my black eyes, my hands with their chewed nails; I question myself about my guilt, sometimes, after a nightmare that's more powerful than usual, a bloody dream, a vision of a hanged man, a woman being prodded by surgical instruments, corpses of drowned teenagers, I scrutinize myself in silence and have no certainty, none; I think of Cruz; I think of Bassam, of Bassam's final expression; I think of Meryem, of Judit, of Saadi the sailor; my regrets fade away on their own, dissipate; I have made use of the world. Life consumes everything—books accompany us, like my two penny thrillers, those proletarians of literature, travel companions, in revolt or resignation, in faith or abandonment.

Men are dogs with empty gazes, they circle in the twilight, chase a ball, fight over a female, over a corner of the kennel, stay stretched out for hours, tongues lolling, waiting to be done in, in a final caress—why, in one instant, does one make a decision, why today, why now, maybe he's the one who decided and not me, Bassam seemed to be looking at me, seated, back straight, in the living room; light from the street projected his shadow on Mounir's closed door, he said nothing, he had seen me come out of my room; the streetlight was reflected on his shaved skull, his face against the light was a shard of sapphire: silent shapes instead of cheekbones, dark shadows around his eyes, motionless; he was waiting, in silence; he waited for God, for the Hour, for me—he stared at me in the night, hands on his knees, a motionless prayer.

I thought I understood what he was asking me; only I could get up, stand firm, in the midst of invisible flames. Maybe our lives are valid for a single instant, a single lucid moment, a single second of courage. I didn't reflect, I didn't think ahead, I knew; Bassam jumped when he heard the click of the knife that I'd picked up from the table: he moved a little, his profile went into shadow, he didn't struggle, didn't cry out, he pressed his hand against my back, to help me maybe, he contracted when the blade sank into his chest, bent over in pain, raised his head to look at me, to send out one final enigma, gratitude, sadness, or surprise, he fell on his side when I withdrew the metal from his heart—I collapsed as well; and dawn was beginning to wheel around us.

Mathias Énard studied Persian and Arabic and spent long periods in the Middle East. A professor of Arabic at the University of Barcelona, he won the Prix des Cinq Continents de la Francophonie and the Prix Edmée de la Rochefoucault for his first novel, *La perfection du tir*. He won several awards for *Zone* (also available in English translation from Open Letter Books), including the Prix du Livre Inter and the Prix Décembre, and won the Prix Liste Goncourt/Le Choix de l'Orient, the Prix littéraire de la Porte Dorée, and the Prix du Roman-News for *Street of Theives*.

Charlotte Mandell has translated fiction, poetry, and philosophy from the French, including works by Proust, Flaubert, Genet, Maupassant, Blanchot, and many other distinguished authors. She has received many accolades and awards for her translations, including a Literature Translation Fellowship from the National Endowment for the Arts for *Zone*, also by Mathias Énard.

Open Letter—the University of Rochester's nonprofit, literary translation press—is one of only a handful of publishing houses dedicated to increasing access to world literature for English readers. Publishing ten titles in translation each year, Open Letter searches for works that are extraordinary and influential, works that we hope will become the classics of tomorrow.

Making world literature available in English is crucial to opening our cultural borders, and its availability plays a vital role in maintaining a healthy and vibrant book culture. Open Letter strives to cultivate an audience for these works by helping readers discover imaginative, stunning works of fiction and poetry, and by creating a constellation of international writing that is engaging, stimulating, and enduring.

Current and forthcoming titles from Open Letter include works from Argentina, Bulgaria, China, France, Greece, Iceland, Latvia, Poland, South Africa, and many other countries.

www.openletterbooks.org